D1531029

For my big sisters, Heidi and Natasha

Also by Kim Curran
Shift
Control
Glaze

DELETE

Kim Curran

PO Box 61593
Irvine, CA 92602
www.xist publishing.com

Ordering Information:
Quantity sales. Special discounts are available on quantity purchases by
corporations, associations, and others. For details, contact the "Special Sales
Department" at the address above.

ISBN: 978-1-62395-731-5
eISBN: 978-1-62395-732-2

PROLOGUE

They say that as you're dying, your life flashes before your eyes. That it's the brain's way of sorting through all the moments in your life, trying to find some way out of your current predicament. Hunting for an experience that might help. Maybe you watched a programme about snakes when you were ten years old, which will come in real handy when a black mamba has sunk its teeth into your leg. Or that time at a wedding when your uncle showed you how to tie a tourniquet with a napkin; well, it might just stop you from bleeding to death.

Everything is supposed to go crystal sharp and slow down, so you have time to think. Time to implement the plan that's going to save your life.

Well, I can tell you, if you're falling from the top of a thousand-foot-high building, there's no TV programme or wise thing any drunk old uncle might have said that's going to help you. Because, let's face it, if you had learned to fly somewhere along the way, then you wouldn't be falling.

And I was falling. Fast. With Frankie Anderson plummeting next to me, her tears peeling away in the wind. As the top of the Shard became a memory, everything that had happened to me over the past six months flashed before my eyes like a zoetrope. Flickering glimpses of experiences.

Aubrey smiling up at me from under a duvet.

Frankie pointing to the stars and explaining how we could change decisions beyond our lifetime.

A single tear falling down Aubrey's cheek when she saw me kissing another girl.

My feet pounding on the pavement as Frankie Forced me to run and run – as she turned me into her puppet, like she had with so many other children before me.

Frankie's laughter when I told her that I knew, that she took broken children and turned them into assassins.

The look on Aubrey's face as she died in my arms.

I'd used a power I didn't understand to impose my will on Frankie and her broken children. I'd made some abandon her, others kill themselves. I'd made her unpick all the threads of her life. And I'd done it all to save Aubrey, the girl that I loved.

But it had come with a cost.

All of those images flashed, blurring together like the streaking city lights. As the concrete rushed up to meet us, I'd Forced Frankie to make a choice: unravel every decision she'd ever made, right back to joining Project Ganymede, or die.

She'd made her choice. And I'd woken up in a world at war.

I'd peeled myself off the concrete in a new reality to find a London I didn't recognise and an Aubrey who didn't recognise me.

As I stood there looking at the ruined city, the question was, how much more was I willing to sacrifice to keep Aubrey safe? And would I ever find my way back home?

KIM CURRAN

CHAPTER ONE

"We're at war?" I said stupidly, struggling to take in what I was seeing.

A shattered London spun around me. The river, a dark abyss cutting through the smoking ruin of my city. St Paul's, a fractured skeleton in front of me. City Hall, nothing more than a pile of twisted metal behind me.

The recorded echo of Big Ben's chimes still rang in the air, played over hidden speakers. The clock tower that held the great bell was gone. Where it and the Houses of Parliament once stood, there was now a black, hungry crater. This wasn't a war; this was the apocalypse.

I turned to look at Aubrey Jones, the only girl I had ever loved. Only moments ago, she was lying in my arms, her blood seeping into a golden carpet. Now, she was standing in front of me, a black helmet tucked under one arm, a patch covering one of her sea-green eyes, looking at me as if I was mad. As if I was a stranger.

I'd been so desperate to bring her back to me, so out of my mind with grief, I hadn't thought about the consequences. No, I realised, as the last, mournful *bong* of Big Ben echoed across the water, that wasn't true. I just hadn't *cared* about the consequences. Without Aubrey, I'd wanted the whole world to burn.

I'd got exactly what I wanted.

"Are you OK, sir?" Aubrey said, and the word "sir" was like a blade in my gut.

My head was dizzy; my limbs strange and alien, like I'd stepped off a roller coaster. I took a step forwards. If I could explain that she knew me, tell her everything that had happened, we could work out another Shift. One that would keep her alive but wouldn't bring this about – I saw a child's red shoe lying next to a crumbling wall, weeds growing through the strap – this horror. There had to be a way out of here. I just had to think.

"You don't look too good," I heard her say as I took another step towards her. Everything swam before my eyes. My knees gave way and I collapsed to the floor. I didn't even have the energy to stand, let alone think.

Zac was the first to reach me. "You're bleeding."

I followed his gaze down to my leg. There was a hole in the black combat trousers I wore. I rubbed at the fabric and my fingers came away damp.

"You've been shot," Aubrey said, not moving a step closer.

I looked from the red stain on my hand to her face. "But I can't feel anything."

"It will be the adrenaline." Zac squatted down next to me, hooked two fingers inside the hole in the trousers and pulled. The fabric tore with a jagged buzz, revealing a puncture wound in my leg the size of a fifty-pence piece and a steady trail of blood. Zac whistled through his teeth. "Turner. Med pack. Now," he said.

A figure standing behind Aubrey jolted to attention and jogged forward. Judging by the black jumpsuit and body armour, I'd assumed she was a Regulator — one of the ex-Shifters who worked at ARES after they'd lost their powers. But when she pulled off her helmet, revealing dark, pretty eyes, a square face and a mop of messy brown hair, I realised she couldn't have been much older than thirteen, fourteen maybe. Far too young to be a Regulator. She struggled to undo a small bag hooked to her belt.

"Give it here," Aubrey said, yanking the pack off the girl and then throwing it to Zac.

I kept staring stupidly at the hole in my leg. Dark, almost black blood oozed out with each pulse. I went to poke my finger in the wound, to see how far it went, to see if it was really there, but Zac slapped my hand away. He unzipped the med pack and pulled out a white gauze dressing.

"Put pressure on it." He put the cotton square on my leg and placed my hand on top of it. Blood stippled through the white after only a few seconds. "Trust you to get shot in the leg and not even notice."

"I guess I've had a lot on my mind," I said, wincing as Zac tied a thin bandage around the gauze and pulled hard. Whatever had been keeping the pain at bay was wearing off. But the fogginess in my mind showed no sign of clearing.

Zac wrapped the remainder of the bandage around my leg four, five times and then tied it off. "That will have to do for now."

Aubrey fidgeted next to us, checking the skies. "Time check?"

The final figure lifted the visor on his helmet and checked an oversized watch strapped over the cuff of his shirt. He too was young, with a plump, red face. I saw a bead of sweat roll down his temple. "Minus eighteen," he said.

"They'll have tracked the Shift by now," the girl Zac had called Turner said, doing a bad job of keeping the panic out of her voice.

"Damn." Aubrey looked down at me. "Can you walk?

"I can try." I reached out my hand for her to help me to my feet. But it was Zac who got me up. I resented his strong arm around my back taking the weight I now found I couldn't put on my leg. I wanted to shake him off, but I didn't have the strength. Pain spread through my leg like heat.

Aubrey reached up and pressed a button on a collar around her neck. "Thirteen, report position."

I jolted as I heard a voice in my ear and realised I, too, was wearing a throat mic and headset.

"Ref TQ 32008," the voice said. "We won't be able to stay around much longer. It's getting hot."

A buzzing screech passed overhead. We all looked up to see a burning trail cut across the sky. A moment later, a dull explosion sounded from a way off.

"Give us fifteen minutes," Aubrey said, staring in the direction of the explosion. I could see a glow of light coming from behind the damaged buildings blocking my view.

"Can we make it in—" A second, louder explosion cut Zac off. It lit up the dark sky, revealing the broken London skyline.

"We'll have to." Aubrey yanked her helmet back on, threw my free arm over her shoulder, and we started to run.

"Wait," I tried to say. "We need to talk."

"No time, sir," Aubrey said, pulling me forward.

The stabbing in my thigh got worse with each step. But I didn't want to let Aubrey know. I tried my best to keep both legs moving as she and Zac half dragged, half carried me along the riverside. I felt the heat of her body against mine, caught the scent of vanilla. I tried not to think about the crushed buildings all around us or the sounds of explosions in the distance. The only thing that mattered to me right now was that she was alive. Everything else could wait.

Turner and the boy jogged ahead across Tower Bridge, stopping every now and then to check we were still with them. The Thames beneath us was inky black, not a single light from the buildings on either side reflected in the surface. The pain was becoming all-consuming and my eyesight was getting dim.

"Hang in there, Com," Zac said. "Not much longer."

We made it across the bridge but there was no slowing of pace. By the time we made it on to Fenchurch Street, my whole body had started to shake.

"He's going into shock," I heard a voice say, dull and distant as if coming from another room. My vision had narrowed to a pinprick of light. My heart pounded in my ears.

"Maybe I should sit down for a second." I hit the ground.

I sensed movement around me. Shouting. Something tugging at my shirt and…

"Wow!" I screamed, as chemicals flooded into my heart. It didn't just beat. It boomed. I looked down to see a large syringe sticking out from between my ribs, Aubrey's hand still on the plunger.

"Still with us, sir?" she said, pulling the needle out. Her face and hair glowed like there was a halo around her. Her green eye was like an emerald. I reached out to touch her face, and she gently guided my hand back down to my side.

"Call me Scott," I said, my words slurring. "Please."

"OK. Are you still with us, Scott?"

"What did you give me?" I said, as Aubrey and Zac got me back on my feet. The pain in my leg had completely vanished, as had the buzzing in my head. I felt amazing.

"Mostly adrenaline."

"Mostly?" Zac asked, raising his eyebrow at Aubrey.

She shrugged. "With a few extra kickers thrown in. For luck."

"Can you stand?" Zac asked.

"I can fly!" I said, trying to catch the vapour trails pouring out of my hands.

Zac laughed and pulled me forward. "I got to get me some of this stuff."

We pushed on, and after a minute, the warm fizzle of whatever Aubrey had given me faded enough that I was able to focus on what was happening. I recognised the road we were running down as Lombard Street. In my reality, it had been lined with gastropubs and glass-fronted offices; now there was nothing but boarded-up buildings and the burned-out wreckages of cars and tanks: the marks of street battles.

We paused for a moment, taking cover behind a crumbling brick wall. The word "Shine" had been scrawled in red paint on the wall. There was nothing shining about this city.

I was starting to feel weak again. Pain crept around the edges, trying to get back in.

It's only pain, a voice in my head said. *You've had worse.*

I forced myself to ignore the ache – locking it away as if behind a wall in my mind – and pressed on. I'd lost track of where we were. With no road signs or familiar landmarks to guide me, I might as well have been in a foreign city. The other thing that made this London feel so alien was that it was empty. Not a soul on the streets, save for me, Aubrey, Zac and their two companions. It was eerie. Like something from a zombie movie.

"Wait here," Aubrey said. "Something doesn't feel right."

I didn't want to let her go, but what choice did I have? I wasn't exactly in any state to run after her. I felt weaker than I could ever remember. And not just from the blood loss. It felt like I hadn't slept in days. Looking down at the way the combat trousers hung around my hips, it looked as if I hadn't eaten much, either. I leant against a wall, and focused on not throwing up.

"How are you doing, sir?"

"I'm fine, Turner," I said, looking up at the girl. "Just a little, you know, shot."

"It will be the comedown from your Shift, too," the boy said in a low voice, crouching next to us. His name tag read "Cooper." "A sixteen!" He whistled through his teeth.

"I've never seen anything like it," Turner said.

"Dur! No one has. No one has ever gone higher than a thirteen before, isn't that right, sir?"

"I… I don't know," I said.

"I scored a nine once. Do you remember that, Turner?"

"Remember it? You tell me about it every single day," the girl replied.

"Yeah," Cooper said, looking dejected, "well, it was pure epic."

"It was pure luck."

Their banter reminded me of how Aubrey and I had been when we first started working together. How she would make fun of me and I would grin dumbly, unable to think of anything remotely witty to say in response.

"Leave the Com alone," Zac said. I'd never been more grateful to anyone.

Cooper blushed even redder, and he and Turner went back to watching for Aubrey's return. They didn't have to wait for long.

"The way is blocked," she said, jogging towards us. "Looks recent."

"An ambush?" Zac asked.

"Feels like it."

"Then we take another route?" Zac looked at me.

"I… I haven't been plotting," I said, the heat of shame stinging my cheeks. That was basic stuff. Even a cadet wouldn't be caught moving through the streets without tracking their route and the alternative paths. But the pain and fog in my head made it hard to focus on what was happening right now, let alone hold on to the alternatives.

"I'll do it," Aubrey said. She pulled her helmet off, closed her eyes and lifted her head, as if turning her face to the sun. Her blonde hair was a little longer than before, with no hint of the red streak. Her fringe fell over the dark patch covering her left eye, and there was a faint trail of a scar cutting across her eyebrow. Her good eye was missing the usual dark make-up that my Aubrey had always worn. It made her look younger. But she was as beautiful as ever. Before I had a chance to gaze at her any longer, we were suddenly standing in a completely different street. Aubrey had made her Shift.

"There." She pointed at an alleyway up ahead. Piles of twisted metal and shattered glass blocked the path between the entrance and us. "That will bring us out onto Prince's Street. And from there we can join up with the rest of the squad."

"What about drones?" Cooper said, and I could tell by the slight quiver in his voice that he was scared. "Isn't this area covered by patrol drones?"

"We should be OK," Zac said, looking off into the distance. "We took out ten of them last week. They'll be using the ones they have left to focus on their territory. It's what I'd do," he added, as if to excuse his mapping abilities. Zac, or at least the Zac I had known, had been one of ARES' most promising Mappers – Shifters who worked out the most likely outcomes of any Shifts – before he went rogue. Some in ARES treated Mappers like psychics, but they couldn't see the future. They were just really good at weighing up the odds.

Aubrey chewed at her lip, scanning the road between us and the alley. "It's the fastest way through. All right, weapons check."

It was only then I noticed Zac and Aubrey had sleek, semi-automatic rifles slung across their backs. They tucked the stocks under their arms, ejected the magazines and slapped them back in, and each flicked off the safety. Cooper and Turner pulled handguns out of holsters and pulled the slides back. In my ARES, Shifters hadn't even been allowed to carry tasers.

"Stay tight," Aubrey said, bringing the gun up to her shoulder.

"Can't the Commandant maybe…" Turner fell silent as Aubrey glared at her.

"Consider the Commandant out of action for the moment," Zac said, not looking at me.

A sense of bitter shame itched in my stomach. I was supposed to be their leader and I was letting them down. They were looking to me for answers and I had none.

I didn't belong here. I had to Shift and get out. Back to my old reality where I wasn't running around with a bullet in my leg and didn't have drones to worry about. But… I looked at Aubrey. She watched me with her one good eye, a curious smile playing about her lips. I smiled back. The Shift could wait. After all, I didn't want to risk making the situation even worse.

I tried to find some hidden reserves of energy as the group set off again, heading for the fallen building.

Zac and Aubrey helped me crawl over girders and rubble to get through to the alley. The pain was biting hard again, and my vision was blurring around the edges. I didn't know how much longer I could keep this up. The alley stank of piss and rotting food, like something had died down here. As we stepped over a large brown stain, I realised I wasn't wrong about that.

When we finally came out the other end, it opened onto a long, wide road.

"They should be up ahead," Turner said, excitedly.

I heard a low *whoomp, whoomp*. Had the drones Cooper had been worrying about found us?

A blur of metal appeared over the top of the empty shops in front of us. A black helicopter with the Union flag painted on its tail hovered overhead.

"Damn," Aubrey said. And reached up to her collar again. "Thirteen squad. We are one hundred metres south of your location. Request drop and wait."

"I regret, no can do," a female voice crackled in return. I could make out the hint of an accent amid the static.

"Then how the hell do you think we're going to get to the Hub, Ladoux?" Aubrey shouted down her mic. "Walk?"

"Relax, Jones," whoever this Ladoux was said. "The Rhino is waiting. Couldn't leave you out in the cold, could we?" Her voice crackled as the reception weakened. "We'll light your way."

"Gee, thanks," Aubrey said.

"What's the Rhino?" I asked.

Aubrey looked at me like I'd asked a very stupid question. She was about to answer when she was cut off by a low, grumbling roar and the sound of metal grinding on concrete. "That," she said jabbing her thumb back over her shoulder, "is the Rhino."

A huge tank rolled around a corner. Its tracks rolled over the remains of a car, flattening it like a tin can. It was so black it seemed to swallow up any light left on the street. There were no windows I could see. No slots in the armour. The only thing breaking the blackness was the Union flag painted on its side. It looked like something out of one of my old videogames. Like something from the future.

The Rhino ground to a halt, cracking the concrete under its weight. A hatch opened in the top and a helmeted head popped up.

"Well," said a lilting voice I recognised. "Are you gonna stand there all day, or are we getting the feck out of here?" A tiny girl clambered out of the hatch to stand on top of the tank. She blew her long, brown fringe out of her eyes.

"Thanks, Cleo," Zac said. "I thought we were going to be walking home tonight."

"Sure, it was no problem. And I've been wanting to get behind the sticks of this baby for a while."

Without any hesitation, Zac, Turner and Cooper scrambled up the side of the tank and dropped in through the hatch. Aubrey hesitated, looking at me. "Are you coming, sir?"

I couldn't move. I stared up at the hulking vehicle and my old classmate, CP Finn, standing on top of it.

"Scott!" The sound of my name snapped me out of it. I looked up at Aubrey, now standing next to CP on the top of the tank. "Are you coming?"

I nodded and stumbled forward. The pain was back and then some, making up for its brief vacation with a vengeance. I tried to bend my leg to climb up onto the tank. And that was all I could remember.

CHAPTER TWO

I faded in and out of consciousness. Swimming to the surface before being pulled back into the darkness. I got a sense of movement: fast and bumpy. We were travelling through the streets of London at breakneck speeds. Faces swam in and out of my view. I caught snatches of muttered voices. They sounded worried. More sudden movement, and then everything was bright, blinding white.

"The Com's been shot!" someone shouted.

The movement stopped, and my boots and trousers were tugged off. A cold hand lay on my leg and the pain was too much to bear. I gave in and sank down into the bliss of sleep.

I dreamt of battles and blood. Tanks and helicopters and fire. I woke to a face inches away from mine. "Aubrey?" I said through cotton-dry lips.

The person laughed. "No. Jones is off being useful somewhere. Whereas I am playing nurse for you." It was Zac.

I struggled to prop myself up on the bed. "Where am I?"

"In the infirmary. It was a close one, sir. You'd lost a lot of blood. Luckily, the doc was able to pump you full again."

I looked down at my arm where a tube filled with dark liquid snaked into the crook of my elbow. Below the IV tube, there was a black symbol inked across my upper arm: a stylised letter S with two double-headed arrows cutting across it. I rubbed at it. It wasn't coming off. It appeared that I had a tattoo. Mum, I thought vaguely, will kill me when she sees this.

I turned my attention to the room.

It was bright white, with plastic sheeting covering rock walls. Wherever we were, we were underground. Why would anyone set up a hospital in a cave? Eight beds were arranged in a circle around the room. Children occupied four of them. Some of the children lay silent, wired up to drips. Others moaned softly in pain, bandages covering various parts of them.

"What happened to them?"

"You can't remember?" Zac said, keeping his voice low.

I shook my head.

"These are some of your old ARES squadron," he said slowly, as if trying to explain something to a child. "You led us in an operation last week to take a bomb factory. You were successful."

"Successful?" I said, looking at the injured kids.

Pain cracked through my head and with it a memory flashed.

I'm running towards a warehouse door ahead, a girl on my left and a boy on my right. I hear a crack and the boy next to me goes down. I keep on running. I think about Shifting, but we have to stick to the plan. It's more important than one boy. I feel a mild sense of annoyance that someone will have to take his place in the plan. I look around to find where the shot came from and see a man, with a red scarf covering his face, standing on the roof overhead. I shout at the girl to cover the left flank and turn to the armed Shifters behind me, pointing up at the man on the roof. They take aim. A moment later and he's falling, limbs splayed, holes in his head and chest. He is dead before he hits the ground in front of me. I step over him and push on.

I press the PTT button at my neck and call in covering fire. There's the sweet sound of rotary guns whirring as the helicopter lays down twin rows of bullets. It cut through the building in front of us. That should sort any remaining snipers.

I'm almost at the door. And I'm smiling. Ready to take on who and whatever is inside. Ready to make them pay.

The pounding in my head faded. That wasn't my memory. It couldn't have been. Who could be that cold? That ruthless? I could still smell the blood and cordite. And the rush – the joy of the fight. It couldn't be me. I blinked the images away, and focused on the room again and the children in it. I recognised one of the faces from the memory: the girl who was running beside me. I realised with a sickening lurch that she was missing an arm.

"Doesn't look like we were successful," I said.

Those children who were conscious looked up at me, their tired eyes filled with excitement.

"Commandant!" the girl said, propping herself up with her only good arm.

The word was picked up by the rest of the kids and echoed throughout the room. They stared at me, eyes wide, not in shock but in awe. As if their favourite pop star had come for a ward visit.

I was the Commandant? The head of ARES? How was that even possible? Nothing made sense in this reality. Children dying in a war I'd brought about? The city destroyed, all because I'd forced Frankie Anderson to undo her decisions. In unravelling all the subtle machinations she'd been carrying out for years – manipulating politicians and businessmen through their love for their children – I'd brought about this war. I'd thought I was stopping a monster Instead, I'd become one.

Sometimes, we have to become the very thing we're fighting against, a voice in my head said.

I shook it away. I wouldn't accept it. More than that, I didn't have to. I was a Shifter, after all.

I lay back down, turning away from Zac and the injured children. I couldn't bear to look at them any longer. I had to think of a decision I could change. Something that wouldn't make everything worse – if that was even possible. I picked over the last six months of my life, plucking at memories and then discarding them, like flicking through an old photo album. But everything I thought of led back to that moment at the top of the golden pyramid with Aubrey lying in my arms, dead. I knew that was crazy. There were a hundred different paths I could have taken. I could make sure Aubrey was never at the Pyramid. I could have chosen not to confront Frankie Anderson – let her carry on using children as political assassins. I could have never gone looking for her in the first place – simply closed the file on Project Ganymede and moved on. Not to mention the hundreds of tiny decisions I could undo, each one creating a new ripple, a new version in reality. Aubrey dying wasn't a fixed moment. It could be avoided. I just needed to find the right pressure point and push. But I couldn't get a grip on any of my memories. Each moment I thought of dissipated, as if I were trying to hold smoke. All because my mind kept returning to the agony I'd felt when I realised I'd lost Aubrey.

"Is he awake?"

I opened my eyes again as a woman walked into the room. She was a dark silhouette against the bright lights of the infirmary. When she stepped clear of the glow of the strip lights, I saw her face. She had a long, thin nose, full lips and clear eyes, chestnut hair pulled up into a messy bun. She was unnaturally beautiful, as if cut from stone. It wasn't possible. It was Frankie Anderson.

I remembered falling, the glass wall of the Shard whipping past my face, Frankie spiralling beside me. She should be dead.

"No!" I screamed. I scrambled to get away from her, rolling off the bed and pulling the drip stand down on top of me.

"It's OK," Zac said. "It's the doc."

"It's her fault," I shouted, struggling to stand up again and failing. "Get her away from me." If she used her power as a Forcer on me again, I would have no chance of escaping.

Frankie moved closer. She was wearing a white lab coat, a stethoscope thrown over her neck and a pair of small, round glasses. She peered at me through them.

"It appears the Commandant is having an RA."

"No," Zac said. "It's probably the drugs wearing off." He crouched down next to me, a serious look on his face.

"Keep your mouth shut, Tyler," he hissed through closed teeth.

He helped me to my feet. I couldn't take my eyes off Frankie.

"I'll be the judge of that," she said, stepping forward. She reached a hand out to touch my eye, and I slapped it away.

"Don't you touch me," I snapped. "You evil, manipulative…"

"Repeat after me," she said, cutting me off. "I am here, I am now."

"What? What are you on about? You did this. This war, all of it is down to you."

She reached into her pocket and pulled out a pen torch, which she shone in my eye. I pushed her hand away again.

"If you keep struggling, I am going to have to sedate you. You are having a reality attack; do you understand what that means?" She pushed her glasses up onto her head, pulling her hair back from her forehead. The Frankie I had known had a scar running below her hairline. It was the same scar I'd seen on the head of every member of Project Ganymede, from the operation that had given them the power to Shift back. But the woman in front of me didn't have it. Her forehead was as smooth as marble.

"I said, do you understand what that means?" she repeated.

I kept staring at where the scar should be. No scar meant no operation. Which meant no power. I took a deep breath and nodded.

"Do you know who I am?"

"You are Frankie Anderson."

"Anderson?" she said, a dark eyebrow hitching. "Captain Black, can you give me a moment with the Commandant?"

Zac hesitated. "I'm not sure…"

"I will have you removed if I have to."

"All right," Zac threw his hands up in defeat "but he's supposed to report to—"

"I'll decide when he's fit enough to report anywhere. Off you go now." She scooted Zac away. He threw me a look from over her shoulder and pressed his finger to his lips. He was telling me to keep my mouth shut.

Frankie twisted the torch off, placed it back in her pocket, and then folded her arms. "I'm Doctor Goodwin. Anderson was my previous husband's name. How did you know that?"

"I've read all your files," I said, scowling at her.

"Which files?"

"From Project Ganymede."

She blinked. "Where have I heard that name? Oh yes, the programme Doctor Lawrence ran before the war. Something about reinitiating the Shifting power. He tried to recruit me."

"Tried to?" I said.

"Yes, but I said no. There were too many unknowables for my liking. I entered medical training instead."

"Oh, yeah?" I said. "Then what about Pandora Worldwide?"

"Never heard of it."

"Liar! You turned children into killers just to play your political games."

She uncrossed her arms and gave me a patient if patronising look. "I can assure you I have absolutely no interest in politics. And my only interaction with children is to see that they get better. Which is what I would like to do for you, if you would let me."

"No." I was so confused. Could it be possible that the decision I'd forced Frankie to undo as we fell from the top of the Shard had led to this? Her as a doctor? Helping children, not using them? I wasn't ready to believe it. "You can't trick me again."

"OK, Commandant Tyler. Let's put your concerns with me aside for a moment. What else do you remember from your old reality?

"There was no war."

She sighed. "No wonder you are struggling to accept the Shift."

"I'm not struggling to accept it! I'm just not going to stay here." I tried to tug the IV out of my arm, when Frankie gently pushed my hands away and did it for me, pressing a small bud of cotton wool over the puncture wound.

"You plan on Shifting to an alternative reality that is closer to your old one?"

I nodded, resenting the whirlwind in my head. I had memories of this Frankie taking care of me – stitching up wounds, patching up my team – swirling in with the memories I had of Frankie sneering at me. Telling her children to beat me up. Forcing me to run till my feet bled.

"Then why haven't you?" she continued. "You got shot in the leg? Why didn't you Shift then? Go on, do it now. Collapse this reality and save us all a lot of pain."

"I... I..." I couldn't answer. I couldn't explain that the only reason I hadn't undone everything and stopped this war from ever starting was because I didn't want to lose my girlfriend.

"Mmm," Frankie said, drumming her fingers on her folded arm. I wanted to hit her. "This is quite fascinating. I've never seen a patient with such a firm hold on an old reality. Are you experiencing any other side effects? Headaches? Hearing voices?" My shocked silence was answer enough. "I see." She placed her glasses back on her nose and pulled a pad and pen out of her pocket "I'm going to write you a script for some antipsychotics. If they don't work, we'll have to try simulator therapy."

I froze. The last time I'd been hooked up to a simulator had been one of the worst experiences of my life. The images I'd seen had driven me to the point where I'd begged to end my life. I still remembered Benjo Green leaning over me, his obese face contorted in a hungry grin, his blade inching ever closer to my eye. And Mr Abbott, my old teacher, coldly watching, waiting for me to die. But that was nothing compared to the things I'd done myself while hooked up to the machines. The ways I'd hurt the people I loved. My sister Katie and my family. I'd done unthinkable, inhuman things. It was the darkness I'd glimpsed in my own soul that haunted me most. I shivered at the memory. Where were Katie and my family now? Out there in the ruined city? Or even worse?

Frankie tore a page off the pad and handed it to me. I grabbed it resentfully. I couldn't read the name of the drug she'd written, but I could see the instruction to take it three times a day. There was no way I was taking her drugs. Or being subject to a simulator again. All I wanted to do was get the hell away from her, find Aubrey and work a way out of here.

"Can I go now?"

"You're lucky. The bullet passed straight through your leg. It could have been much worse. Perhaps it was much worse?" She raised her eyebrows as if expecting me to answer. "If you Shifted to save your life, it would explain the force of your Shift. I understand it registered a sixteen? The hypnic jerk is a powerful defence mechanism."

That made sense. The hypnic jerk – the reflex reaction that in normal people sends a signal to make their limbs twitch, but in Shifters sends a signal to the brain to Shift – had saved my life before. It was a Shifter's ultimate defence mechanism.

"Can I go now?" I repeated. Even looking at her was making me dizzy with confusion.

"Take these for the pain." She threw me a small orange tube. White pills rattled around inside. "And remember: you are here. You are now."

I recognised the phrase from training. It was what we were supposed to tell ourselves if we were having a reality attack. But I didn't want to be here or now.

Frankie turned, reaching up to adjust the drip next to one of the kid's beds. "Patching up children and sending them back out to fight," she said with another sigh, "exactly what I trained for."

I took this as a yes. I yanked on a pile of clothes I guessed must have been left for me along with my boots, and limped for the door before she had a chance to say anything else.

"Goodbye, sir," a girl said, as I reached for the doorknob.

I stopped. I knew which kid it was. The one without her arm. I couldn't face her. I threw the door open and left without a word.

CHAPTER THREE

I walked out into a tunnel illuminated with a sickly green light. It looked and smelt like something from a fairground haunted house.

"I didn't think she would let you go," Zac said, stepping out from a shadow. "Last kid I saw had a reality attack, they hooked him up for three days solid. And even then..." He shrugged.

"I'm not having a reality attack." I said, looking at the pills Frankie had given me. The label said Tramadol. I didn't trust her as far as I could throw her, but the pain was a distraction I didn't need. I popped the lid off with my thumb and dry-swallowed two of the white tablets.

"Whatever. We're wanted in the command room." He nodded to the left and led the way up the tunnel.

It sloped gently upward, and the damp smell lessened as the tunnel grew wider.

We passed a few adults dressed in combats with military insignia on their arms. Each person greeted me with a sharp salute and a glowing smile. "Congratulations, sir," and "good work," they said, over and over, until I was sick of hearing it. Each of them looked at me like I was something special. A hero, even.

Zac chattered the whole way about my earlier Shift and what had been going on. About how we'd blown up an enemy base and how I was probably going to get a commendation for it, if they didn't haul me over the coals for disobeying an order.

None of it sounded familiar. But unless I wanted to end up in Frankie's hands, I was going to have to keep my mouth shut. I just needed enough time to find Aubrey again.

The tunnel opened up into a cathedral-sized space of heavy grey concrete. I stepped out and stared at the roof overhead. Four great pillars standing on a circular floor held up the domed ceiling. The floor itself was covered in black-and-white tiles that created an image of a cartwheel of arrows pointing in all directions. As well as the tunnel we'd exited, two more led off of the central hall, pointing north and west.

"Welcome to the Hub. Home of the S3."

"S3?" I said, my jaw hanging open in wonder. I knew, somehow, that this whole place was deep under the streets of London. How long, I wondered, had this place taken to build? How long had we been at war?

"The SSS?" Zac hissed, looking around to check no one had heard me. "The Special Shifting Service? You really can't remember?"

I shrugged. "Guess not."

Green-tinged light illuminated the room, which was filled with bustling people: soldiers dressed in various shades of camo and armour; kids in black jumpsuits; and a host of other personnel, all moving with determined purpose.

I remembered the handful of NSOs – non-Shifting Officers – we'd had at ARES. Most of them were ex-service specialists brought in for our protection. But this was something else. There had to be two if not three hundred people here. Each of them very much still in service.

Zac shook his head. "I'd keep that to yourself for now. Come on, they'll be waiting." He headed towards a tunnel on the right.

At the bottom was a metal door with a red light above it. Zac paused and stood aside, letting me go first. I tugged at the handle. It was shut tight. There was an electronic pad on the side of the door.

"Let me." Zac pressed his hand against the lock.

"Captain Black. Access level four," an electronic voice chirped, and the door opened.

The room looked like the control of a rocket launch: screens lined the far wall, showing live video feed and streams of data; men and women sat behind desks, wearing headsets and tapping frantically away on keyboards. I recognised a few of the faces from *my* ARES as I was starting to think of the old reality. I wondered where my friend Jake was. I prayed that somehow he and his sister

Rosalie had gotten themselves away from London and out of this mess.

To the side of the screens was a large circular table where Turner and Cooper stood, looking as confused as I was.

"What's going on?" I asked.

"The Red Hand have pushed deeper into the city," Turner said, pointing at the table. "I guess they didn't appreciate us tramping around their area yesterday."

The top of the table was a large touchscreen, like the tablets we'd used at ARES, only on a much bigger scale. It showed a map of London with the familiar loop of the Thames in the centre. Bright red squares were overlaid in what I assumed were strategic positions.

Zac leaned over and dragged a square so it covered an area in the east of the city. "That means they hold everywhere south of the Marsh Wall now." He drew a line with his finger from one edge of the loop in the river to the other.

"And we," a man said from behind me, "can't allow that."

I knew that voice. I'd both feared and loved it. But hearing it now wasn't possible. He was dead. I'd watched him die.

I turned around to see a man whose face was a mass of scars, with one milky eye.

"Cain?" I said, stunned to see my old fighting instructor alive and, apart from a few new scars, well. The last time I'd seen him, he'd been lying in a pool of his own blood, missing part of his brain.

"Tyler," Cain said, the only person not to address me as sir or Commandant. "I hear congratulations are in order after last night. Although we will need to have a word about you failing to follow orders. Again."

I scanned his face, hoping for some kind of answer, and my eyes lingered on the scar across his forehead. The scar combined with the golden S pinned to his collar reminded me with a cold dread that Cain was an adult Shifter. That he was carrying part of a kid's brain. In this reality, did Cain know the truth behind Project Ganymede? Did anyone know? And was the man behind the project still alive?

"Is Abbott here?" I said, a sudden hot anger rushing through me.

There was a ripple of uncertainty in the group behind me, and I noticed a few of the intelligence officers tore themselves away from the screens to look my way.

"Abbott?" Cain said, his mismatched eyes tightening.

I knew I'd slipped up and considered Shifting to undo having asked the question. But I needed to know. I nodded.

"Abbott died in the attack on Old Street," Cain said. "I would have thought you would have remembered that, Tyler. Being as it was you who dragged his body out of the rubble."

So, Abbot was dead. And with him, I assumed, his attempt to restart the Ganymede programme. I was glad he was dead. Glad in a way that scared me a little.

I tried to think of something to say to cover my mistake, some excuse I could make that would stop everyone staring at me. But I had nothing.

Zac came to my rescue. "Commandant Tyler is going through a bit of an adjustment after yesterday."

Cain's face softened. "Unsurprising, really. I hear it was a big Shift."

"Sixteen on the Lawrence scale, sir," Cooper said.

Cain raised a ragged eyebrow. "I didn't know the scale went up that high. Well, you'll find your feet soon enough, Tyler." He slapped my shoulder with his massive hand.

"Of course," I said, coughing to hide my embarrassment.

Find Aubrey, I said to myself. Find Aubrey and you can work a way out of here. Till then, I needed to play along. I turned back to the table. "What do we do?"

"We wait," Cain said. "We've got someone on the inside, and once we have their report, we'll be able to see what we're up against. Then we go in hard." He dragged a large black circle to cover all the red squares on the screen. "In the meantime," Cain said, "I suggest you go get yourself cleaned up. You look like shit. And can someone get the Commandant an S3 uniform? I know you're attached to the old kit, Tyler, but ARES is over now. You're in the army now, boy."

I looked down at what I wore and noticed the splatter of blood over the white ARES badge on my chest. It wasn't my blood.

"Do you know where I can find Au... ah, Captain Jones?"

"The new transfer? She's out on a mission," Cain said.

"Right. Can you get her to, um, report to me as soon as she returns?"

"Report to you, sure thing, Tyler," Cain said with a sly smile. "Now get out of my sight."

"I'll drive you home, sir," Zac said. He looked at me kindly and I realised, with a weird feeling of guilt and annoyance, that in this reality, he and I were friends.

"OK," I said, uncomfortably aware of the curious looks I was getting from the people in the room. They were all expecting something of me. "As soon as you get the report back on the Red Hand, I want to know." This seemed to work. They returned to whatever they had been doing, and Zac and I slipped away.

We walked back across the Hub and towards a set of silver doors. Behind the doors was a small metal room, which looked to be made of the same solid material. I followed Zac as he stepped inside and turned to face the way we'd come. The doors slid back into place, throwing us into near darkness. Before I could ask what was going on, the room jolted and I had the sense we were ascending. It was a lift. There were no counters ticking down floor numbers to let me know how far up we were going, but judging by the popping of my ears, it was a long way to the surface.

"Feels like Shifting, doesn't it?" Zac said

The massive lift shuddered to a stop and the doors inched open again, revealing what looked like an aircraft hangar. I saw the Rhino in the far corner and next to it a row of sleek, black armoured cars and various other vehicles that looked decades ahead of anything I'd ever seen. All of them, including the Rhino, had a Union flag painted on them somewhere. Only now that I looked closer, I realised that instead of a red and white cross on a blue background, the flag was on a black background.

"Look at the state of her!" an angry voice carried across the room.

I looked to where the voice was coming from to see a man with a long, lanky ponytail slide out from underneath the Rhino. He stood up and I could see he wore a Led Zeppelin T-shirt underneath his black overalls and rubbed an oily rag in his hands.

"Carl?" I said, walking towards him.

It was my old head of IT. Only instead of computers, it seemed he was in charge of the machines here.

"You were supposed to bring her in for an overhaul a week ago," Carl said.

"Don't call it a her," CP said. She was sitting on top of the tank's tracks, swinging her legs back and forth. "It's so creepy when you call it that. It's a machine. Not a woman."

Carl opened and closed his mouth, then decided against complaining. "Well, you're lucky she… it didn't sustain more damage the way you pounded it."

"We were in a bit of a hurry. Isn't that right, Com?" She smiled over at me, pulling off a swift salute: two fingers brushing against her temple.

Carl spun around and fumbled a salute, slapping himself in the face with his rag.

"How's the leg?" CP said.

I looked down. "Still attached, thanks, Cleo," I said, her name from this reality coming too easily. It was good to see her. Of all the people here, she seemed to be the only one who hadn't changed. "And thanks. For getting me back to base before I bled out."

"Not a bother," she said, blushing under her fringe.

Seeing her blush reminded me of how she used to act around my other old classmate. "Is Jake around?" I asked, a longing to see his crooked smile and mess up his hair welling up in me. Even though Jake was five years younger than me, I still considered him as one of my best friends.

"Jake, sir?" CP said.

"Jake Bailey? About your age. Sandy hair. Dark eyes."

She twisted her face to the side, thinking. "I remember a Jake from training, a year or so above me. But I haven't seen him since he graduated. I think he failed his final tests, so he'll be out on civvy street."

"Oh, right." So Jake wasn't part of ARES – or S3, as we were now called. I guessed that that was a good thing.

"I can put a request out to find him, if you need," she said, pulling out her tablet.

"No, that's fine. Thank you." As much as I was sad about not seeing him, I was glad to think he wasn't caught up in this nightmare. I hoped that he and his sister Rosalie were far away from the capital.

Carl's cough snapped me out of my thoughts about Jake. "It's good to see you, too, Carl."

"I, um, we've never met, sir."

I was really going to have to keep my mouth shut. "No, of course. It's only I've heard so much about you."

Carl beamed. "Good to meet you too, sir. Did you get my report on the upgrade ideas I had for the girls?"

CP groaned.

"I mean, the vehicles. Tech combined with the power to Shift presents some pretty exciting weaponry possibility. We've already proven it can work with the quantum grenades. And I also sent you a report on some further ideas on the defences for the Hub."

"Don't tell me. You want to bring in some sharks?"

Carl blinked. "Sharks, sir?"

I waved him away. "Don't worry about it."

"Oh, right. Well, some of the legacy systems are a bit antiquated, and many were disabled after the last war, but–"

"I'm sure the Com will look forward to hearing all about your ideas at a later stage," Zac said. "But for now, he needs to get some rest."

"Oh, yes. Of course. But if you have a few minutes, I could explain my idea for a quantum cannon."

"Later, Carl," Zac said, pulling me away.

"See ya, sir," CP said.

"See ya, Cleo," I said.

"We'll talk later, then, sir," Carl shouted after us as we walked away.

"Well, he hasn't changed," I said.

Zac laughed. "Wait till he starts going on about his plans for a robot army."

We walked towards a huge set of stainless steel doors, easily twenty feet high, embedded in the grey concrete. Zac slammed a yellow button and slowly the doors inched open, revealing a row of large spikes protruding out of the bottom, making it look like a portcullis.

Two soldiers stood on guard on the other side. They turned to us as we ducked under the door, avoiding the spikes.

"It's you, sir," one of the soldiers said, a bright smile on his shiny face. "We heard about the level sixteen. That's the highest so far, am I right?" He looked over at his friend while I stared, wide-eyed.

"Um..."

"How do you do it?" the other guard asked.

"Well, I just... you know... do?" It was weak, but it seemed to suffice. In fact, they nodded as if what I'd said was in fact totally profound, rather than being utter nonsense.

I flinched as the door started to descend again.

"What do you think of the new defences, sir?" the first guard said. "Ten inches thick, able to withstand a bomb strike. It's official; the Hub is the safest place in Britain."

"Very impressive." I smiled grimly at the guards. They returned my smile with glowing pride. I felt sick.

Zac saved me from any more of the adoration of my fans. "If you're quite done wasting the Commandant's time…"

The guards muttered their apologies and went back to their guard duty.

"Wait here," Zac said, "I don't like to park it in the hangar. You never know what modifications Carl might make."

I didn't get a chance to ask what "it" was before Zac went jogging off away from the doors. I walked forward, leaving the soldiers and the defences behind, and onto the street.

We were somewhere in one of London's more upmarket areas, guessing by the looming white buildings in the Palladian style: all stone columns and pediments. The hulking great lump of grey concrete that was the first level of the Hub had been squeezed in between two buildings, which must have been at least three hundred years old.

I could see a small park up ahead, an oasis of nature in a city of stone. Pale morning sun shone through the rustling leaves and I saw a squirrel dash across a branch. It was good to be out in the open air, even if I could smell the cloying sweetness of burning. The recycled air in the Hub had made my eyes dry and my throat scratchy, like when you've been on an airplane for too long.

A low rumbling sounded and I jumped, scanning the sky to check for another helicopter or drone. There was nothing but the felt-grey clouds.

The rumbling grew louder and a sleek black car pulled around a corner. The door opened.

"Get in," Zac said, then added an awkward "sir" as an afterthought.

I climbed into the seat and closed the door. "One thing, Zac," I said. "You can quit it with the 'sir,' OK?"

"Sure thing, Tyler," Zac said with a crooked smile. "Like old times, hey?"

He slammed the accelerator and the vehicle leapt forward.

"Sure," I said, looking through the holes in the metal plates and out onto streets I didn't know. "Just like old times."

CHAPTER FOUR

I didn't know where we were going, and I was content to let Zac drive. I sat back, hardly able to see anything outside. Every now and then, I would catch a glimpse of a face in a window. But they always turned away, terrified, and scuttled back into hiding. What had this war done to these people? What had *I* done to them? Guilt coiled around my spine like a snake pulling tighter and tighter.

The only sign that anyone still lived in these streets was graffiti on walls and across fences. Most of it appeared pro-army; images of brave British soldiers fighting off enemies. But there were a few scrawled phrases that didn't see quite so keen on the war effort. "Screw. This. War." was written in six-foot-high letters on the side of a derelict building. I couldn't agree more.

There was also that word again. Shine. I'd seen it when we had been running through the streets. And here it was once more, sprayed in red paint over and over.

"What does that mean?" I said, nodding at the graffiti.

"Shine?" Zac said. "No idea. It's been appearing more and more lately." He shrugged and looked back to the road. And then groaned.

"What is it?"

"Roadblock."

Zac pulled to a halt in front of a red-and-white barrier. An armed solider sauntered over to the car and knocked on the side window.

Zac sighed and rolled it down. "Good morning, Private," he said with forced cheeriness.

The private leant forward and peered through the window. "It's still curfew... Oh." He stopped, seeing our uniforms for the first time. "S3, is it?" He didn't sound too impressed.

"Yup," Zac said, showing him a tattoo on his right arm – the same tattoo I had – as if it was ID enough.

The soldier sniffed and straightened up. "On you go then." He waved us through the barrier.

"Well, he didn't seem too friendly," I said when we were clear.

"The army pretty much hate us."

"But I thought we are the army?"

"We're special forces," Zac said with a grin. "We get all the cool toys and missions, while they get sent off to foreign countries to get their balls blown off. Poor bastards."

We drove through another three roadblocks, the soldiers on duty looking less and less happy to see us each time, before Zac pulled up outside a block of modern, glass-fronted flats and killed the engine. The silence after the roar of the car was unsettling, emphasising the quietness of the streets.

"Where is everyone?" I said.

"There's still half an hour till curfew ends." He tapped at the watch on his wrist; it read 5.33am. "So they're either inside, or sneaking about and hoping nobody catches them," Zac said, opening his door.

I waited, assuming he was stopping to get something. But he walked around the front and opened my door, too.

"Well, are you getting out?"

"But… I don't live here," I said, stepping out of the car and looking up at the building. The pale, dirty skies reflected in the windows made it look a stone obelisk. It must have been one of the only buildings I'd seen that was still intact.

"Um, yeah you do," Zac said, resting a hand on my shoulder. "Penthouse suite, buddy."

I followed him towards an armed guard protecting the entrance. The man stiffened upon my approach, jerking his gun to his chest. I ignored him, sick of guns and men snapping to attention whenever they saw me, and pushed through the doors.

Inside were a large reception desk and a water fountain with a statue of a leaping fish in the middle. The fountain burbled in a way I guessed was supposed to be relaxing, but really just made me want to use the bathroom.

"Good morning, Mr Tyler," the woman who appeared at reception said. She was unnaturally cheery for this time of the morning. "It's been a while. I hope everything is well."

"Yeah, sure," I muttered.

"I took a few messages for you while you were away." She reached into a small cubbyhole behind the desk and handed me a pile of envelopes. I tucked them under my arm without even looking at them.

"Thanks."

"Well, then, have a great day." She smiled a beaming plastic smile and walked back into the room from where she'd appeared.

"Come on," Zac said, tugging at my arm.

He led me over to a set of golden lifts. The doors slid open automatically without having to be called, and we stepped inside. I stared at the numbers as they counted up. Zac watched me the whole time, the corner of his mouth curled.

"Cut it out, would you?" I said.

"What?"

"The mysterious smile. It's annoying."

"Hey, I'm sorry, but it's kind of funny, you know?" he said, looking straight ahead.

"What is?"

"You. Not remembering, being all..." he looked up, trying to find the right word.

"All what?" I said, with a sigh. "All stupid?"

"No, being all shy and hating the attention. Like when it all first started. It's sort of nice to have you back."

The elevator pinged open on the top floor, and I stepped out before I could read too much into what Zac was saying.

On either end of the corridor, large windows looked out onto the city to the east and west.

"Wow, I really live here?" I said, walking towards the window and looking down at the river beneath us. In the dull grey light of morning, it was almost possible to pretend London was whole again from up here.

"Yep. All the top brass were moved here when the war first started. When they didn't think London would ever come under attack. Now you're the only one left."

"Why?"

"They didn't think it was safe."

"And were they right?" I said, remembering the shattered glass buildings I'd seen yesterday.

"It's palladium-based glass," Zac said, knocking on the window with a bent knuckle. "It can withstand a force of up to two hundred thousand pounds per square inch. There are sentry guns on the roof with motion trackers that have a one hundred-meter-range sensitivity. And surface-to-air missiles positioned all around to take out any aerial attacks. But even then... probably not. I mean, where is safe these days? The brass keep asking you to move into the Hub with the rest of the S3. But you insisted. Said something about not running away and being a beacon for hope."

"God, I'm a real dick, aren't I?"

Zac didn't answer. He smiled and walked me towards the only door on the floor, marked with a large, silver number one. I dug in my pockets for a key. But they were empty.

"It's DNA-sensitive. Only you can open it," Zac said, pointing at a small silver panel on the side of the door.

"Oh, right."

I placed my hand on the panel. It was cold, sucking the warmth out of my hand. Something scratched across my palm and, after a second, the door swung open with a clunk. I looked down at my hand, where a thin red line cut across my palm.

"It takes a skin sample," Zac said in explanation.

"Welcome home, Commandant Tyler," a female, computerised voice said as I stepped through the door.

I groaned at my own arrogance. "Mum? Katie?" I called out.

"Scott," Zac said, "you live alone."

I turned around to face him. "What? Then where are they?"

All humour had left his expression. "Your parents were moved north when the attacks started."

"And Katie?" I said, fear tightening my chest.

"Well, I guess she's in training."

"Training? You don't mean… Katie is a Shifter?" I said, grabbing my head in my hands, not wanting to believe it.

There had been a moment a few days ago when I thought that maybe Katie might be a Shifter, too. But I'd hoped, prayed, it had been my imagination. All I wanted for my little sister was a normal, stable life, where the biggest things she had to worry about were her exam results and whether some boy liked her. Not this. I thought about what my life had become since the day I'd met Aubrey. How crazy it all was. How close to crazy I'd become because of it. This life was the last thing I wanted for Katie.

"Probably," Zac said. "Every relative of a Shifter is tested, you know, to see. But don't worry, Scotty. The Shifter academy is probably one of the safest places in the country after the Hub. She'll be fine. Besides, you went into training a sorry shell of a kid, and" – he slapped me on the shoulder – "look at you now."

I must have looked pretty pathetic, as he started to laugh.

"Thanks," I said. "I guess."

I walked farther into the room and looked around. Could this flat really be mine? It was too clean for a start, not a thing out of place. And too big for one person alone. It had an open-plan living room and kitchen that was bigger that our whole ground floor at home. I'd dreamed of having a place of my own. Somewhere that Mum and Dad couldn't bother me. Now that I did have it, all I wanted was for Katie to come jumping out from the built-in cupboard, shouting, "Surprise!"

"Can I go and see her?" I asked.

"Your sister? Sure, I guess. I mean, you're the Commandant. You can do pretty much whatever you want."

Me, the Commandant. In charge of all the Shifters. I couldn't quite get over that. I put the letters the receptionist had given me down on a glass coffee table and picked up a notebook. I opened it to read a page filled with my scratchy handwriting, but I didn't really understand any of it. There was a list of names. A request to form a new squadron dated a week ago.

I turned the page around to face Zac. "What's this about?"

"Thirteen squadron? That's your new S3 unit. Handpicked from the best of the S3, including myself, naturally."

I ignored Zac's bragging. "Tell me about the S3."

"The Special Shifting Service. It's kind of like the SAS but, you know, with Shifters. We're divided into thirty squadrons of ten. Shifters, soldiers, all working together for the greater good. S3 is the only mixed unit of its kind in the country. It's kinda an experiment to see if it can work."

"And can it?"

"It's only been operational for a few months, so I guess we'll see. The Minister for Defence seems to think so. He moved his operations to the Hub last week."

I put the pad down and looked for anything that struck me as familiar in the room. There was nothing. Not a picture. Not an ornament that was part of my old life. This other me was a complete mystery.

"I still can't get over this," Zac said. "You seriously can't remember a thing?"

"Nope."

"Well, I guess it's been a tough few days. Hell, it's been a tough few years. It will come back to you."

"What if it doesn't? What if I can't ever remember?"

"Then you fake it till you make it, Scott. You're still you, still the same powers, no matter what you can or can't remember."

I wasn't convinced. I didn't know who this Scott Tyler was. I wandered over to the bookshelves. They were filled with what looked like military strategy books. *The Art of War* by Sun Tzu. *On War* by Carl von Clausewitz. They all looked pretty well read. Where were my comic books and tatty SF novels?

"I think it's best if I go. Leave you alone," Zac said.

"No," I said forcefully, surprising even myself. "I mean, stay a bit. Maybe you can help me remember."

"If you're sure," Zac shrugged, and then vaulted over a low grey sofa, landing lying down. He reached for a remote control and fired up an enormous TV fixed to the wall.

It was tuned to a news channel, broadcasting a report about the British army's latest victory in the Middle East. It showed footage of men and women wearing orange jumpsuits, bags over their heads and their arms tied behind their backs, being shepherded into waiting trucks by soldiers.

"Prop," Zac said, flicking over to another news channel. "More prop. Do you have any games?"

"I have no idea. And what's prop?"

"Propaganda. All the channels are pumping it out 24/7, keeping everyone believing that the good guys are winning the fight."

"And are we?" I said, easing into an armchair.

He glanced up from the screen and sucked his teeth. "That depends."

"On what?"

"On who you think the good guys are."

"Are you saying we're not?"

"No!" Zac said, sitting up. "God, no." He looked around, as if nervous that we were being listened to. "It's only that it's not as simple as all that."

"So tell me. From the start. Who are we fighting and why?"

Zac sighed. And began.

CHAPTER FIVE

"No one really knows what started it. There wasn't a single incident, like a duke getting shot or someone invading Poland. If there was, we probably could have done something about it. It sort of grew and grew. And before we realised we were actually fighting a war, it was too late. Some people think it began with 9/11 and the way the West reacted with the air strikes on the Middle East. The Arab states were pretty miffed, as you can guess, and stopped all the oil flow to the west. After that, we were scrabbling around looking for alternative fuels. Fracking everywhere we could, destroying landscapes to get at the liquid oil deep in the earth. Which was what made the Green lot crazy. At the same time, Scotland voted to become independent and planned on whacking *their* oil prices up."

"That explains the flag," I said, realising what was wrong with the flags I'd seen painted on the Rhino and the vehicles. "It's missing the St Andrew's Cross."

"Yeah, they stripped it off after Scotland devolved. Only, the British government overruled the Scottish vote and kind of invaded. As you can imagine, that didn't go down well with the Scots. Or the Irish or the Welsh. Or pretty much anyone, really. And by that point, we were being attacked on all sides."

"What do you mean? We're not only fighting one enemy?"

"Not at the start," Zac said, kicking his shoes off and putting his feet up on the arm of the sofa. "In the early days, it was like everyone was after us. Anarchists, Islamist groups, even the Communists got back in the trying-to-kill-us game. There were air raids and bomb strikes. Two hundred thousand people died in the first year. We've lost count since."

I shook my head. It was impossible to take this all in.

Zac sniffed and carried on. "They say there was a nuke strike on Britain back in 2010, only some Shifter managed to avert it. Not sure if I believe it; more prop, if you ask me. But it did make Shifters popular with the great British public."

"They know about Shifters?"

"Know about us? They love us! Especially you. Come on, Scott, don't tell me you don't remember your ad campaign."

"No. Way."

Zac burst out laughing. "It was hysterical. You, standing in a field somewhere, with the British flag flapping behind your head, looking all heroic. So cheesy. Anyway, it worked. People started to see us as symbols of defiance. If a bunch of kids could stand up to the enemy, so could they. And slowly, we started winning. We had help, of course. The Americans, the French. And now it looks as if we've almost got the Emperor of China on our side."

"Hang on, there's an Emperor now? What happened to President Tsing?" I said, remembering the old man I'd met with his Shifting guard, the *Banjai Gonsi*.

"He died, and what with all the chaos, the people decided they needed an Emperor again. So his son, Tzen, was appointed. Or anointed. I don't know how it works. Anyway, he's due to sign a treaty making them our ally. And then, no one will mess with us."

"So it could all be over soon?"

"Only, we'll still have the Red Hand to deal with." I didn't like the look on Zac's face. All the time he'd been talking about death, he'd hardly shown any emotion, as if he had become desensitised to it all. But one mention of these Red Hand and he looked genuinely afraid. "They're a new religion that sprang up after the war. No one really knows where it started or what they believe in. It's something about trusting completely in God. What we do know is that they hate us."

"Us as in the British?"

"No, us as in Shifters. They say we're an abomination and as such should be destroyed. They're the ones who were behind the attack on Old Street." His face scrunched in disgust. "We lost seventy-three Shifters in that attack."

I listened to him, trying desperately to find some glimmer of something familiar in what he said. But it only left me feeling even more confused and sick.

So much death. And all because of me. Because I stopped Frankie controlling all those politicians. She'd said herself that if she hadn't been manipulating and guiding them, they'd bring chaos down on the planet. And she was right.

I couldn't wait for Aubrey any more. I had to make this right now. I covered my face with my hands and reached out for a decision I could change that would undo all of this. But I had to be so careful, so absolutely certain, that whatever reality I brought about next wasn't worse than this one. I thought about my decision to confront Frankie at the party. When I led Aubrey and the rest to the Pyramid, I'd made them promise to focus so we could all get out of there if needed. I could wipe that decision away. Let Frankie get away with it all. I didn't care, so long as I was back there with Aubrey.

I held that moment in my mind and pushed. But nothing.

My power wasn't working. Panic bubbled in my stomach. What if it wasn't fear stopping me after all? What if entropy was catching up with me? If I lost my power to Shift before I had a chance to fix this, I'd be stuck here, knowing that I was responsible for it all. It was unthinkable.

I risked testing it on something small, something that could have no effect. I reached into my pocket. My fingers found a small coin, a five-pence piece. I rested it on my thumb, focused on the two options and flicked.

"Tails." I caught it and opened my hand. It lay heads up. I focused on Shifting my choice.

"What's that?" Zac said.

"What did I just say?" I asked him.

"You said heads. What are you doing?"

I slipped the coin into my pocket. "Just testing something."

That meant my power to Shift worked. So, why wasn't I able to change the decision that led us to the Pyramid that night? Why wasn't I able to Shift us out of all of this crap?

"I'm sorry, is all this talk of anarchy in the UK boring you?" Zac said.

"No," I turned back to him. "It's so much to take in, you know?"

"I guess," he shrugged. "I've had a few years to get used to the idea. But now, for serious, you need to go get changed and get some more sleep. The war will still be here when you wake up."

"Not if I can stop it," I said.

Zac laughed, loud but sharp. "Good luck trying. ARES have had Shifters on the case ever since all of this began. And they only seem to make it worse. The war has become a singularity. Too many people pinning it in place. Personally, I think we need to ride it out."

"Still think if you avoid using your power, you can escape entropy?"

Zac's face crumpled in confusion. "What? No. Is that a thing?"

"No," I said quickly. "I mean, I don't think it is. But you do. I mean, did. I mean, I don't know." I stood up, as much to stop the conversation as to do what I'd come here to do. "Where's the bathroom?"

"How should I know? You've never let me up here before."

He reached for the remote again as I wandered through the flat, opening doors. I finally found the bathroom: a room as big as my bedroom at home, with light grey tiles lining floor and ceiling and a huge shower head suspended in the centre. I peeled off my clothes, noticing the aches and the series of bruises across my body. They ranged from bright purple to greenish yellow. I caught a glimpse of myself in the large mirror hanging over the sink. Ribs sticking out, hip bones jutting. When was the last time I had eaten? I also rubbed at the tattooed S on my arm. Did we all have this? I wondered. Marking us out as Shifters? It seemed that in this reality, there was no need to hide our power. Instead, it was being put to good use protecting the country. Maybe Shifters in this reality were proud of who they were, whereas I'd always been strangely ashamed of my power. And I knew that Aubrey felt the same. We'd promised each other that once we'd found all the members of Ganymede, we'd quit and go about our lives. Well, there was no chance of that happening in this reality.

I threw the switch for the shower and stood under it, letting the high-pressure water pound on my skin. It hurt and felt good for it. I grabbed a bar of soap and scrubbed at my skin, trying to wash off the ground-in dirt, which had stained my skin. As I started to feel if not exactly human, then at least one rung up from vegetable, there was a knocking on the door.

"Alright," I shouted. "I'm finishing." I regretfully turned off the shower. Zac hadn't stopped banging.

"What?" I said, throwing open the door as soon as I'd found a towel to wrap around me.

"We're needed at HQ now," Zac said, his face grim and grey. "It's the Red Hand."

KIM CURRAN

CHAPTER SIX

The lights flashed red in the Hub when we returned. A level three alert, I knew somehow. People were rushing back and forth: soldiers kitting themselves up, support staff pushing computer equipment around. Zac and I headed straight for the command room.

Sergeant Cain waved me over to where he stood with Cooper and Turner. Cooper was sucking on a gold medallion while Turner nervously fiddled with the equipment on her belt.

"What's happened?" I said.

"The Red Hand have sent us a little message." Cain pressed a button and an image started playing out on the screen.

A woman sat in a dark room, with a bag over her head. People stood in the shadows behind her, red scarves pulled over their faces. One of them tugged the bag off, revealing the woman was in her late twenties with blonde, curly hair. She blinked in the light.

"That's Lieutenant Sarah Edwards," Cain said. "She was one of two S3 spies we had under cover in the Red Hand."

"Looks like she was found out," Zac said.

"The video went live half an hour ago and has already had three thousand hits," Turner said.

"You stand accused of crimes against God's will," a muffled voice from the video said. It was clearly going through a vocoder, which gave it an eerie robotic quality.

"I don't know what you mean," Edwards said.

A scarved figure stepped forwards, squatted down in front of Edwards and took her face in their hand. Edwards tried to pull herself free, but their grip was too strong.

"You are an operative for the British army. You have been spying on us," the robotic voice said.

Even with the grainy film quality and the low light I could see Edwards eyes widen in fear. "No… I, I was…"

They slapped her hard across the face, silencing her attempts at defending herself. "Don't deny it! One of your fellow rats has already given you up!" That voice was starting to unnerve me, like nails on a blackboard.

Edwards shook her head.

"What's that?" the interrogator said. "Your country can't hear you." They pulled Edwards by the hair till she faced forward, staring into the camera.

"Yes, you stupid bitch. I've been spying on you. And I hope they find you and kill you using the information I've given them.

The dark figure let go of Edwards' hair. "Thank you for your co-operation."

It was hard to see what was happening, but I could hear Edwards shouting. A dark hand holding something metallic reached around her neck. Her screams became high-pitched and incomprehensible. Then there was a blur of movement, a flash of light, and Edwards went silent. The figure stepped aside, revealing Edwards slumped in the chair, her head flopped against her chest, a steady flow of blood pooling on the floor around her feet.

The dark figure strode towards the camera, eyes covered by dark glasses, face completely hidden by their scarf.

"She is the first to be found guilty," they said, straight into the camera. "We have one more of your operatives. We will kill him within the hour unless you free our men. There is no bargaining. No conditions. An exchange of lives. It is God's will."

The figure held up their right hand and I could see it was covered in blood. They pressed it against the lens of the camera, leaving a red smudge that obscured everything else. And then the video went blank.

I swallowed down the bile that had risen into my throat. "Are we going to make the exchange?" I said.

"Of course not, Tyler. We don't negotiate with terrorists. But we do know their location, thanks to Edwards, and the air force are going to strike within the hour."

"But what about the other spy? What will happen to him?"

"We get him back." Cain smiled and handed me a file. A picture of a square-jawed, sharp-eyed young man looked up at me. The name read Captain Hedges.

"He looks familiar," I said.

"He should do. He was one of ARES' finest. I trained him myself. From what little intel we've got, they've tortured him."

"What can he tell?"

"Mission objectives. Base locations. But it's not what he can tell them that concerns us as much as what he can tell us."

"Which is?"

"Whatever he was about to reveal before he was caught. He was only able to transmit a fragment of a message: 'X73. Attack.' Our team are trying to decipher it now. Hedges may know what it means. We need that intel."

"So what do we do?"

"We go in there and we get him. In and out before the air force brings the rain. And you," Cain said, shoving something into my chest, "are leading the extraction. Get your squad together. We've got five minutes."

The thing in my hands was a black flak jacket. Gone were the ARES letters.

"Zac?"

"Here, sir," he said, stepping forwards, formality on show once more. "The rest of Thirteen are on standby."

"OK, right. The squad. Get them. And are Aubrey and Cleo back yet?"

"Still out on their mission," Zac said.

"I am afraid you will need to put up with my flying instead, sir."

I turned to see a woman with dark, curled hair tucked neatly under a red beret. She wore bright red lipstick to match, which I was pretty sure couldn't be regulation. She carried her helmet under an arm and I was able to read her name off the tag on the side. Ladoux. She had been the one on the other end of the mic when Aubrey called for an evac. Her accent was clearer now – a subtle sing-song of French.

"Flying Officer Ladoux reporting for duty, sir." She pulled off a sharp, textbook salute. Behind her stood three other soldiers: two men and one woman. Like Ladoux, they carried their helmets under their arms and were dressed in combats, flak jackets and red berets. Each had a fresh number thirteen in white paint in the side of their helmets. They stood in various poses of readiness, but none of them had the twitchy nervousness I'd expected from a bunch of people about to go up against a bunch of armed crazies. It was clear that they'd all seen action before.

Ladoux snapped her arm back to her side. "Gunship all but fired up and ready to go, sir."

"Right, thanks, Ladoux," I said.

One of the men stepped forward. He was chewing gum as if his life depended on it and had the wide-eyed stare of a man who hadn't slept in weeks. "Gunner Unwin ready to go, sir. This sounds like a classic point-and-shoot situation. You point. I shoot." He grinned, happy with what I guessed was a well-practised joke.

The woman behind him clipped him around the head. "Stop showing off, Unwin." She was a broad woman who looked to be in her late forties, judging by the streaks of grey in her brown hair and creases around her bright grey eyes. "Trooper Ward, sir. And this is Sapper Williamson." She pointed at the last solider, a man in his late twenties with soft brown eyes and a spattering of freckles across his nose. He smiled, showing dazzlingly white teeth, and saluted.

"Can I say it's a great honour to serve with you?" Ward continued. "We won't let you down. Isn't that right, Unwin?" She fixed him with a matronly glare.

Unwin nodded. "One hundred percent, sir."

Cooper and Turner fell into position next to Zac. My squad. Shifters and soldiers. Children and adults. All itching for a fight.

"OK," I said, addressing the Shifters. "Standard procedure. You follow my lead, keep all the alternatives open to you so you can Shift. But remember, you don't Shift to save your own arse. We're a team here. You Shift for the greater good. *Ad verum via.* You got it?"

"*Ad verum via,*" the entire squad, including the soldiers, shouted. It seemed that it was not the first time they'd heard ARES' old motto. Towards the true way.

"Right," I said, gathering myself. "And you lot," I said, addressing the soldiers. "Try and keep up."

The squad all pulled off a salute. "Sir, yes, sir!" they shouted. Cooper and Turner copied it, a moment late.

"We know the drill sir," Ladoux said after the echo of their shout died down.

It was weird. As much as I didn't recognise where I was or what was going on, this all felt strangely familiar. Like I'd done it many times before. Perhaps it was all that training at ARES kicking in. Or maybe some of the me from this reality was starting to return.

"It's oh seven hundred. You've got under an hour before the air strike," Cain said. "Reports are they're heavily armed, with at least one hundred men guarding the building. You're to get in and get out, fast. You are not to engage with the enemy. Your only priority is to get Hedges out alive; do you understand me?"

I remembered the kids in the ward. "Let's hope this goes a bit smoother than our last mission."

Cain leant forward and lowered his voice so the others couldn't hear. "War is never smooth, Tyler. You keep your head about you and you'll be fine." He squeezed my shoulder and then pushed me away. "Get to it."

I pulled the flak jacket on and headed for the exit, the squad falling into place behind me. A helmet was thrust into my hands, and I strapped it on without even needing to fiddle for the straps. I was aware of the crackle of white noise in my ear, which must have been coming from an earpiece embedded in the helmet. I reached my hand up to my collar, as I'd see Aubrey doing, and sure enough, I found a button.

"How long should it take us to get there? I asked Ladoux.

"No more than ten minutes, Com." Her accent made the word "Com" sound like "comb". What was a French woman doing serving with the British special services? I wondered.

Zac checked his watch. "That only leaves fifty minutes before the strike."

"Plenty of time," Unwin said. "We'll be in and out like a virgin on his wedding night."

"Unwin!" Ward said, shaking her head.

"Sorry, Mum," Unwin said.

I looked at the two of them, wondering if Ward really was his mother. But as Unwin was black and Ward was white, I assumed it must be a nickname for the older woman. She certainly was keeping him in check like a mum, though. Something about the warmth behind her stern stare reminded me of my own mother.

We all rode up in the lift together. The team were almost indistinguishable now in their visored helmets and black fatigues. Adrenaline bubbled through my blood, making my muscles twitch. I curled my hands into fists. This felt good. All the fear and doubt of the past few hours were vanishing, replaced with a sense of control. I reached into my pocket and pulled out the tube of painkillers. I didn't want any distractions. I swallowed three tablets just to be sure.

"Let's go."

The doors were already opening as we approached, and out on the street, a black helicopter was waiting. Ladoux ran ahead, hopping into the pilot's seat. After a few moments, the blades of the copter started to spin, blowing litter into dancing spirals. I climbed in, ducking to avoid the downdraft of the blades. The rest followed, and we all strapped ourselves in as the bird took off.

I looked down on a London I could hardly recognise. The damage was not restricted to the centre – it spread as far as I could see. Buildings lay in crumpled heaps. Bridges crossing the Thames were buckled and some completely gone. This city, the city I called my home, had taken a battering.

All was still beneath us, no lights on in offices or houses lit up to welcome people home. But I could see, far to the north, pinpoints of lights marking out streets. Where life carried on as usual.

The copter buzzed through the grey skies, heading west into a low-wattage sun. It dropped low, and I could make out the reflection of the whirring blades in the rippling water.

"We got company," Ladoux said, yanking the controls to the left.

"Rocket!" Zac shouted.

I clung on as a trail of fire came from a rooftop and headed straight for us.

Ladoux pulled back on the stick, easing the copter into a vertical climb. The rocket soared beneath us, heading straight for a building on the other side of the river. The shockwave from the explosion hit us a few seconds later, making the copter shake. But Ladoux was in total control. She righted the bird and guided it closer to the riverbank.

"Nice flying, Ladoux," Zac said.

She simply smiled in response.

"Since when has the Red Hand had SAMs?" Unwin said, looking back out of the window at where the rocket had struck.

SAMs. Surface-to-air missiles. I didn't know if I knew that from this reality or from playing too much *Duty Calls*.

"When they hit a supply truck last week," Zac said.

Unwin sucked his teeth. "Man, hitting us with our own weapons is cheating."

"I guess their god is all out of lightning bolts," Williamson said, which got a chuckle from everyone in the copter. All except, I noticed, Ladoux. Perhaps the mention of lightning while flying wasn't amusing.

"I won't be able to set down here," she said sternly. "So you'll need to jump."

I pulled back the doors and looked down. It was a ten-foot drop to the pavement below. Which might not be so bad if the copter didn't keep lurching left and right.

Zac clambered towards me, and without a moment's hesitation, he stepped out onto the skid of the copter and leapt off. He landed in a crouch on the pavement below, then straightened up and smiled at me.

Well, if he was going to show off...

I took a deep breath and stepped out into the air. The shock of landing passed all the way up my shins, my spine and even into my teeth. On my injured leg, I hadn't made such a graceful job of it as Zac, and it took me a moment before I could stand up.

The rest of Thirteen squad followed, dropping out of the helicopter like conkers falling from a tree. Cooper and Turner came last, leaping out at the same time. The copter peeled away, leaving us standing in front of the huge tower block.

CHAPTER SEVEN

"I'll put down somewhere and then come find you," Ladoux said over the radio. "Break some balls."

This was the S3's way of saying good luck, I knew somehow. The words "good luck" themselves had become a bad omen, although I couldn't remember why.

We moved silently in crouched runs, keeping to the shadows, coming to a stop behind a cluster of bushes.

The Red Hand's base was a deserted council block, eighteen floors high. It had once been painted a pale blue, as if that would somehow make it blend into the sky.

"Looks like they have Hedges on the tenth floor," Zac whispered, pointing up at the windows.

"What makes you say that?" I asked.

Zac pushed down the visor on my helmet and pressed a button on the side, turning everything a pale blue. As my eyes adjusted, I could make out Zac in front of me, his body marked out by a red glow.

"Heat vision," he said.

I could see the red of the outlines of the members of the squad around me and, when I turned to look at the building, fuzzy orange figures moving around behind the glass. Without me needing to do anything, the image zoomed in, reacting to my irises focusing, maybe. Zac was right; I could see two figures carrying the cold, black outlines of weapons, pacing in front of a man huddled on the floor, his back pressed up against the windows, purple strips around his wrists. Handcuffs, I guessed.

I scanned the rest of the building: five men on the bottom floor. Two on the roof with RPGs, if I guessed the shapes of the things slung across their backs correctly, and double sentries on the sixth, eighth and twelfth floors. Fifteen men in total. Hardly the small army Cain had told us to expect.

I pushed the visor up. "Right. Unwin, Williamson and Ward, I want you to stay here and provide cover. Turner, Cooper and Black," I said, turning to Zac, "you're with me."

The three soldiers lowered their visors and raised their weapons. I did the same, pressing the button on the side of my helmet to cycle through the vision options – thermo, night vision, x-ray – till it was clear to see and I set off. We moved in silence, communicating in hand signals, which I was surprised to realise I knew. A jab of a hand to indicate move forward, a clenched fist by the side of the head to tell the others to stop. I guess I must have picked them up from watching too many war movies.

I thought about every step I was taking, each time I ducked rather than dodged, holding all the moments in my mind in case I needed to Shift. And I knew the rest of the team around me were doing exactly the same thing.

I held my fist up and we all stopped behind a small metal building. On the third floor, there was a large, arched window. The only thing in the entire building not made out of hard, sharp edges.

I pointed it out to Zac. "Can we get up there?"

"Sure thing." Zac shrugged off his backpack and pulled out a grappling hook attached to a long rope. He slotted it into the barrel of a gun.

I crept out from behind the cover of the wall, Zac, Turner and Cooper behind me, and headed for the building. Zac took aim and with a click, the grapple soared into the air and over the top of the building. Zac tugged twice on the rope and nodded for Cooper to go up. The boy pulled a gold medallion out from under his collar, kissed it, and then grabbed hold of the rope. He braced his feet against the glass surface of the building and started to walk up.

Turner watched him, chewing on the side of her finger, gasping for air every time he slipped or made a wrong move. After a minute, he was at the third floor, next to the large window. He wrapped his foot around the rope and hung there, one hand free.

He pulled out a small blue hammer and laid his head and a hand against the glass, like a safe cracker listening for the telltale clicks, moved a few times till he found a place he was happy with, then hit the spot above his fingers with the hammer. At first, he only succeeded in smashing a hole in the glass. Cooper sighed into his helmet. Then there was that strange, jolting sensation when someone makes a Shift. The glass shattered, falling like rain around us in a shower of diamonds. It was kind of beautiful to watch.

Cooper stood on the window ledge and waved Turner up. She clambered up the rope after him, and Zac and I quickly followed.

We were in an empty flat. It reeked of dead animals, and a stained mattress lay on the floor. All the interior walls had been knocked through, creating one large, unliveable space. Graffiti covered every surface, including that word I'd seen earlier. "Shine."

Cooper had his head out of the window, gathering up the rope, when an explosion shook the building. I watched him fall, his hands clawing at the air. Then suddenly, he was hanging half in, half out of the window. Turner had Shifted and grabbed him by his flak jacket.

"Thanks," he said as she pulled him through.

"You owe me," she said, dusting her hand on her leg.

"Consider it payback from when I warned you about Matt."

"You didn't warn me," Turner said. "You set me up with him!"

"Oh, yeah. But only because I was hoping he'd make me look—"

Their banter was cut off by the cracking of gunfire.

"I guess the Red Hand know we're here," I said. "We'd better move fast."

Without needing direction, my team spread out to cover both the window we'd come in and the door I was about to exit through. I was poised to open the door when I felt a hand on my arm. Cooper held up a thin, black tube, about eight inches long – a fibre-optic camera. He attached one end of the tube to his tablet and slid the other end through the small gap under the door. A moment later, a grey image appeared on his screen. The corridor outside. The camera moved to the left, revealing the way was clear. To the right, two large figures stood with their backs to the camera. Behind them, I was pretty sure despite the grainy image, was a sentry gun.

I patted my pockets and found what I knew would be there. A quantum grenade.

"A cat?" Zac said. "Good thinking."

We called the grenades the "cat in the box", after our lessons about Schrödinger. It was designed to go off in a variety of ways. Sometimes it would explode like a normal grenade, other times it gave off a flash of blinding light, depending on which button on the clip we pressed. The random nature gave Shifters the advantage, as we were able to Shift through the various options till the one most advantageous to us worked. I clicked the dial on the clip with my thumb, thinking about all the options open to me. And then settled on flash.

The door creaked open so loudly, I expected the men to turn around to investigate. But looking at them in the screen, they were still facing the opposite way. I'd have to get their attention for the flash grenade to work.

I threw open the door and stepped out. "Oi!" I shouted, at the same time throwing the grenade in a small arc so it came bouncing to a stop next to their feet.

They turned around and looked from me to the grenade, just as it erupted in white light.

Only then did I realise the men were wearing helmets, stolen from the army by the looks of things, which included visors that protected against flash grenades. Before they had a chance to run at me, I Shifted, this time going for the sleeping gas.

With that weird flipping in the stomach I'd missed so much, I was standing in front of two men who were slowly sinking to the ground, the Morphothane gas taking them down before they even had a chance to turn around. I waited for the gas to dissipate, then gestured for the team to come out.

We stepped over the sleeping guards, Cooper and Turner stripping them of their stolen helmets and armour before I even had to say a word. I pointed at Zac and then to the sentry gun. He was to stay here and cover this corridor. He nodded, a little too enthusiastically, I thought. I could hardly blame him. Even I was starting to have fun.

I didn't want to admit it, but it was true. I was getting the kick of all kicks out of this. I could never remember having felt so calm and in control in my life. I guess it was adrenaline taking over. Whatever it was, I liked it.

Cooper, Turner and I pressed on, through a door marked "In Case of Emergencies" and up the staircase. Only seven flights to go.

The sounds of gunfire hadn't abated from outside, and every now and then, there was another explosion. We ran up the staircase, taking two steps at a time, till we came to the tenth floor. I nodded at Cooper, watching as he pulled the same trick with the camera. His eager smile reminded me of Jake. I wondered again where he was now his life wasn't being controlled by a government agency. I'd track him down as soon as I was back at base.

The tenth-floor corridor was empty. This door opened with a creak and I slid out, holding a hand up to the other two, telling them to wait.

Voices came from up ahead, loud and angry. I crept closer, till I could hear what they were saying. From what I could gather, it was two members of the Red Hand arguing.

"Why don't we kill him and get out of here?"

"Slate said we were to keep him alive."

"Then leave him here. I didn't sign up to get bloody bombed!"

Bombed? I thought. Did they know about the air strike?

"What did you sign up for, then? All that stuff we said at our initiation about trusting in God? Don't you believe anymore, brother?"

"What good will God do me if I get my bloody head blown off?"

I took a few steps closer to the open doorway. I risked the tiniest of glances around the door. It was another flat that had been converted into an open space. Exposed wooden frames were all that was left of the walls. Two large men stood with their noses an inch apart; a man was bound and gagged on the floor behind them. Hedges. Jackpot.

I strode forward and pulled out my gun.

"You should have listened to your brother," I said and fired, sending two bullets into the chest of the man on the left.

The second man dove for cover while letting off a spray of bullets. I ducked back around the doorway, as the frame next to me exploded in a shower of plaster and wood splinters. Eventually, the gunfire stopped and a clicking noise filled the space. The man was empty.

I straightened up and raced through the door before he had a chance to reload. It was a risky move. But hey, if it didn't work out, I'd Shift and take the more sensible option.

It did work out. As the man tried to replace the magazine of his machine gun, I jumped up, grabbing hold of an exposed heating pipe overhead, and swung, hitting him in the face with the heavy soles of both of my boots. He let out a loud *oof* and toppled over. I landed on his chest, with a knee on his throat. I leant forward till I heard a wet crunching sound. The man went still.

I clambered off him and looked around to see if there was anyone else here. Only Hedges and me.

"Clear," I shouted. A moment later, Turner and Cooper crept into the room.

I walked over to Hedges. He stared at the man on the floor, and I couldn't tell if it was disgust or relief on his face. I pulled the gag out of his mouth.

He coughed, gasping for air. "Thank you," he said, through puffed lips. It looked like he was missing a few teeth, and his left eye was swollen completely closed. It seems Cain had been right about the torture.

"You're safe now," I said, pulling out my knife and slicing through his bindings.

The sounds of gunfire outside lessened. But it wasn't over. "You know the drill. You follow me closely. You don't take your eyes off me, you hear? So, stay sharp. Stay focused and you will get out of here." I helped Hedges to his feet.

As I turned, there was a grunt and a gunshot. The man I'd shot had used the last of his breath to try to complete his duty. Hedges looked down and patted his body, trying to find the wound. But there was none.

On the floor, in front of us, lay a body. Cooper had instinctively leapt in front of the bullet.

I crouched down and pulled his helmet off. His eyes were wide and staring, looking desperately for a way out. Turner knelt down on the other side and took his hand.

"You'll be OK, Coops." She was lying. The boy was dying. But any minute now, the hypnic would kick in and Cooper would find a way to Shift himself back to life. Maybe he'd have pushed Hedges out of the way or have been on the other side of the room when the gun was fired. He sure as hell wouldn't have sacrificed his life for some mission.

I couldn't allow that. We had a job to do. I held Cooper's face in my hands and stared into his eyes.

"It's OK," I said, Fixing him – stopping him from undoing any of his decisions. "It will all be OK. You did good."

He smiled up at me, grateful I was there at his last moment. Not knowing that I was the one killing him.

He jerked, his limbs twitching, and then went still. I laid him on the floor and closed his eyes.

CHAPTER EIGHT

Turner bent over Cooper's body, rocking.

"On your feet, Private," I said. We didn't have time for this. "On your feet." I yanked her to standing. When I saw the look of pain on her face, something in me softened. "Come on," I said, patting her on the shoulder. "There's nothing we can do now."

She sniffed back the tears, repositioned her gun strap and followed me out the door.

I helped Hedges down the stairs, as he was struggling to stand. There were raw, red marks on his arms and legs and bloodstains on his shirt. How much had the Red Hand put him through? How close had he been to breaking?

When we got to the third floor, Zac fell back into position without saying a word. And without explaining the three new bodies lying dead in the corridor. He'd clearly had some action of his own.

We slipped out of the window; Zac and Turner helping Hedges make the leap down to the ground.

It was silent outside now. Not a single gunshot. We crept around to the front of the building as Unwin staggered around the corner, groaning and swearing. Williamson came after him, a steady stream of blood pouring down the side of his face. Between them they were carrying the limp body of Ward. Her grey eyes stared straight up at the sky.

They laid her on the floor, and Unwin let out a steady stream of angry swears.

"They had a rocket launcher," Williamson said, using the cuff of his sleeve to wipe away some of the blood.

This had not been the in-and-out extraction we had planned. I checked my watch: less than fifteen minutes to get out before the air strike. "Where's Ladoux?"

"Speak of the devil," Unwin said, nodding behind me.

I turned to see Ladoux jogging across a patch of grass. She ran straight past us and stopped in front of Hedges. She pulled him into a quick hug.

Hedges winced. Embarrassed at this public show of affection or because her embrace had caused him pain, I wasn't sure.

Ladoux let him go and then smoothed down the front of her shirt. "They didn't hurt you too much?"

Hedges shook his head.

"Unwin and I are fine too, by the way," Williamson said. "Just in case you were wondering. Ward and Cooper not so much."

Ladoux looked down at Ward's body, her smile vanishing in an instant. "Where's Coops? What happened?"

"We almost got our arses handed to us is what happened. They knew we were coming," Unwin said, throwing a fresh piece of gum into his mouth.

"How is that possible?" Zac said.

"I don't know. But they were ready," Williamson said.

"Well, you got what we came for," Ladoux said, looking back at Hedges.

"Oh, sure. Mission accomplished. Whoopy-freaking-do!" Unwin said.

"Not yet," I said. "We still need to get Hedges back for—" I didn't have a chance to finish. Zac shoved me hard in the chest, there was a loud snap, and I felt white searing pain cut across my arm. Zac and I both hit the ground. We were under fire.

We rolled behind the smoking car to get some kind of cover.

"Get back!" I yelled at the team. They herded Hedges around the side of the building. We weren't in the clear yet.

"Up there," Zac said, pointing to the top of the building.

I flipped my visor into place and zoomed in on the figure. They were slim – a woman or child, maybe – holding a small pistol and pulling the trigger over and over, while they screamed in rage. The gun had stopped firing, the cartridge clearly empty, and yet they kept pulling the trigger. My visor flipped through filters till the person came into focus. It was a teenager. I couldn't tell which gender, thanks to the red hoodie they wore pulled up over a baseball cap. But I could see the tears pouring down their face.

I stood up, took aim, and fired. A single shot to the head and the figure crumpled to the ground. We waited to see if we were in the clear. Everything was silent apart from the crackle of fire coming from the burning building. Slowly, we stood up and stepped forward. It was over.

"Ten minutes," Zac said, meaning how long we had till the air force would get to work. Not that the strike was needed any more. The Red Hand had cleared out long ago, leaving only a small defence team behind. But I would be happy to see this block go up in flames anyway.

I nodded. "Let's get back to the bird."

Ladoux led us to where she'd landed the copter. Unwin and Williamson carried Ward's body and laid it in the cockpit. Turner dug out a blanket from her pack and covered the woman with it.

We stood for a while before getting back on board, looking towards the tower block. The strike would be coming any minute. I wondered if there were still some of the Red Hand in there and was surprised at how completely OK I would be if there were. They deserved to burn, I thought. Someone tugged on my arm. I yanked it away, irritated at whoever was there.

It was Turner. She held a white gauze bandage in her hand. "Your arm, sir."

The scrape was deep. Blood oozed steadily out of it, soaking into my uniform. I nodded at her to continue.

She worked quickly, cutting away my sleeve so she could get access to the wound. She mopped at it, throwing each soaked swab to the floor, then pulled out a tube.

"This may sting," she said, as she poured a line of glistening liquid into the cut.

She wasn't kidding. I had to bite down on my lip to stop myself from whimpering in pain. It was worse than the cut itself. She wrapped a bandage around my arm, tying it off in a neat bow.

"Thank you," I said.

"No problem," she said, packing up her equipment. She was about to walk away when she paused. "Cooper's body."

The strike was due any moment. "I'm sorry."

She nodded and forced a smile.

I felt Cooper's loss harder than made sense. As far as I was aware, I'd only met him yesterday. And yet there was a part of me that counted him as a friend, that had fought alongside him. The death of Ward hurt, too. I knew nothing about her. Had she been a mother? A wife? I would never know now. All I knew was that she was a good solider.

I looked at the rest of my squad. Unwin, the gunner – who even now was trying to make a joke, but his smile didn't reach his eyes – passed Turner a cigarette. She took it with a shaking hand and chugged on it, sending a cloud of blue smoke into the sky. Next to them, Williamson saw to the cut on his forehead, trying to hide how much pain he was in. Ladoux stared ahead, flicking the lid of a lighter open and closed. *Flick*. Open. *Flack*. Closed. Over and over, and yet she didn't smoke. And Hedges, frail and haunted, sat on the floor, unable to stay standing any more.

I looked from squad member to squad member, taking in as much as I could about them. Noticing how Williamson bit his nails and how the thin tan mark around Ladoux's fourth finger meant she used to wear a wedding ring. Had she lost her husband to the war? Tiny little details that made up the person.

I felt a wave of pride for my squad swell in my chest. "You did good," I said. "You all did good."

I was glad to hear the sound of the planes arriving to hide the choke in my throat.

We flew home into glorious mid-morning sunshine, as if the weather itself mocked us. The atmosphere in the copter on the return trip was heavy and numb. The rush of excitement was gone, leaving the cold reality of what had happened. We had won. The bad guys were dead or defeated. The good guys saved.

But at what cost?

Zac stared out of the window at the streets below, his angular features illuminated by the sunlight. I guess I could see what girls saw in Zac. What Aubrey probably saw in Zac, with his square jaw and Roman nose. It didn't make it any easier knowing he'd saved my life. Was that my blood flecked over his face or an enemy's?

I squeezed the bandage around my arm, feeling the sticky wetness of the blood seeping through, but I couldn't feel anything. Either the anaesthetic was doing its job or the adrenaline was. It wouldn't be long before they both wore off and the pain came back.

It's only pain, that voice in my head said again.

The copter banked hard and I had to hold on to a strap to stop myself from sliding.

"Set down in three," Ladoux said.

We dropped altitude fast, making my stomach flip so hard I thought someone had Shifted. I even looked around, hopeful that the world had changed. Everything was as it had been.

Whatever had taken over me back there in the battle was starting to fade, too. What was I doing? Leading men on missions when I should be working out a way to get the hell out of this reality. And yet I felt like I owed them all something. Felt responsible for them all.

Ladoux set the helicopter down and we piled out, the blades already slowing. Zac helped Hedges out, and walked him back into the Hub. Hedges really needed to go to the infirmary, but Cain told us he needed to be debriefed on whatever the hell X73 might mean first.

I let Zac and the rest walk ahead of me, grateful for this moment of peace. If the turmoil in my mind could ever be called peace.

My hands shook so hard, my fingers were a blur. I needed to keep it together for a little longer. Enough to get me through the next hour. The next day. Enough for me to find Aubrey and get us all out of here.

We rode the lift down in silence. Turner was fighting to hold back her sobs. Zac wrapped an arm around her, and she buried herself in his chest. Unwin too was trying hard to hide his tears. Williamson just let them flow. Ladoux, however, looked straight ahead, her expression as cold as my own. I swallowed a couple more of Frankie's painkillers.

The lights had returned to pale green and the alarm had been silenced. In its place was a stir of excited voices. As I stepped into the Hub, I couldn't believe what I saw. Everyone was smiling and laughing, as if I'd walked into a cocktail party rather than a military headquarters. A group of people were gathered in the middle, peering over each other's shoulders. A hand reached up to be high-fived by members of the group.

"What the hell is going on here?" I shouted, my voice cutting through the laughter. "What kind of animals are you people?"

The group parted as I walked forward, revealing Aubrey standing in the middle of the group, a smile frozen on her face.

CHAPTER NINE

The buzz of excitement silenced like a scratched record. The group who had all been gazing at Aubrey in delight turned to me, cowed and nervous. Eyes darted between the two of us like spectators at a tennis match.

"Captain Jones brought in the Red Hand's second in command," CP said, stepping forward. Her face was flushed and her fringe plastered to her face with sweat. "We were in and out before they knew what was happening. Nobody got as much as a scratch. You should have seen it, sir. She was incredible." CP's smile was spread so wide, it looked as if her head might flip in two. Aubrey had been smiling, but under the force of my stare, it faded into a complete blank.

"He's in the cells, Commandant," she said quietly. "Awaiting interrogation."

The group, sensing my anger, all suddenly found something more important to be doing, leaving me standing in front of Aubrey, CP at her side, and my squad behind me.

"Tyler," Zac said, a subtle warning in his voice.

I couldn't remember having ever felt anger like this. Hot and indignant and all directed at the girl I knew I loved.

"Nice work, Tyler." The slap on my back was so hard, I spun around, fists instinctively raised, ready to fight.

To his credit, Cain didn't even flinch. He merely looked me up and down.

"Two successes in a single day. Good work."

"Success," I said, the word hissing between my teeth. "You call the death of two people a success?"

"Extraction complete. I'd call that a success. The losses were…"

"Don't you dare," I shouted. "Don't you dare say collateral damage or wrap this up in military speak. They were my team and they're dead because of me."

Cain grabbed me by the arm and pulled me into the corner, away from Aubrey and the people watching. "Because of the enemy, Tyler. The enemy. They're the ones who killed our people. Not you."

"I led them in there. I let them die and for what? To recover one spy, who probably doesn't even know anything?"

The pain in my leg and head was back, and with it, the cold, sickening realisation of what I'd done. Of who I'd become. I hadn't recognised myself back at the tower, giving orders, making life-and-death decisions as easily as choosing what to have for breakfast. I'd killed a boy for the sake of the mission. It might not have been my bullet in his chest, but it might as well have been my finger on the trigger.

"You did your duty, Tyler. As you've done time and time before and as you'll do again."

I shook Cain off me, still quaking with anger. I couldn't look at him. Because he was right: I had done this before. I sensed it, like a guilty memory surfacing after you've tried to hide it. The *me* I was here, he was ruthless and focused. He was a killer. And all because he believed in doing his duty.

"Do we have a problem, Tyler?" Cain said.

I finally looked at him. "No. We're good."

He nodded and patted me on the shoulder. "It's always tough losing men. But their sacrifice won't be forgotten. It was all for the greater good."

"*Ad verum via*," I mumbled.

"Exactly. And with the intel Hedges has, we might be able to crush the Red Hand once and for all."

We both looked over at Hedges. He must have been strong and handsome once, but now he looked like a shell of a man, his face a bruised ruin, half-starved and broken. Could a man like this really be so important?

You take power where you can find it, the buzzing voice in my head said.

Power. Duty. Choices. I felt as pinned as when Frankie had taken over me. Only now, I was the one stopping me. I needed help. And I'd just flipped out at the one person I believed could help me.

Aubrey stared at me, her gaze fixed and unreadable.

I walked over to her. "I'm sorry," I said. "I should have congratulated you. It's only that..."

"You have no reason to explain yourself to me, Commandant," she said, which wasn't the same as saying I didn't need to apologise.

"Still, I'm sorry."

She nodded. But there was no softening in her expression. "Our guest is waiting. We should probably see what he has to say for himself."

She spun around, her large boots squeaking on the tiled floor of the Hub, and headed for a tunnel.

I glanced around at the group who were doing a pretty terrible job of pretending they hadn't been watching the whole exchange. My squad had been watching too, although judging by the expressions on their faces, they were as annoyed as I was. Only Zac smiled.

"Permission to fall out?" he said.

"Yes, of course. Fall out," I said, waving them away with my hand.

When I looked back, Aubrey was disappearing through a doorway. "Hang on," I called, struggling to catch up with her thanks to my throbbing leg.

She slowed her pace and waited for me.

"Thanks," I said. "I still haven't quite found my way around here." I reached into my pocket and swallowed two pills straight from the bottle.

"Zac said you were having trouble."

I found myself irritated by the idea that she and Zac had been talking about me, and jealousy added to the mix of emotions rushing through me. Maybe now wasn't the time to be baring my soul to her. It could wait till later.

The tunnel sloped downwards, getting darker and damper the deeper we went. The walls became smoother, covered in a slick layer of water breaking through the cracks.

"How far down do you think we are?" I asked.

"Oh, about a hundred feet. It's an old tunnel system that was used during the last war as a shelter. After the strike on Old Street, ARES moved in here and started building."

We turned another corner. There was a row of rough wooden doors; they looked old, way older than the rest of the Hub. Black metal hinges had been hammered into place with nails as big as my thumbnail.

"What are these rooms?" I asked, peering through a small window covered by thick metal bars.

"Cells. They're hundreds of years old. CP told me they used to keep those too evil for the Tower of London locked up down here. Chuck 'em in the cells and leave 'em to rot. No reprieve. No buying your way out."

I ran my hand against the surface of the wood. "How many do you think died down here?"

"Who knows? Hundreds? Thousands, maybe?"

"And on this our country was built."

She stopped to look at me with a quizzical, confused expression. "Don't you believe in what we're doing?"

"Of course I do," I said, quickly. "We have to defend ourselves, right? Protect the country. I get that. It's just..."

"Just what?"

I looked down at my feet. "I lost Cooper today. He was just a kid."

"I'm sorry to hear that. But Cooper wasn't much younger than you."

"Exactly! And I'm a kid."

Aubrey let out a small snort of air and the corner of her mouth hitched in a grin.

"What?" I said.

"Nothing." She carried on walking. "You're not like I imagined."

I'm not like I imagined, I wanted to say. I wanted to blurt everything out. To tell her that we loved each other. That there was a better place for us all. But the words refused to come. So instead, I focused on not tripping over on the uneven ground.

"This is it." She'd stopped in front of a large wooden door. A new chrome lock had been drilled into it, complete with a palm reader. Aubrey nodded at me.

"What?" I said, not knowing what I was supposed to do.

"Only senior officers have authorisation."

"Oh, yeah. Right." I placed my hand on the reader, waited for verification.

"Commandant Tyler. All area access," the familiar electronic voice chirped as the door opened.

Inside was a small damp room hewn out of the rock. Sitting chained to a chair was a muscle-bound young man. I scanned his tattoos: swastikas on each knuckle, a bulldog on his right arm, a crown on his left. His face was quadrisected by a red St George's Cross. I noticed a ring on his little finger that had a gold lion on it, that he'd recently gone down a belt notch, and a hundred other tiny details about him, including the fact he'd cut his head shaving it. It was a weird experience, this heightened awareness. It must be all part of the training from this reality.

"This," Aubrey said, "is George Burnley. Otherwise known as the Brute."

The "Brute" was drooling, his eyes staring into space.

"You've cuffed him?"

"Of course."

"He's a Shifter, then?" I said, stepping forward. "Bit old, isn't he?"

"He's sixteen," Aubrey said, "and responsible for the deaths of at least seven ARES officers, not to mention a series of vicious racial attacks."

Suddenly, I wasn't so worried about why we were fighting and what we lost. Because if it was to stop animals like this, then it was worth it.

Aubrey closed the door behind us. "He was recruited into the Red Hand from a neo-Nazi group called the English Defence League that sprang up at the beginning of the war. They believed the government brought the war on us by allowing foreigners in the country." The disgust was clear in Aubrey's voice. "We rounded up most of them in the early days. But George here proved useful to the Red Hand. He's an explosives expert."

"You take power where you can find it?"

"Something like that."

He had a nasty gash across his cheek, which was oozing gently. "Was that your handiwork?" I said, pointing at the cut.

"He didn't want to come quietly," Aubrey said.

"They never do," I said. "Right, uncuff him. We're not going to get any sense out of him in this state."

"But what if he Shifts?"

I smiled. "Fixer, remember?"

"Sure, I remember," she said, pulling out a key from a pouch on her belt. "I wasn't sure you did."

She undid George's cuffs and then stepped away hastily.

He blinked his eyes and smacked his lips together, as if waking up from a long sleep. He went from drowsy to rage in a matter of seconds, trying and failing to break free of the chains. He strained at his bindings, the muscles on his arms bulging.

"There's no point," I said. "The chain isn't going anywhere and neither are you. Unless you cooperate."

"I will never cooperate with you scum who are destroying this nation."

"Then you will stay here and rot," Aubrey said.

He let loose a torrent of such foul abuse directed at Aubrey that I reacted without thinking. I punched him in the throat, leaving him gasping for air.

"If you ever, ever," I shouted, "speak to her like that again, I will tear your tongue out, do you understand me?"

"I'd like to see you try," he croaked, holding onto his throat.

"Now, Captain Jones is going to ask you some questions and you are going to answer them civilly or," I pulled the knife I'd used to cut Hedges' bindings and ran the tip across the red lines on George's face, "I will remove each of your tattoos. One by one."

He went cross-eyed looking down at my blade.

When I pulled it away, I saw the change in him. Gone was the big-man act, leaving only a scared teenage boy, sitting abandoned in a cell.

"What do you want to know?"

"X73," Aubrey said.

George's bulldog face wrinkled in confusion. "I don't know what that is."

"Don't lie to us," I shouted, spraying his face with spittle.

He blinked. "I've never heard of it. I'm telling the truth." And the desperation in his eyes made me believe him.

"What about the attack they are planning?" Aubrey said, walking to stand behind him.

"I don't know. They said something about a programme and a virus. I thought they might be planning on hacking S3's computers. But they don't let me in on the strategy stuff. I'm only there to blow things up, you know?"

Aubrey laid her hands on his shoulders and leant in close to his ear. "If you are lying to us, this will go badly for you."

He tried to twist around in his chair to look at her. "I swear on my life. I ain't lying."

"Your life isn't worth spit," Aubrey said, quietly. "If you want to keep it, you need to give us something."

"I... heard they had a spy in S3."

This didn't come as a surprise to me. They'd known about our raid on the tower after all. "Who?"

"I don't know. I heard they'd turned a loyal member of the S3. But I swear that's all I heard."

"And what about Slate, your leader?" Aubrey said.

I recognised the name from the argument between the two guards at the tower.

"I've never met Slate. No one has, as far as I can tell. But there are rumours that Slate's a Shifter, too."

Did that mean there were more adult Shifters out there? Maybe one of the men from Project Ganymede? I remembered the men Aubrey and I had rounded up. None of them had struck me as the type to lead an army.

"If you give us the identity of Slate, I'll see what I can do about giving you a cell with a view."

"I've never met her."

"Her?" Aubrey said.

"Yes. That's all I know. That Slate is a woman."

A woman and a Shifter? Could it be Frankie? Could she be tricking everyone yet again? It sounded exactly like her.

"That's all I know. I promise ya. Can I go home now?" George looked pathetically at me, a single tear running down the tattoo on his face.

"I wouldn't hold out too much hope for that," Aubrey said, slapping the cuffs back on him. After a moment, he slumped again in his chair.

I followed her out of the room. "What do we do with him now?"

"He'll be processed. Probably executed."

I didn't care he was a teenager. He was a killer. The justice of his punishment gave me a sense of calm. "Good," I said.

Are you so very different? that niggling, gnawing voice said again. I pushed it away.

"I have an idea of who Slate might be."

Aubrey stopped and turned to me. "Who?"

"Frankie Anderson." She looked confused. "You probably know her as Francesca Goodwin."

"The doctor?" Aubrey said, her eyes wide. "What makes you think that?"

"Let's say I've had dealings with her in the past."

"But George said Slate was a Shifter. The doctor went through entropy years ago."

The lack of scar made me believe Frankie hadn't been a part of Project Ganymede. But there were other ways to hold on to your power. I knew thanks to Benjo Green. And who better than a doctor to work that out? "I think she might have found a way around it."

"OK. But if the Red Hand have infiltrated the division, how do we know who we can trust?"

She was right. Someone had told the Red Hand we were coming earlier, I was sure of it. "I don't know. But we have to tell someone. Sergeant Cain?"

"No," Aubrey said. "We need to take it higher than him. We need to take it to the Minister of Defence."

CHAPTER TEN

We stood in front of an enormous metal door covered in bolts and dials. Aubrey hesitated next to me, as if waiting for me to do something. Then, with the tiniest of shakes of her head, stepped forward and pushed a button.

Machinery whirred in response.

"Identify," a computerised voice snapped.

"Captain Jones and Commandant Tyler," Aubrey said, with only the slightest of pauses. The door hissed and slid open.

The room inside looked exactly like I'd imagined the interior of Number Ten Downing Street to look. Dark wood panels, a large oak desk with green banker's lamps. It looked like the Minister of Defence had made himself a home from home.

Two guards stood to attention, guns held to their chests. They didn't even acknowledge our presence as we stepped into the room.

A slim, dark-haired man stood with his back to the door, bending down over something on the table. Somehow, I knew this was his way of proving he was unafraid. A paranoid man would always sit facing the door. A man with nothing to fear wouldn't even look up when another person entered the room. Which made me wonder: what were all the bolts on the door and armed guards for?

This man was trying to manipulate appearances and hide the truth. Just like me.

He slowly straightened and turned around. I recognised Benjamin Vine, the Prime Minister from an old, old reality. In that reality, Vine's daughter had been killed by Ella – one of Frankie's puppets. Pushed off a cliff on a school holiday as Frankie put her pieces in place. That loss had driven him into politics and all the way to the top job. What had made him become a minister this time? Had his daughter died in the war?

He had always looked as if the responsibility of power weighed heavily on him. And now, it looked to be crushing him. His hair was greying at the temples, his skin pale and pasty, there were purple circles under his eyes. The eyes themselves, though, were sharp and bright. His suit had seen better days. Without even thinking, I scanned it and noticed the smudge of ink on his cuff, the faint patches of dust on his knees. Had he been praying?

The level of awareness I was experiencing ever since the battle was scaring me. It was as if my eyes didn't belong to me anymore. More of the version of me from this reality overriding my conscious thoughts.

"Ah, Commandant Tyler," Vine said, clicking the button on a silver pen and placing it carefully on the table so it lined up perfectly with the sheet of paper he'd been writing on. "Good of you to visit me. I hear you have been very busy."

Vine's eyes took in my bruises, passing over me and then looking to Aubrey.

"And you must be Captain Jones. Congratulations on the mission. Zero casualties. Impressive. We're glad to have you on board."

A strange stab of competitive jealousy jabbed at me. I'd failed where Aubrey had shone, and I didn't like it. I pushed the alien feeling away.

"Thank you, sir," Aubrey said. "Glad to be useful. Speaking of which, we gathered some intelligence from the man we took in tonight."

He walked around his desk and lowered himself into his chair. "And you have brought this direct to me because…?"

"Because we think there might be a Red Hand spy in the division."

"Oh, undoubtedly. I would be disappointed in our enemy if they didn't have eyes on us at all times."

Aubrey and I shared a look. Vine seemed to be taking the news that the S3 had been compromised very lightly.

"We think it's Slate," Aubrey said.

Vine's demeanour changed. He lent back in his chair, placing both hands on his lap. "Slate? Here? Are you sure?"

"No," Aubrey said. "But George told us that Slate is a Shifter, and Commandant Tyler..." Aubrey trailed off and looked to me.

"It's Doctor Goodwin," I said, utterly confident.

Vine leant forward again. "And what makes you believe this?"

"She's a Shifter."

"She *was* a Shifter."

"I believe she still is. And more than that..." I hesitated. *Don't tell them,* that voice warned.

I ignored it. "She's a Forcer."

Vine reached up slowly and stroked his chin. "A Forcer? As in, she is able to push her ideas on other people? Are you sure, Tyler?"

"Positive."

Aubrey let out a small gasp. "I thought Forcers were a rumour. Something propaganda made up."

"There are reports in ARES' files about the existence of Forcers in the past," Vine said, his stare burning my cheeks. "As well as experiments they conducted in trying to trigger the power. But all have been a failure."

"Not all of them."

"I have known Doctor Goodwin for nearly twenty years. Don't you think I would have noticed if she was a Forcer?"

"That's why she's so clever. She manipulates people indirectly. So you never see her hand at work."

He repositioned the pen, which had rolled slightly to the right of the pad. "You yourself have worked with her for two years and yet you've only come to this decision now?"

"I've had a change of... heart."

He didn't seem to be buying any of this. "There is a simple way for us to rebut this. Rhys, have Doctor Goodwin meet us in the simulator room, will you?"

The guard clicked his heels, spun around and opened the door. Vine stood up, carefully buttoning his jacket using both hands. His movements were almost infuriatingly controlled and slow, each action only as big as it needed to be. It was as if he was working through a mental checklist: stand, check; suit button, check.

Aubrey and I waited as he walked past us and out into the corridor. The second guard fell into place behind the Minister and we brought up the rear.

There was the slightest hint of a limp in how Vine walked: a small scuff of his left foot with each careful stride. I wondered if it was an old injury or a fresh one. How much was Vine hiding?

My hands shook by my sides. I wasn't sure which I was more nervous about: confronting Frankie again or seeing the simulator room?

I lost track of how many lefts and rights we'd taken. I even stopped trying to keep hold of the options as I normally did when walking around strange places, so I could Shift if I'd hit a wrong turn. Instead, I focused on not losing sight of Vine in front of me and in hiding my shaking knees from Aubrey. All I could work out was that we were being led farther away from the Hub than I'd been yet. And, I was sensing, even deeper beneath the ground.

Vine finally halted in front of a door. It had a palm lock on it like all the doors here. Vine laid his hand on it, and it swung open. Inside was a small room, with a single white leather chair in the middle. It looked like something out of a dentist's surgery. Or an execution chamber. Above it hung a large silver dome with a trail of clear wires hanging out of it, like tentacles on an octopus.

Frankie and the guard were already waiting inside.

"What is this about, Minister?" she said. "I have patients to attend to."

"Just a routine procedure, Doctor. Would you please take a seat?"

He moved aside, gesturing to the simulator.

Frankie saw me. "Ah, Commandant. Am I to assume that you have something to do with this?" She turned to the Minister. "You are aware Mr Tyler is suffering from an extreme reality attack?"

Vine looked over to me, a curious look on his face. "I will deal with Tyler later. For now, would you please take a seat?" There was iron in his voice that suggested she should not make him ask again.

"This is ridiculous," Frankie said, slipping into the simulator seat. "You know this machine only works on Shifters?"

"It will only take a moment of your time." Vine walked towards the machinery next to the chair and ran his hands across the control console. "Captain Jones, if you could assist me…"

Aubrey approached the machine and pulled the helmet down over Frankie's head. She attached the electrodes to Frankie's skin and strapped her legs and arms in place. Aubrey had done this before, it was clear. When she had finished, she stepped aside.

"Thank you," Vine said. "And you are a Spotter, am I correct?"

"Yes, sir."

A Spotter was a Shifter who had the ability to sense when someone was Shifting, without the need for technology. And Aubrey was one of the best.

"Good. I'd like a second opinion in case the machinery does not give us conclusive answers." With that, he flicked a switch.

The machine whirred and hummed. Frankie's hands clenched on the rests of the chair and her body went stiff.

"A Forcer, if such a thing exists," Vine said, turning the dial up on the machine, "would be a Shifter of preternatural power. They would score a… what was the level of the Shift you performed yesterday, Commandant?"

"A sixteen, sir," I said.

"A sixteen. Impressive. We would have to assume that a Forcer then would be at least able to reach those levels, yes."

"I… I don't know." I was suddenly worried he would work out that I was a Forcer. For some reason, I knew I had to keep that secret. More than me not knowing what was going on. More than wanting to get out of here. No one could know about that side of my power.

Frankie was convulsing now, her limbs thrashing. If I was right, she was facing her very worst fears in there.

"The machine is registering a zero?" Vine said. "Do you concur?"

"She's not Shifting, if that's what you mean," Aubrey said, clearly uncomfortable with what we were doing to Frankie.

"Let's turn up the test, to make sure." He twisted again.

Frankie's scream was high and desperate. Whatever she was going through, it was terrifying.

"Stop it!" Aubrey shouted, moving towards Frankie.

Vine grabbed Aubrey by the arm, holding her back. "Still zero," he said, reading from a screen on the simulator. "Let's give her a few minutes more. So the Commandant can be convinced." He didn't take his eyes off me.

Frankie's screams had turned to sobs. I knew what she was going though. I'd been there myself. She was begging for someone to kill her. For someone to end the pain. It was at this point when Abbott had subjected me to the simulators that the power to Force had awoken in me. With a word, I'd been able to make Abbott kill himself, Benjo Green munch down on a tray filled with surgical tools, and guards lie down and go to sleep.

I watched Frankie kicking and thrashing. Was she manipulating us even now? Was she managing to resist the desire to Shift herself out of the situation? All the time, the lights on the machine never moved.

She let out a cry of terror. I couldn't watch any more.

"Stop it," I said.

"I'm sorry, what was that, Commandant Tyler?" Vine said. "I couldn't quite hear you."

"I said 'stop it', OK?"

Vine hit the switches and Frankie went limp in the chair. Aubrey quickly pushed the helmet away from Frankie's head and unfastened the straps. Frankie's unconscious face was pale and streaked with tears. Vine laid a hand on her wrist, patting it like soothing an elderly relative.

He turned to me. "Satisfied, Commandant?"

I was satisfied that Frankie wasn't a Shifter. But I wasn't satisfied that she wasn't this Slate George had been talking about. Maybe he'd been confused. Maybe he meant an ex-Shifter. I was going to keep watching her, no matter what.

"It's a shame, really." Vine pulled out a white handkerchief and wiped his hands on it. "To think of the possibilities, were we able to put a Forcer in the Igloo. As it is, we're in desperate need of a new Fixer. And the only other one we have in the division is you, Commandant Tyler." He pushed the white cloth back into the pocket of his jacket. "But of course, we'd have to be truly desperate to consider that."

I didn't know what this Igloo was or why Vine needed a Fixer for it. Something about the blank way he looked at me made me realise I couldn't let him know that.

Luckily, it seemed Aubrey had never heard of it either. "What is the Igloo, sir?"

"The Igloo, Captain Jones, is the only thing standing between us and a nuclear strike."

CHAPTER ELEVEN

The room was brilliantly white, even brighter than the infirmary, with a vast, domed ceiling and curved walls. I saw now why they called it the Igloo.

As my eyes adjusted to the glare, I made out hexagonal panels covering the walls and ceilings. It reminded me of an observatory. Or like being inside a huge satellite dish.

Frankie had reluctantly led us here. I could sense her anger towards me in every sharp glance and clipped word. She kept her distance, which was fine by me.

Vine walked into the centre of the room and stopped next to a large white box that looked like an oversized sarcophagus: wider at the top than at the bottom with a slight bulge at the top for a head.

"This" – he laid his hand on the coffin-like box – "is the heart of the Igloo – the Eskimo."

The box had a glass window at the head. What I saw through it made my head spin.

I recognised that face: the dark eyes that stared out unseeing through the glass, those purple lips stretched across a too-wide face. His flesh gathered in pools around his jaw onto the silver pillow propping his head up.

The Eskimo – the man apparently responsible for the safety of the country – was Benjo Green. The man who had tried to eat me. Twice. The man I'd broken out of ARES to help me defeat Frankie. The man who had held on to his Shifter power by consuming the brains of other Shifters.

What little hair he'd had had been shaved off, and his head was covered in rows of silver electrodes. Only, they didn't look as if they were stuck on. They looked as if they had been drilled into his skull.

"Is he conscious?" I asked.

"Of course," Frankie snapped. "If he was unconscious, he'd hardly be able to Fix. We keep him pumped full of amphetamines to make sure of it. But all non-essential areas of his brain have been put into a comatose state. It's a very delicate balance of chemicals."

Chemicals. That seemed to be her answer for everything. I thought of the painkillers in my pocket; the ache in my leg was gnawing.

"How does it work?" Aubrey asked.

"The machine" – Vine looked up at the ceiling – "amplifies his brain waves, extending the focus and reach of his Fixing ability."

Seeing Benjo like this – reduced to nothing more than a cog in a machine – made me realise how Vine and the rest of this reality truly saw Shifters. Not heroes as Zac had said, but tools to be used. Like me and my team. Expendable. And yet, as much as the uneasiness squirmed in my stomach like an eel, I respected it, too. I was as sickened with myself as I was Vine.

"What I am about to tell you is beyond classified." Vine pulled at a thread on one of his buttons. "You may have heard rumours about a nuclear strike on this country?"

Aubrey and I exchanged looks and then nodded.

"It's correct. The strike happened in September 2010. We understand," Vine continued, "that it wiped out the whole of London, killing millions upon millions in minutes. We don't know who was responsible. Our best bet is that it was an ex-Russian nuke auctioned off to the highest bidder. What we do know is that there was a Shift registered on that day. A Shift that was off the charts. Way, way above even your abilities, Commandant Tyler. From the information our scientists have been able to gather, we have been able to deduce that there was a Shifter on their side. Who, upon seeing the unparalleled death... well, we're not entirely sure, but we presume they altered a choice that somehow led to the strike. What choice they unmade, we will never know. But we do know that we can't have them or any other Shifter on their side – on any side – altering the delicate confluence of choices that led to them standing down with the strike. So, Mr Green here stops that strike from happening and ensures that the overall reality in which this country endures stays firmly in place."

I was unable to take my eyes off Benjo's sunken face. The man who had been one of the biggest threats to Shifters was now our saviour. "How long has he been here?"

"Three years," Vine said. "We arrested Mr Green for, well, you don't need to know the details, other than to say he was given a choice: death by lethal injection or this. He made the right choice."

I laid my hand on the glass. I hated Benjo. Yet I couldn't help but feel sorry for him. He'd become the lab rat he'd always feared.

"And you don't think he has long left?" Aubrey said, peering down on him, disgust curling her lips.

Frankie adjusted the controls on the machine. "We've been monitoring his brain activity, and we don't think he can stand the strain for much longer."

"And you want to do *this* to another Fixer?" Aubrey said.

"It's not a matter of wanting, Captain Jones," Vine said. "It's a case of needing. Without this deterrent, we will be vulnerable."

I stared at Benjo. His black, button eyes, which used to glint with a twisted, terrifying intelligence, were now dead and blank. How much, I wondered, was he aware of? Did he sense us here? Did he want to break free and punish everyone?

A shudder passed through me. I was a Fixer. Would they put me in there? Drain me till I was nothing more than a shell? Then any chance of undoing my decisions would be over for ever. No, there had to be another way to end the war.

"Perhaps we will find a Fixer in our new batch of recruits. Has your sister shown any potential in that regard?" Vine continued without looking at me.

"My sister? You mean Katie? What has she got to do with anything?" I said.

"Well, we had hoped she might turn out to be another Fixer. I'll have a full report once the cadets have gone through the final stage of their training next week..."

Vine carried on talking but I couldn't hear what he was saying, as the blood pounding in my head drowned it out. What if Katie was a Fixer like me? What if they took her and put her in this machine?

"I have to see her," I said, cutting Vine off.

He looked a little shocked at my rudeness – he was obviously not used to people interrupting him.

"Well, if you think that it would help this situation."

I had to bite down on my lip to stop myself from shouting that there was no way Katie was ever going to end up helping in "this situation". I'd tear this whole place to the ground before I would allow Katie to come anywhere near it. I glanced at Benjo, his black eyes staring at nothing, at everything. This punishment, if that's what it was, was the least he deserved. But there was no chance in hell I was going to let Katie end up the same way. I'd give myself up to this machine first.

I swallowed, pushing the rage deep down. "I have to see her," I repeated.

"You will need to complete your report on the prisoner first," he said.

"I can do that, sir," Aubrey said.

I was overcome with gratitude and warmth for Aubrey. I knew I could trust her: in this reality and in every reality. There was nothing I couldn't deal with as long as she was with me. I believed that together, we could find a way home. A way back for us both. But it would have to wait. Vine and Benjo and Aubrey all of this could wait. For now, I had only one concern: my little sister.

"Very well," Vine said. "You are dismissed."

I took one last look at Benjo and left.

CHAPTER TWELVE

The corridor walls looked like they were moving in and out like great lungs, expanding and then contracting in on me. I reached out and touched the wall on my left to make sure it was solid, that it was only my head messing with me. The slick dampness seemed to seep through my fingertips and up my arm to settle around my heart like a cold fist.

I forced myself to walk on till I got to the too-bright lights of the Hub. Throngs of S3 staff scurried around like ants. Everyone had a purpose, everyone knew where they were going. Everyone but me.

The tightness in my chest intensified. Pain shot down my left arm. I was having a heart attack. I was dying...

"Commandant?" a soft voice said. I felt a warm hand take my clammy palm.

CP was looking up at me, her large blue eyes peering out from under her long fringe, concern twisting her tiny mouth.

"Commandant, are you OK?" she said.

I laid a hand on her shoulder, marvelling at how her frail frame felt so solid, so real. She helped me straighten up.

"Yes, of course," I said, changing my desperate grip on her shoulder to a reassuring pat. "I'm tired, is all."

I tried to smile. But whatever expression took hold of my face only seemed to make CP look even more concerned.

"Can I get you something? A cup of tea? My Nan always said that a cup of tea would sort anyone right out."

I laughed and some of the tightness lessened. "She was a wise woman, your Nan."

"She'd want to get some food inside you too, sir. You look like a scarecrow."

I was reminded of how much I thought CP and Katie would get on.

"There is something you can do for me," I said, rolling my shoulders and straightening my clothes. "Are you staying in the academy?"

"No, sir. I moved into the barracks here when I graduated last month." She tapped the first class symbol on her arm proudly. "Although I do miss it some."

"Fancy paying a visit, then?"

CP blinked. "You want me to take you to the academy?"

"Well, as Commandant, I should probably do an inspection, you know? And as you were... well, as you were there most recently, you could fill me in on anything that's changed."

I could tell she didn't believe a word of it. But she wasn't going to question a superior officer. God bless the British army.

"Of course, sir. Shall we go now?"

"Yes," I said, taking a full breath at last.

I let her go first, then wiped my damp palms on my trousers, hoping nobody would notice.

The academy, it turned out, was in Hampton Court, south-west of the city. CP had commandeered a car and she insisted on driving.

"You're in no fit state, sir," she said.

It took less than thirty minutes to get there with CP behind the wheel. I risked looking at the speedometer at one point and wished I hadn't. It was easing into over a hundred miles per hour. She chatted cheerily the whole way, about the mission to capture George and how amazing Aubrey had been, about her time in training. I let it all wash over me, making the necessary noises of interest to let her know I was paying attention. It was nice to experience something so familiar, so normal, amid everything else that was going on.

We snaked along empty roads clinging to the river till the red-brick building with its twisting turrets appeared over a bridge. Once home to King Henry VIII and now home to a bunch of kids with special powers. I wondered if there were Shifters in Tudor times? And if so, were they conscripted to fight for the crown or were they left to live normal lives?

A handful of kids were doing drills in the yard as we drove in through the large, black gates. They marched up and down, their little hands pumping. The stone beasts that lined the entrance into the palace stared haughtily on.

An older girl of around eighteen shouted out instructions. I could hear the cracking of gunfire from somewhere nearby. I guess they were teaching Shifters to shoot now.

CP strode towards the large doors while I held back, watching how the expressions of the cadets changed from serious determination to distracted delight at seeing their old classmate, and then to outright curiosity at seeing me. A couple stopped marching to point and were promptly slammed into by the kids behind them. The marching descended into a chaotic mess of shoving and muttering.

We walked through the doors to the sound of the older girl now yelling for order.

Inside, there were more kids, weaving around the staircases in silent single-file rows. Even when Sir Richard had been in charge, I'd never seen discipline like this. They looked more like robots than children.

As I followed CP into the centre of the hallway, the cadets slowed their pace and many stopped altogether to see who we were. A whisper began and was picked up and repeated throughout the room: *Commandant.*

"What's going on here?" a familiar voice shouted. "Don't you all have somewhere to be?"

Richard Morgan, my old commandant and son of Sir Richard, the old head of ARES, pushed his way through the groups of staring children. His jaw nearly hit the ground when he turned his gaze on me.

"C-Commandant Tyler," he stuttered. "I wasn't expecting…"

"Dick!" I said, genuinely pleased to see him.

He flushed at the ripple of laughter that passed through the group. "Excuse me?" he said, his nostrils flaring as he tried to restrain the anger from having been embarrassed by a senior officer.

I took pity on him. "Mr Morgan," I said, after quickly scanning his arm to check he had no rank. Dick had gone through entropy already, which made him an NSO – a Non-Shifting Officer. I walked forward to meet him, my hand outstretched. "It's good to see you again," I said.

He took my hand, looking at me sideways. "Well, naturally."

"Naturally," I said, unable to keep the smile off my face. Same old Dick.

"So, are you here to do an inspection? You'll find everything in shipshape order."

"Ah…" I'd only come here to try and find Katie. I scanned the gathering of cadets to see if I could spot her among the curious faces. She was nowhere to be seen. "Yes, that would be good. Only if it won't inconvenience you."

"Anything for the famous Commandant Tyler," he said, but it was through gritted teeth.

"You can stay here," I said to CP, who looked relieved that she didn't have to be subjected to any more of Morgan's lessons.

I followed him up the stairs and the tour began.

He droned on for a good thirty minutes about the history of the building and how ARES moved the training here after the strike on Old Street, punctuated with – I counted – five mentions of his father's name.

His father, it turned out, had been the Minister of Defence until a year ago when he retired. But, Dick assured me, he was still very much hands-on with the war effort. I remembered what a blustering fool Sir Richard had been, and couldn't help but wonder if the war could have ended already if he hadn't been in charge.

I was getting tired of Morgan's waffle and was about to ask him to shut up when we finally came to the training room.

It was a large, square metal building, about thirty yards by thirty yards, and it looked totally out of place amid the historic brickwork. I could hear the sounds of shouting coming from inside.

"This area used to be the tilting yard," Morgan said, opening a door, "where they used to joust. But we had this structure put up, as we needed the space."

Inside, I was faced with a row of children going through a series of fighting moves. Morgan placed his finger over his lips, telling me to keep quiet, and then led me up a staircase and onto a raised metal walkway for a better look. There

126

must have been at least a hundred, maybe more; all stood in neat lines as the instructor at the front yelled out orders. They moved in perfect synchronicity, punching and kicking, a loud "huh" rising up with the finish of each sequence.

As I watched, a memory hit me.

My thighs are burning from the stance and my hands are shaking. I'm struggling to keep up with the older kids on either side of me. Sergeant Cain is barking orders and I'm so scared he'll see me and pick me out again. Last time, a girl beat me up and everyone laughed. Not this time. I have to do well. I have to be better than all of the rest. I cannot fail.

That fear, the fear of getting it wrong and crashing out of ARES was so powerful, it was like experiencing it fresh for the first time. Tears pricked at my eyes and I had to dig my nails into my palms to stop myself from crying. Because what scared me most, more than that remembered terror, was that it was not *my* memory. It was *his*. The me from this reality. His past was leaching over into mine. The two realities fighting for dominance in my mind. The one reality in which I'd been a part of ARES since I was a little kid, growing up to become a warrior, a leader of men. And the other, my memories, where I had joined only a year ago and didn't know the first thing about how to command.

That meant I was starting to accept this reality. If I didn't fight it, it would take over me and I would lose myself completely.

"Everything OK, Commandant Tyler?" Morgan said.

"Yes. Fine," I said, looking down at my hand and the red half-moon marks in my palm. "What's next?"

"The final phase of the programme."

"Which is?"

"The simulators."

CHAPTER THIRTEEN

Simulators. Twice in one day. I sucked back two more pills, not so much to quieten the pain in my leg but because the floating, numbing feeling they gave me helped. The bottle was getting empty. I'd have to find another doctor to re-prescribe them, as there was no way I was going to talk to Frankie again.

At least the simulator room here was a little less intimidating than the one back at the Hub. It looked more like a games room than an execution chamber. A row of black leather chairs lined the wall, the kind that had been the envy of boys at my school three lifetimes ago. Only these kids weren't playing *Duty Calls*. Helmets with trailing wires were pulled down over their heads, so all I could see was the lower half of their faces. Jaws were clenched in fear or pain. Or both.

Three adults wearing lab coats moved silently from bay to bay, making notes on clipboards.

"What are you doing to them?" I asked.

"Oh, you know. Making them face their greatest fears, fight for their lives. Same old, same old. The main difference from when you and I went through the tests is that we've become more sophisticated at registering their scores. You can see the read-outs there."

Morgan pointed to a screen behind each station. LED lights flicked up and down like the display on a stereo. Some were edging into the red, while others barely made it out of the green zone. As the lights danced, another memory struck me.

It's over. My body is shaking and I fight back the urge to be sick. The things I've seen are worse than I could have ever imagined. But it's over now. I'm alone in the darkness. And I'm safe.

Someone pulls the helmet off my head and I have to squint at the sudden light. When my eyes adjust, I see them, smiling.

A bead of water drips down my temple and I catch it in the corner of my mouth with my tongue. I lick the dampness away and taste salt. Sweat or a tear, I don't know. It doesn't matter. I've passed.

I gasped at the freshness of the memory, and the nausea that had threatened to overtake me then hits me again now. The terror of what I'd been through mixed with the joy of knowing I'd passed.

The kids were going through what I'd been through. What every ARES officer had been through. Part of me wanted to rip all the wires off their heads and save these kids from whatever mental torture they were experiencing. But another part of me, a part that was growing stronger and stronger, knew that this was how it was done. It was cruel, maybe, but necessary. And it wasn't as if it caused them any physical damage.

War is about sacrifice. These kids needed to learn that. If the kids didn't pass, then we couldn't have them dragging the rest of us down. It was the way things were. You were useful or you were out.

"What kind of numbers are you getting?" I said.

"We've got a good batch this year. Some of the cadets are registering sevens and eights. We only had a twenty-five percent dropout rate."

"And what happens to those cadets?"

"They're sent to the reintegration programme, naturally."

"Naturally," I said. And I meant it.

A kid screamed and tore at their headset. A tester ran over and tried to stop them from pulling it off. Their lights had stayed green. They'd flunked.

"Of course, nobody has come close to your score of eleven, sir," he said, an edge of bitterness clipping his words. "We had hoped that maybe your sister… but she's proving challenging."

131

The mention of my sister's name changed something in me. Reminded me why I was here.

"About Katie. I would like to see her."

"Well, I'm sure you know the policy about cadets fraternising with their family."

I continued to smile. Trying to keep my expression unreadable while fear bubbled away in my stomach. What if he wouldn't let me see Katie? What was I going to do then?

"But," Morgan continued, "as you of all people are hardly likely to distract Ms Tyler from the true path..."

I smiled. "Well, quite." My voice was low and steady. I almost didn't recognise it.

Morgan led me down a tight corridor and we stopped in front of a door. I could see through the window that there was a class going on inside. Physics, I guessed, as my old teacher Mr Jarvis was at the front fiddling with a laser. My heart almost crashed out of my chest when I saw Katie sitting at the back of the classroom, staring out of the window.

Morgan opened the door.

"Apologies for the interruption, Mr Jarvis. Can we have a word with Katie Tyler, please?"

Katie turned at the sound of her name and looked at Morgan with a totally unimpressed expression on her face. It was the expression she normally reserved for me.

"What is it?" she said.

"Ms Tyler!" Mr Jarvis snapped. "Show Mr Morgan some respect."

I laid my hand on Morgan's shoulder and moved him out of the way so I could have a clearer view of my sister. She looked paler than usual, and her long light-brown hair had been cropped to above her shoulders.

I beamed and waved her over to me. The attitude she'd been directing at Morgan vanished. Her face turned to stone.

"Commandant Tyler would like to speak with you, so if you could gather up your things..." Morgan said.

Stiffly, Katie pushed herself up out of her seat and picked up her bag. All the eyes in the room followed her as she walked through the class and towards the door, her arms stiff by her sides.

"Katie," I said, scared at the change in my sister. Where was the Katie who would roll her eyes and call me a twat? Who would test out her latest karate moves on me? I didn't recognise this quaking creature.

"Commandant," she said, her voice barely a whisper. She clicked her heels together and saluted.

The classroom burbled, amused and curious at the same time.

"Is there somewhere I can talk to Ka... Cadet Tyler?"

"The room across the hall should be free," Mr Jarvis said, looking from me to his student.

"Well, show the Commandant the way, then, Tyler," Morgan snapped, pushing Katie forward. "And if I find that you have been causing trouble again, there will be consequences."

Katie gave him the dirtiest side eye I'd ever seen her give and stomped through the door.

I nodded to Morgan and Mr Jarvis, and followed her out.

The opposite room was almost identical to the one we'd left, but instead of oil paintings of Tudors, the walls were covered with etchings of famous Shifters, including Lord Cuthbert Morgan-Fairfax, the man who had set up ARES, and, I was mortified to realise, a picture of me. It was the image Zac had described: me standing in a field, the British flag waving behind me. Although I thought I looked more constipated than heroic.

Light spilled through the leaded windows, throwing Katie into shadow and making diamond-shaped patterns on the floor. She stood, her hands clasped behind her, facing away from the door.

"Katie," I said. "It's OK. It's me." I laid my hand on her shoulder and she flinched. "Don't you know me?"

She turned, ever so slowly, and finally looked at me.

"I guess."

"I'm your brother."

"Like I could ever forget it," she said, her nose scrunching up like I stank. "*Why can't you be more like your brother? Your brother never gave us this trouble.* Not a day goes past when someone doesn't compare me to you. So, yeah, I know you're my brother." She rolled her shoulder to shake off my hand.

There was so much bitterness in her voice I could hardly stand it. Katie was being forced to live up to *my* standard? When I'd become so used to living in *her* shadow? Everything in this reality was turned on its head.

"I'm sorry," I said, not sure what else to say.

She laughed through her nose. "*You're* sorry? Sure."

"Look, Katie, I'm guessing I deserve this, like maybe I haven't been around much. But I'm here now and I'm trying to help you. So, if you could stop being such a bitch for a minute, that would be great."

Katie and I had always had what could be called an antagonistic relationship. But really, it was usual brother-and-sister stuff. I'd push her, she'd push back. I'd tease her, she'd come up with a devastating putdown that crushed me. But whatever was happening here was something else. I guessed the other Scott didn't know her the way I did.

Her eyes widened in shock and she opened and closed her mouth, trying to think of something to say. "Help me? How?"

I had been thinking the whole way over here about what I was going to do. How I could actually help her. If I pulled her out of training – if that was even something I had the power to do – it might look suspicious. But there was a way that Katie could get out without causing any concern.

"You need to fail," I said.

"I what?"

"I know that probably goes against every bone in your body to not come out on top. But it's really important that you don't graduate."

She tilted her head and looked at me. "And why should I listen to you?"

I didn't have an answer for that. "Um... because I love you and I want the best for you?"

This seemed to shock her. "You don't even know me."

"I do," I pleaded with her. "And I'm going to take care of you, I promise. You have to believe me."

She chewed on her bottom lip, considering my words. "When I was really little, you were fun. You'd come home from training at the weekends and holidays and we'd play together. We'd build pirate forts and you'd make me walk the plank; do you remember that?"

I smiled. "How could I forget? You broke your leg and then didn't tell Mum on me."

"And I remember how you stayed with me in the hospital and refused to let go of my hand."

That memory was faint for me. I could mostly only remember the guilt and the fear that I'd killed my little sister.

"You used to look after me. You used to be fun. And then the war started and you turned into..."

"Into what?"

"Into you!" Katie's eyes tightened and a sardonic smile twisted her mouth. She was pleased about something. "Mr

'By-the-rules'." She shook her head. "Mr 'My-duty-comes-first'."

"I'm sorry, Katie. I thought I was protecting you. And I'm going to go on protecting you."

Which was true. Whatever I had done in this reality, I believed I had done it to keep Katie and my family and everyone I ever cared about safe. But it had meant that in protecting them, I'd stopped caring about them.

"By making sure I don't enlist? Well, you shouldn't have bothered. There is no way I want to become an officer and spend another second being compared to you."

"So, you're not planning joining S3?"

"Why do you think I've been working so hard to make sure nobody sees how good I am?"

I shook my head, trying to understand what she was saying. "What do you mean?"

"I've been flunking every class, every test. And it's really hard! I could beat every kid in this place without so much as raising a sweat. And trying to hold back my power when they make you do stupid things like climb poles… it's exhausting. But I want to get out of here."

"And I want that, too!"

"But you're literally the poster boy for this crap!" She pointed at the image of me tacked to the wall.

"I'm not anymore. I can't explain why. But I don't want this for you. I never wanted my life for you, Katie. All I want is for you to be safe and happy and for us to be a family again."

She snorted. "You've been doing a pretty shit job of that lately."

I didn't have an excuse for that. How could I explain to her that I wasn't the brother she knew? The brother she knew was an institutionalised dick, more concerned with doing his duty to his country than to his family. Whereas I... I was just a regular dick who didn't want to see his little sister hurt.

"I know. And I'm sorry. And when this is all over, I will explain. But right now, I need you to keep it up. If you don't make the grade, then they let you go, right?"

"But there are tests."

"Then fail them."

"There are rumours here that these are not the kind of tests you fail." She looked up at me. "What are they like?"

The memory of Frankie thrashing in the machine blended with older memories. Memories that belonged to him.

All I could recall was pain. "They hurt."

Katie took a ragged breath and stepped away.

"But it's only pain, Katie. You can handle it. They push you to try to find your limits, so give in. Let them think you're weak."

She chewed on her bottom lip so hard, I was worried she might draw blood. "But what if..."

"What?"

"A man came here a while ago. He was asking questions about Fixers."

That must have been one of Vine's men looking for a replacement for the Igloo. "And are you one? A Fixer, I mean?"

"I don't know. Sometimes, I think, maybe. Like sometimes, I get so bored of all the changes and I want things to stay still and silent. And when I focus on that…"

"People around you can't Shift?"

She shrugged, her small shoulders hunching over.

"Look, I guess you don't really know me, but I know you. And you're the smartest, toughest person I know." I bent down so our faces were level, and took her hand in mine. "But you can't let them know you're a Fixer. You have to find a way to cheat the tests." I closed my eyes and saw Katie lying in the coffin, her eyes staring blankly. "You have to."

"You're scaring me, Scott," she said. The first time she'd used my name.

I opened my eyes and looked at her. "Everything will be OK. I promise. Hang in for a little longer and then I'll come and get you and make sure you're safe."

"Safe?" Katie said. "Who's ever safe with the war going on?"

"I'll make sure you get sent home, to Mum and Dad."

"Mum *and* Dad?" she said. "Don't you mean Mum *or* Dad? They live in different countries now, Scott. Or don't you remember that, either?"

So, they'd finally had the balls to split up. Well, maybe that was a good thing. "Wherever you want to go, Katie, I'll get you there."

She tightened her grip in my hand. "You left me here," she said, tears glittering in the corner of her eyes. "You said you'd come and you never did. Three years, Scott and you never came."

I couldn't bear to see Katie cry. It cut straight through me. I would give anything, do anything to make her tears stop. But now, there was nothing I could do.

I pulled her into a hug. She resisted at first, and then gave in, wrapping her arms around me.

"I'm sorry, Katie," I whispered into her ear. "But I'll find a way to make it all OK. I promise. I'll get us all out of here."

"I'm so scared, Scott," she answered.

"Me, too."

There was no one else in the world I could admit that to. Not even Aubrey. Only my brave, brilliant little sister. Her arms tightened around my neck. We stayed like that for a few moments, neither of us willing to let the other go.

There was a small knock on the door. Reluctantly, I broke from Katie's hug.

"Commandant?" CP stood at the door, looking anxious.

"What is it?" I said, my voice croaking.

"A call has come in from the Hub. You're needed back there now."

I looked at Katie, hoping she could read in my eyes everything I wanted to say to her. That I loved her. That I'd return for her and if I couldn't find a way to undo everything I'd caused, we'd carve out some kind of life together here.

CP coughed. "It sounded pretty urgent, sir."

"I'll come back," I whispered in Katie's ear.

"You'd better."

KIM CURRAN

CHAPTER FOURTEEN

Cain and the whole of Thirteen squad were in the command room, along with Hedges. He was looking better than earlier, his cuts cleaned up and back in S3 uniform. There was a steely glint in his eyes now, too. Revenge, I wondered? Voices were raised and it seemed that Cain and Hedges were disagreeing about something.

Aubrey looked up as I came in. Her jaw was tight, her skin pale. She was worried about something. And it wasn't me.

Zac stood next to Williamson, both too engrossed in the data on the screen to notice me. Turner stood in the corner, her eyes puffy and red; she'd been crying again. Ladoux leaned on the edge of the table, her red beret pulled low over one eye.

"Take your time, Tyler. Don't worry about us," Cain said as I approached.

"Bring me up to speed," I said, ignoring Cain's sarcasm. I wasn't in the mood for his crap.

"I know what X73 is," Hedges said.

"George was wrong," Aubrey said. "It's not a computer virus."

"It's a biological virus."

I closed my eyes at hearing Frankie's voice behind me. It appeared there was no escape from her in this place.

"Thank you for joining us, Doctor Goodwin," Cain said as Frankie came to stand at the table next to him.

"I thought you were avoiding me, Sergeant Cain," Frankie said. "Or is there another reason you've missed your last two psych evals?"

The two stared at each other, and I got a twinge of pleasure at the idea that Cain didn't trust her either. But then he looked away, his expression becoming that of a chastised child. Why would Cain feel guilty about avoiding a psych eval? And then I remembered. How adult Shifters had a tendency to go crazy. I forced myself to look at his scar, remembering what it really meant. He didn't seem to be on the verge of megalomania, like a lot of the men from Project Ganymede I'd tracked down had been. But there was always time. Was that bomb still planted in his cortex, I wondered? Did he know about it or what the true cost of keeping his powers was? In my reality, when Cain had found out the truth about Project Ganymede, it had destroyed him.

I turned my gaze to Frankie's forehead. Smooth and undamaged. I had to accept the facts: she wasn't a Shifter now. She didn't have the power to control me. But that didn't mean she could be trusted. She could still be Slate.

Just because the Minister of Defence trusted her didn't mean I had to. After all, plenty of powerful men had fallen under Frankie's spell before. I wasn't willing to believe that in undoing a single choice, a person could change this much.

And yet... I remembered what it felt like when the me from this place took hold. How easy it was to make the hard choices. How completely sure I felt that they were the right things to do. Maybe the Frankie I confronted at the Pyramid had felt the same? Maybe she had been doing what she believed to be her duty, too? She'd said that once she'd started down the path, she knew there was no way back. When I Forced her to unravel her life right back to her decision to volunteer for Project Ganymede, had I stopped her in taking the first step?

Cain coughed, pulling my attention back to the room. "What can you tell us about this virus?"

Frankie smiled at Cain and eased him out of the way so she could get to the table. She pushed some buttons on the screen, and a 3D image of a DNA strand appeared. The double helix of molecules spun on its axis. We all leant in to see.

"I present to you the X731608 virus. A highly virulent hybrid of nanotechnology and the Ebola virus."

She pulled up some images marked "Test Subjects". There was a collective grunt of disgust and I had to turn away from the pictures of children with blood pouring from their eyes and noses.

"Make them go away," CP said. She too was unable to look at the pictures.

"So, it attacks people's brains? Nice," Zac said, closing each of the images with a push of his finger.

"Within a matter of seconds, yes," Frankie said. "It was engineered to target the orbitofrontal cortex and will eat through the frontal lobe within ten seconds of infection. And spreads faster and wider than any virus I've ever seen, up to thirty miles in an hour."

The group shared a worried look.

"And what do the Red Hand want with it?" Cain said.

Frankie took a deep breath before speaking again. "It was designed to target a specific chromosome. A particular region of chromosome fifteen, to be exact, which has been identified for being associated with disorders such as epilepsy and autism. And" – she paused and looked straight at me – "Shifting."

The realisation of what that meant passed over me like an icy breeze.

"You're saying this virus targets Shifters?" CP said. She looked as horrified as I felt.

"That's exactly what I'm saying."

A ripple of understanding moved through the group. If X73 got into the wrong hands, it could kill half of the people in this room. Not to mention the rest of the Shifters in the country.

Cain swallowed so loudly, I heard it on the other side of the table. Of course, I thought, he's as much at risk as the rest of us. "Where did it come from?"

"As far as I understand," Frankie said, "it was created at the start of the war by Doctor Lawrence and his team. They were tasked with understanding the source of Shifting."

Lawrence; I knew that name. He was the man who had originally set up Project Ganymede.

"In identifying the gene responsible for the power, they were also able to engineer a virus to target it: X73."

"And the Red Hand know about it?" I asked.

"Yes," Hedges said. "Sarah and I heard them talking about it."

I caught the slightest flicker of emotion from Ladoux at the mention of the dead woman's name. Was it guilt that she'd been unable to save her from the Red Hand?

"Is there an antidote?" Zac said.

"Not that I know of," Frankie said.

Worried mutters passed through the group. Unwin and Williamson whispered to each other. Aubrey rested her hand on CP's shoulder, reassuring the young girl. The tendons on Hedges' jaw jutted sharply, as if he was biting down hard, fighting to keep his emotions in check. Ladoux just stared at the DNA strand as it spun in neat circles. She was holding her lighter again, rubbing her thumb over the surface. I could see now that it had a faded engraving on the brass case.

"The question is, do they want X73 to use it, or," Zac looked to Cain "to stop us from using it?"

"Yes," Aubrey said. "If George was telling the truth, their leader is a Shifter. Maybe she's as keen to see this out of the way as we are?"

"She could be an ex-Shifter." I tried not to look at Frankie.

"In which case, the virus would still be effective," Frankie said. "Entropy doesn't affect our genes, you know? Only our power."

And our personality, I wanted to say.

"First thing," Cain said, cutting through the murmurs in the group, "we need to work out if they do have it. Where was the virus stored?"

Frankie called up the info on the files. "A medical facility in Sussex, according to this."

"Sussex," Hedges said as if he was surprised, leaning on the desk with his closed fists. "The Red Hand thought it was stored here."

Details on the facility appeared next to the image of the virus, including a picture of a large silver dome sticking out of the ground. Frankie zoomed in on the building, and we could clearly see a sign in front of the structure.

Do not enter. Government Medical Research Facility.

"Gee, a big sign. That's bound to keep the Red Hand away." Williamson rolled his eyes.

"Actually, it's got top-level security," Zac said, scanning through the rest of the data. "Eye scans. DNA-encrypted access. Will we even be able to get in there?"

"Unrestricted-access individuals only," Aubrey said, tapping at a line in the file. "That means you, Commandant."

Our eyes met and I felt that rush of connection. Maybe now was the time to tell her what was really going on. I could walk out of this room with her, and neither of us would ever need to walk back in. With a thought, I could end it all. Then I remembered the image of the dying children. No, getting out of here could wait till I'd finished this mission. Just one last job.

"When do I leave?"

"Ladoux, is the copter ready?" Cain said. She was still watching the helix spin and spin. "Ladoux!"

She snapped out of it. "This thing is evil," she said. "It shouldn't even exist."

"Which is exactly why we're going to get to it before the Red Hand do," Cain said.

"If it's not already too late," Zac replied.

Something didn't feel right. If the Red Hand knew about this virus, we could be walking into a trap.

I know.

I sensed him there, the other me, in the shadows of my mind. He was amused by everything, mocking my failure to keep up. What was I missing? I scanned the files again, looking for something.

You won't find it there, I sensed him.

I pushed him away. The more I let him in, the more I lost of myself. If he had worked it out, I could, too.

I returned my focus to the room. Unwin and Williamson were already checking their weapons. CP stood next to me, chewing on her nails. Turner, who hadn't said a word throughout the entire exchange, was hunting for something in one of her pockets. Whatever it was, she seemed to find it in her left pouch. She pulled a clenched fist out and slipped the object into her breast pocket. I saw a glint of gold. The rest were looking to me, waiting for their orders. Even Cain seemed to be expecting me to have an answer.

"If they had it, we'd know," I said. "They'd have sent us another of their little messages to make sure of it."

Zac's eyes blinked as he thought through the options. "The Com's right. We might still have time."

"Right, Tyler," Cain said. "I want you to take a small team and go and check it out."

"Agreed," I said. "Black, Unwin, Williamson and…" I hesitated before saying Aubrey's name. I was caught between wanting to protect her and wanting to stay close to her. "Jones," I finished. "Suit up."

Turner took the news that she wasn't coming on the mission with a small nod. I didn't think she was up to being on duty, anyway. CP muttered about it not being fair that she didn't get to go.

"I suggest you take the good doctor with you, too."

"No!" I said, glaring at Cain.

He raised a ragged eyebrow. "Do we have a problem, Tyler?"

"I don't think a civilian should be on the mission," I said hurriedly.

"Please," Frankie said. "I was a solider for ten years. I've seen as much action as you. And you need me. What if the virus is released? Who will treat you?"

"I thought you said there was no antidote."

"No. But you can either die screaming or I can help ease the process."

We stared at each other, neither willing to back down or show the slightest crack of weakness.

"I think a Shifter-targeting, flesh-eating virus getting into the hands of the enemy takes priority over whatever problem you have with the doctor, don't you, Tyler?" Cain said.

I turned my glare on him. In my anger, I felt a familiar buzz of power, different to how it felt to Shift. It was the same feeling I got when I'd broken free of Frankie's hold. I knew I could Force Cain. I could make him listen to me. And yet, maybe he was right.

Besides, if she came with us, I could keep an eye on her. "OK." I turned away, letting the power drain away.

Hedges stepped forward, fists clenched by his side, clearly trying to conceal the pain he was still in. "Permission to join the squad, Commandant."

I'd read Hedges' files on the way to extract him. He had an exemplary record, had proved himself in combat on at least eight missions, and his profile made a point of his 160 IQ. He would be a good asset, but he had a lot of healing to do first. And not only physical.

"We'd be proud to have you," I said, ignoring Frankie's gasp and Ladoux's sudden turn of head, "but not today. There will be other missions, Hedges. This war isn't over yet."

Hedges nodded his understanding.

Ladoux squeezed his shoulder. "He's right," she said. "You need to stay here." Then she leant in and whispered in his ear so quietly that I couldn't hear. And yet, I found I was able to read her lips. *"You will have your revenge soon enough."*

I coughed, hiding my discomfort at having witnessed that private moment. "Right, what else do I need to know?"

"We'll need to follow hazmat procedures," Frankie said. "You can't go into a place like this and start blowing things up." This was directed at me.

"What do you need?" I asked, ignoring the implication that I was only good for one thing.

She listed a series of things, including hazmat suits for the whole team.

I clicked my fingers at Unwin and Williamson, who jolted to attention and ran off to get what was needed. "OK. But once we're on the ground, you follow my lead, do you understand?"

Frankie nodded, resentfully.

I leant in so that only she could hear "If I get the tiniest suspicion that you are screwing with me, I will finish you."

"You might have everyone else fooled, Commandant Tyler," she said, softly. "But I have been working with sick Shifters for fifteen years. I know a reality attack when I see one. So the question is, how much longer can you hold on before you break altogether? You should let me help you before it's too late."

Could I trust her? The woman who had once taken everything from me was now offering to help me. Could she help me find a way home? No, I didn't believe it.

I tuned away from her and addressed the squad. "We leave in ten."

CHAPTER FIFTEEN

The landscape below us changed from the grey slate of the scarred city to a patchwork of yellows and greens as we flew out into the countryside. Out here, where nature carried on like always, it was almost possible to believe the war wasn't happening.

Aubrey peered down, a small smile on her face. She'd said she'd been based in Brighton before they'd moved her to London. So was this where she'd grown up? Amid the rolling hills of the Sussex countryside? I remembered what *my* Aubrey had said about her childhood, how she'd been taken into the agency at the age of seven, how her mum had killed herself. I wondered how different this Aubrey's early life had been.

I recognised the landscape from my youth, too. Mum and Dad had taken Katie and me to a holiday village out here once. Somewhere to offload us onto a bunch of organised kids' activities, while they relaxed in the log cabin's hot tubs. But we hadn't minded. Some of my best memories of my childhood had been there.

The rhythmic *whoosh* of the blades settled in time with my calming pulse. It felt right to be up here, on my way to another mission. I felt like I had purpose. Focus. I was where I was supposed to be.

I tried to push that thought away. To fight to hold onto my past and stop it from blending in with this present. But it was becoming harder and harder. Had those memories of childhood trips to the forest been his or mine? I wasn't sure anymore.

Unwin, Williamson and Zac chattered the whole way, trading stories and insults. Williamson was dry to the point of scathing. But anytime he said anything that came close to upsetting someone, he softened it with one of his dazzling smiles. Unwin, who seemed to be the brunt of most of the jokes, was taking it all in good humour. Aubrey listened, smiling at the bawdy humour, without joining in.

That was, till Unwin nudged Williamson and nodded to her. "Hey, Williamson, did you hear the one about why women make better soldiers?"

Aubrey cut him off before he had a chance to deliver the punchline. "Because our brains aren't located in our combats?"

Unwin laughed and tried to rile her again. "How did you lose your eye, Captain? Did you poke it out with an eyeliner pencil?"

"I told someone I'd rather tear my eye out than have to serve with you, Unwin. And then I got sent here. So..." She shrugged.

Zac and Williamson rocked with laughter. Unwin tried to come back with something, then gave up and laughed along. "Nice one, Jones."

Frankie appeared to be bored of the trip. She sat with her eyes closed and head resting against a metal strut behind her. If it wasn't for the fact that she periodically opened her eyes to check her watch, you might think she was sleeping. She was dressed in the same black jumpsuit as the rest of us, but instead of regulation boots, she was still wearing her pumps.

"We're coming up on the location," Ladoux said over the radio. "I'm not picking anything up on visual."

Zac clambered over Williamson's leg and slid the door open, causing the wind to whip around the cabin. A bump of turbulence knocked him forward.

Williamson grabbed hold of Zac's arm, stopping him from toppling forward. "Try not to die."

Zac smiled in gratitude and took hold of the safety bar before stepping out to the foot rail. He flipped down his visor to focus on the landscape below.

"I can't see anything, either," Zac said after a while, and pulled himself back inside.

"There," Aubrey said, pointing out the window, "Between those two copses of trees."

I looked where she directed and caught a glimpse of sunlight reflecting on a metallic surface.

"Set us down between the trees," I said.

Unwin and Williamson checked their equipment for what must have been the thousandth time. The more time I spent with them, the more I noticed the little adjustments they'd made to their kit. Unwin had "Point and Shoot" painted on the side of his helmet, while Williamson had drawn what I assumed was a unicorn on the back of his flak jacket. It was shooting laser beams out of its eyes. Aubrey, too, had made subtle adjustments, the most noticeable of which were the purple laces she had threaded through her boots.

Ladoux's uniform was neat and untouched: every button buttoned, every crease perfectly pressed. Her small rebellion was the make-up – her vivid red lipstick perfectly matching her beret. I wondered why someone who took so much care over her appearance had decided to join the British army and be destined to a life in combats and boots. I looked at my own uniform and noticed that, like Ladoux, I didn't have a thread out of place. The two of us had that in common: playing by the rules.

"Put down in three," Ladoux's voice came across the mics.

Right, I said to myself. Focus.

I didn't wait for the blades to stop spinning before I jumped out into damp grass, the downdraft tugging at my clothes. My boots sank into the ground and the long grass came up to my knees. My trousers were instantly damp.

The others leapt out after me, and each looked down at the ground unhappily.

"Is this a swamp?" Unwin said as he slowly sank into the mud "No one told me anything about swamps."

"It's a marsh," Aubrey said.

"It's a nightmare," Williamson said, struggling to free his boots.

"The land is too unstable," Ladoux said. "I'll find higher ground and regroup." Then she pulled back on the controls and peeled away, leaving us alone in the sea of green.

It was hard going, fighting against the mud, weighed down by all our equipment. Frankie made a small squealing noise as her foot disappeared into the soil and then tried to hide it with a cough.

"First time on fieldwork?" Aubrey asked.

"Well, um, yes," she said.

"You'll learn fast enough. Fieldwork blows."

I blinked at the familiarity. Aubrey, *my Aubrey*, had said the very same thing. I must have been staring, as she looked at me with her good eye. "Everything OK, sir?"

I gave a thumbs up and pressed on, trying to focus on the present rather than being lost in the rush of memories that Aubrey's words had unlocked.

The rest of the squad appeared to be enjoying themselves. Chatter passed between Unwin and Williamson, and they laughed.

I caught Williamson's eye. "We did our basic training here," he said. "Ward lost her boots."

"And didn't shut up about it for the rest of the weekend," Unwin said. "She ended up killing and skinning a squirrel, just to have something to wrap her feet in." The two soldiers smiled at the memory of their lost friend.

"How long did you serve together?" Aubrey asked.

"Two years," Williamson said.

"Only five months for me," Unwin said. "But she used to look after me. That's why I called her... called her Mum." He fought to control the emotion in his voice.

"Yeah, she was more of a mum to me than mine ever was," Williamson said. "Mine was a cow."

"Yours, too?" Zac said.

I'd never known Zac had any problems with his mother. For that matter, I'd never known anything about Zac's life other than that he was an enormous pain in my arse. But this was not the time to be baring our souls.

"Focus," I said in a warning tone.

Unwin swallowed hard and sniffed, responding instantly to my command. Williamson nodded in agreement, and his expression became serious. Having that effect on them reminded me of how I'd Forced the guards at Greyfield's to obey. A strange mix of power and guilt. I don't know why the squad listened to me, only that they would. They would jump in front of a bullet if I told them. Loyalty. Power. Were they the same thing?

Do you know why they follow me? He was here again. He was always here. *Because they know I will do what needs to be done. They know if I let them die, it will be because their death will have meaning. If I let them live, it will be for the same reason. They know I can make the choices they're too selfish or too scared or too caught up in their small world to make.*

I remembered Cooper and how I'd held him in my arms, making sure he died, because the mission required it. Maybe he and I weren't that different after all.

No, I thought. We are different. I had to believe that if I was going to hold on to myself. I blocked him out and focused on the feel of the mud sucking against my boots.

Finally, the ground became more solid and progress was easier. Once clear of the marsh, Aubrey and Zac picked up the pace, jogging ahead to the edge of a thicket of trees. They worked perfectly as a team without a word from me. I felt a hot curl of nausea in my stomach, watching them together, so easy in each other's company. And yet I welcomed it, because I knew, without doubt, that the jealousy belonged to me and only to me. It was a small victory.

I held up a fist, halting the rest of the squad behind me. They responded by spreading out, and seconds later, I could hardly see them, their camo blending into the undergrowth. Even Frankie knew what to do, pressing her body into the mossy ground.

"It's clear." Zac was on the other side of the copse of chestnut trees, beckoning us forward.

The squad were on their feet in an instant, moss and bushes suddenly becoming humans again.

They moved through the forest without so much as stepping on a twig. I, on the other hand, stumbled a few times and even hit myself in the face with a branch. But I Shifted to cover up my clumsiness.

Weren't you trained… at all?

That annoying, nagging voice in my head made its return. It was like he was sitting on my shoulder, ready to point out everything I was doing wrong.

"Will you piss off, OK?" I muttered.

"You alright, Com?" Williamson said, looking at me worriedly.

"Yes, just this… this bramble." I swiped at a nearby shrub, trying to cover my mistake.

I had to block him out. Even if it meant sacrificing the sharpness I'd had at the Red Hand base.

When we cleared the trees, I saw the very top of a silver dome rising out of a hillock. It reflected the trees all around it, creating its own kind of camouflage.

Zac was leaning casually against the "Do not enter" sign, readjusting his glove as if he was leaning at a bus stop, waiting for his ride home.

Aubrey stood in front of the door. "You're up, Com."

I joined her and looked down at the entry system. A palm reader similar to the one at my flat and an eye scanner. I laid my hand on the pad and pressed my eye against the black eyepiece.

Blue light flashed and I felt a scraping across the palm of my hand, deeper than the sample taken at home.

The door swung open.

I looked down at my hand, where a deep red scratch ran from my thumb to my little finger. They certainly weren't taking any chances here. I shook away the mild stinging sensation.

I turned back to the door. "Masks on," I shouted.

The team responded by pulling on their masks, the green-glass eyes making them look like sad ghosts. I was about to tell Aubrey to take point when I was hit with an unsettling sense of déjà vu. I knew this place. I'd been here before; I was sure of it.

I took in the landscape. I recognised those trees, that rock formation and, above all, this building. I knew that once inside, we'd find a long corridor leading to a small laboratory. But I didn't know how I knew. An uneasy sensation prickled at the back of my head.

"Something's not right," I said, my voice muffled by the mask.

"We should go in," Ladoux said, eagerly.

"Wait." I needed to work out what to do.

Aubrey and the rest of the team looked at me, awaiting orders.

"You think it's a trap?" Zac said.

I didn't know what I thought. I hesitated, looking between the trees and the bunker. "Let me go first."

Aubrey stepped out of the way as I pushed open the door. My memory – if it had been a memory – was right. I stood in a narrow corridor, and I had to stoop to avoid banging my head on the low ceiling lights. It led to a small white lab, silver workbenches in the middle, an assortment of bulky equipment, and shelves filled with glass beakers. On the far wall, there was a freezer. I opened the glass door, the black suction seal making a soft popping noise. There were rows upon rows of small vials in polystyrene holders. I pulled out one at random, a clear liquid with the name "Zaire Ebola virus" printed on across the vial. The next was labelled "meningoencephalitis". The third held a dark purple liquid. "X731608" was written on a white label in tidy red ink. The substance swirled as if there was something alive inside. I placed the vial back and closed the door.

There was no one here. No immediate threat. Maybe I was being paranoid. But something felt wrong.

"Clear," I said into my mic, still somewhat uncertain.

Zac came first, followed by Frankie and the rest of the squad. Frankie looked much more at home here, despite the fact that she'd lost a shoe back in the marsh. "OK, start packing everything up. And be very, *very* careful. A single drop of this stuff, and..." She didn't need to finish.

The squad set about emptying the freezers into two white polystyrene boxes we'd brought. I ran my gloved hand over the metallic surface of a workbench, trying to shake off the sense of disquiet.

"You OK?" Zac said quietly, standing next to me, covering up his mic so no one else could hear.

"I don't know. I..." I couldn't explain why everything felt so wrong.

I didn't have to.

There was a strange bouncing, scraping sound overhead, something moving through the air ducts. We all looked up, following the progress of the sound till it settled over a grate in the ceiling.

Williamson was the first to work it out. "Grenade!" he shouted, twisting his body away from the duct to cover a box, his first instinct to protect the mission.

It was too late. The grenade exploded in a flash of blinding light and tore the ceiling to shreds. The shockwave hit and threw me off my feet, sending me crashing into a freezer, which shattered beneath me. I slid off the door and onto my feet, the explosion still ringing in my ears, and tried to assess the damage.

Frankie, who had been standing directly under the grate, was gone, nothing more than a red stain where she had been. Unwin was missing half his face but was still alive, although I doubted he would stay that way for long. All that was left of Williamson was his torso still protecting the box of vials. What was unmistakably an arm lay on the workbench, still holding a single vial.

As well as blood everywhere, there was seeping purple liquid. The virus was out. I had a matter of seconds. I closed my eyes, fighting off the unconsciousness that my body was willing on me, and focused. The world flipped.

I was standing beside a tree, looking down on the facility. Unwin was standing next to me, his gas mask off and gun pointed at the silver dome. I remembered I'd given the order to pull back as soon as Aubrey had opened the door. The Shift had worked. Relief flowed through me. I wouldn't allow us to mess up again.

"It looks clear," Unwin said. "Are you sure it's a trap?"

His young face was whole and undamaged once more. "Absolutely certain."

I checked the whole team were still here. Zac and Williamson were standing with their backs against trees, waiting patiently on my next order. Aubrey was adjusting the straps on her gas mask.

I scanned the hillock for any sign of movement. There was a glint from behind a clump of stones about one hundred yards away. I thought through my options, trying to work out the best way to progress. We needed to get the vials, but I knew they were waiting for us.

"Why don't I..." Frankie said, stepping out from the cover of the trees.

There was a loud crack, as if she'd stepped on a twig. She stopped, then slumped to the floor, a single red hole in her forehead.

I considered leaving her like that. But instead, I focused again. And everything flipped.

This time, I'd left the squad covering the bunker while Zac, Frankie and I went into the lab alone.

Zac guarded the corridor while I helped Frankie with the freezers. I kept staring back up at the grate where the grenade had landed.

"If you were to focus on what you are doing, Commandant, we could get this done quicker," Frankie complained.

I raised my eyebrow. This was the problem with working with civilians. They had no idea how lucky they were.

I looked back to the grate. They were out there, waiting. The team covering the outside was all that was stopping them from making their move. A team, or a lone operator maybe? They'd strike as we exited. It's what I'd do.

"OK," Frankie said. "That's the last one."

I nodded. "We're coming out," I said into the mic. "I want covering fire focused on three o'clock from the entrance of the bunker." The gunshot that killed Frankie had come from that direction.

"Roger that," Unwin said. They knew not to question my orders, even if they didn't make sense.

We walked down the corridor, Zac and I carrying the boxes filled with sloshing vials of X73.

"On my count," I said. "Three... Two ..."

On one, I threw open the door as the gunfire sounded. I pushed Frankie and then Zac forward, forcing them to run as fast as they could for the trees, and I followed, zigzagging left and right. If it was a sniper, I wasn't going to be an easy target.

We were close to making the cover of the trees when a branch in front of me splintered, showering me in bark and sap. I threw the box forward and followed by throwing myself over it. Zac threw himself next to me.

The gunfire died down.

"You were right, sir. There's definitely someone out there," Unwin said, helping me to my feet.

"Only one?" Zac said, breathing heavily, brushing leaves off his uniform.

"Maybe they thought that's all that would be needed," Aubrey said. "A single sniper to take us all out and then run off with the virus."

"Then why blow up the facility?" I said.

"But they didn't…" Frankie began. The others shared knowing looks, and she caught on. "You've Shifted?"

"Yes."

"And you can remember?" she asked.

"Yes."

"Interesting."

I fixed her with a stare that suggested she might want to keep her mouth shut or I would do it for her.

"What happened to us before?" Williamson asked.

"You don't want to know." I handed my box of vials to Williamson as Unwin refused to touch it.

There was a loud snap and I turned, my hand drawing my gun without even realising.

It was Ladoux, finally joining us. She walked down the verge, hands out, palms up to show she was no threat. As she came closer, her expression went icy cold.

"You have the vials?"

"Thanks to the Com," Unwin said.

Ladoux turned to me, her face blank and strange. Then something caught her eye. A flash of purple amid the green. One of the vials must have fallen out of the box when we'd dived for cover. Ladoux and I went to pick it up at the same time. She got there first. She held it up to the light, as if looking at a precious stone. "When will men learn not to play at God?"

Frankie took it off her. "Without 'man playing at God', we wouldn't have penicillin or antibiotics. Not all science is evil." She put the vial back in the box.

Ladoux didn't look convinced. In fact, she looked angry. I didn't have time to work out why.

I gave the boxes to her and Williamson, as Unwin downright refused to touch it.

"You three, head back to the helicopter. Frankie, you go with them."

I needed to get to whoever had been firing at us, work out what they knew and what other plans they had in store. I also wanted to work out why I was so sure I'd been to this place before.

"I'm going to get the sniper."

KIM CURRAN

CHAPTER SIXTEEN

I watched Frankie, Ladoux and the two men head back through the trees. Ladoux kept turning back. Was it the very existence of the virus that had unsettled her so much? I would talk with her later. I turned my attention to where the shots had come from.

"Need backup?" Zac said.

"Only if you haven't got anything better to be doing," I said.

"Well, I had planned on finishing a heartbreaking poem about the horrors of war I've been working on," he said, picking at a bit of bark. "But it can wait." He gave his lazy salute.

"I'll come, too," Aubrey said. "We can triangulate them."

"Good idea," I said. "Like *Jurassic Park*."

She stared at me blankly.

"You know, the three dinosaurs? Clever girl? No?" I was getting nothing but confused expressions. "Forget it. Let's go."

The three of us spread out. Aubrey was to loop around on the right, Zac on the left, while I was going to walk straight out. I had all the variations held in my mind in case I needed to Shift. It was a bit like memorising a hand of cards, trying to hold a sequence straight. A slip of concentration, one decision made without thinking it through, and I could be in serious trouble. The biggest fear was being shot in the head. In that case, there was nothing that could save you, not even the hypnic jerk – the Shifter's reboot function. I was hoping it wasn't going to come to that.

On my mark, we split off. I moved fast, running from cover to cover, but I was trying to make myself seen, to distract whoever was up there from Aubrey and Zac coming around from the sides.

I stopped behind a tree to check my pistol was loaded, then ran again. I moved in short sprints, up the hill and towards the clump of rocks from where I'd seen the flash of light.

There was definitely someone there. I saw a hand resting on a rock twenty yards away. I slowed, taking cover behind another tree. If I could shoot their hand, then I'd disarm them. I raised my pistol and took aim. As I was about to squeeze the trigger, they stood up.

It was a teenager: a tall, skinny boy with shaved hair. He wore a mismatch of dark green clothes and, I could see, the symbol of the Red Hand printed on his shoulder. He held a sniper rifle in his hands. I froze. The barrel was pointed straight at my head. He lowered the gun a couple of inches.

"Are we good to go?" he said, his hands twitching around the stock of the gun. I was surprised, given how fidgety he was, that he'd been able to shoot straight at all. "Are we good?" he said again when I hadn't replied.

"I don't know what you mean," I said, stepping forward.

The gun was pointing to the left of me, but all it would take was a second and it would be directed at my face again.

"The virus, Tyler." He knew who I was. And it seemed I was supposed to know him. "Are we still going ahead with the plan?" There was a mixture of fear and hope in his voice.

"No," I said. "The plan is cancelled. The vials have been secured."

"Thank God," he said, dropping the gun to his side, his face relaxing in relief.

I stared at him, more confused and more scared than I had been since I arrived.

"Are you alone?" I said looking around.

"Yes, just like you instructed."

"Like I instructed?" I said.

Bile rose in my throat. How could that be possible? How could I have been involved in something like this?

But wasn't me. It was him. That's why he knew what had been going on, why this place had felt so familiar. He'd been here before. He was working with the Red Hand. He was working against us.

I tried to match this realisation with the Commandant Tyler everyone seemed to think I was. War hero. Leader. And all the time, he'd been on the side of our enemies.

You don't understand.

What is there to understand? I thought, furious at the ghost of him. Furious at myself. *You're a traitor.*

It's more complicated than that.

I hit my head with my hand, trying to displace his spirit. It didn't matter what his plans had been, I was in charge now. And there was no way I was letting him get away with this.

"Tyler?"

I realised the boy had been calling my name, louder and louder.

"What?" I snapped.

He jerked, flinching at my words. "What's the next move, Tyler?"

"I... I don't know."

"Am I to blow up the lab, still?"

"No," I said.

"But Slate said I was to wait until everyone was inside and–"

"Slate can go screw herself," I said, my hand flexing around the grip of my gun. I still hadn't holstered it.

The kid bent over and began dismantling his rifle. "Whatever. I'm getting sick of these games. I joined the

Red Hand because I believed God wanted me to *do* something. And all I've been doing is sitting on my arse." I guessed he couldn't remember throwing the grenade or shooting Frankie in the head. "I'm heading back."

A twig snapped to my left. In my shock, I'd forgotten about Zac and Aubrey. I couldn't let this boy talk to them. I couldn't have them know that I had been involved in this. The boy turned at the sound.

The kick in my hand was harder than I had expected, shooting from the hip as I was. The boy had a second to look surprised and confused, then folded to the floor. Blood pooled out from the bullet hole in his temple.

I'd reacted purely on instinct. I hadn't even remembered that I was still holding the pistol. It was as if the gun had shot itself.

I looked down at the smoking gun in my hand and then to the boy. I didn't know which sickened me more, the sight of his empty eyes or the fact that I had killed him in cold blood.

"Are you OK?" Zac said, rushing out from the right.

"Yes," I said. "Everything is OK." I holstered the gun and fiddled with my belt, trying to hide my shaking hands.

Zac looked down at the boy. "I saw you talking; what did he say?"

Footsteps approached. Aubrey looked panicked and scared as she raced towards me, then smiled when she saw that I was OK. I looked away. I couldn't face her after what I had done.

"What happened?" she said.

"He left me no choice," I said.

Aubrey laid her hand on my arm as she came close. The simple kindness of the gesture made me feel even worse. Then she crouched down and went through the sniper's pockets. I prayed there was nothing there tying me to him. "He's clean," she said, standing up.

"Was he alone?" Zac said.

"Yes." I rolled the boy over with the tip of my boot so that he looked into the ground rather than accusingly at me. "It's time we got back."

Zac picked up the sniper rifle and looked at it for a moment. The barrel was slightly loose. He finished the job the boy had started, stripping it down in a matter of seconds and throwing it into a bag that lay behind the rocks.

"Are you sure you're OK?" Aubrey said, looking at me.

"Yes, and can you stop asking me?"

"Then why are you crying?" Aubrey asked.

I reached up to feel my cheek. It was damp.

"The helicopter will be waiting," I said, spinning on my heel and walking away from them and the dead boy.

CHAPTER SEVENTEEN

"You're back?" Hedges limped over to us as we entered the Hub.

"Don't look so surprised," Williamson said. "We're good, you know."

"Damn good," Unwin said. And the two men high-fived.

"No, it's just that... I'm happy to see you. You secured the vials?"

"Yes, we have them," Ladoux said, and there was still a cold edge of bitterness in her voice. Anger that the virus had ever been created, I assumed.

"That's good. *Really* good." Hedges fixed Ladoux with a look. What the hell was going on between those two? It was more than something as simple as romance. But I was too tired to work it out.

"Good job, Tyler," Cain said, slapping me on the back. I was too tired for that, too. "Vials recovered. Zero casualties. Good job."

Zero casualties. Unless you counted the boy lying in a pool of mud on a hilltop, which apparently the army didn't.

"And just in time, too," Cain continued. "We couldn't have Emperor Tzen finding out about the existence of this stuff on his visit tomorrow."

"What do you mean?" Ladoux said.

"Emperor Tzen's a Shifter. This virus was designed to kill–"

"I understand that," Ladoux said, irritated. "What do you mean about a visit?"

"The Emperor of China is coming here tomorrow," Hedges said, a broad grin on his bruised face.

"Does that mean..." Zac said, his eyes wide.

"The treaty?" Aubrey said.

"The end of the war?" Ladoux said, staring at Hedges who nodded slowly.

"All in good time, all in good time." Cain smiled, unable to hide his excitement. "For now, we need to ensure these vials are destroyed. I was thinking we could fire up the incinerator, Doctor Goodwin?"

"That should do nicely," Frankie said. She went to take the boxes off Zac and Williamson, who had been carrying them.

"Here," Hedges said, getting to them first. "Let me. It's about the only use I can be at the moment."

Frankie nodded and Hedges followed her out of the room, carrying a white box under each arm.

"The rest of you, fall out," Cain said.

The squad saluted, and I was about to leave when I felt an arm on mine.

"Can I have a word, Commandant?" Aubrey said, as we exited the command room.

"Of course."

We waited for Zac and the others to head back up the tunnel towards the Hub. Unwin whispered something about having tracked down some booze somewhere and they were planning on celebrating the success of the mission.

"What is it, Captain Jones?"

Aubrey tilted her head, her eye fixed on me. "Well, you can start with who you are," she said.

"What do you mean? I'm Scott Tyler, I mean, Commandant Tyler."

"Nice try," she said, 'but the Commandant Tyler I've heard about doesn't cry over the body of an enemy."

I swallowed, my Adam's apple pushing against my throat mic. "I'm having a bit of trouble adjusting. It's just the reality attack. I'll be fine," I said, ashamed of myself.

"Still? You shouldn't be on duty while you're in this state." Aubrey rested her hand on my arm again and turned me to face her.

Her touch seemed to bring me back to myself. "I don't know what to do, Aubrey."

She flinched a little at the use of her name. "Well, you should report to the doc and get signed off for a start."

"No," I said, pulling my arm away. Frankie was the last person I was going to turn to.

"But you're putting lives at risk."

"Did I risk anyone today? Or did I, in fact, stop you all from dying, time and time again?" I slammed my hand into my fist emphasising my point.

She blinked. "I guess I should be thanking you, then?"

"Yes. Yes, you should," I said, rage building. I fought to control it, to control him. He was getting stronger with every passing moment, while I was losing more of myself. If I didn't do something soon, it would be too late. I would be stuck here.

I looked at Aubrey and the treacherous thought crept in – the reason I hadn't tried harder to Shift back to the old reality. I would be stuck here, but would that be such a bad thing?

I hated myself for it. I wanted to hold on to her and myself at the same time. But only one of them was possible.

"But that doesn't change the fact that you need treatment," Aubrey said. "You're forgetting basic procedure, and if your memories don't come back–"

"Don't you get it?" I said, running my hand across my head in frustration. "I don't want them to come back!"

Aubrey looked at me, her eyebrows drawn in together over the top of her patch. "Why not?"

"Because it was better," I said with a sigh, feeling the weight that had been crushing me lighten. Even saying it felt good. "It was better. And I can't lose it."

"Better how?" she said.

"No war. No bombs. No... this." I waved my hands around at the Hub, at the soldiers and armed kids and, by extension, the torn streets above.

"Are you talking about before the war? But you can only have been about six."

"No, I mean in the other reality, where I come from. Where there was no war and you and I were..."

"You and I were what?" she said, a small smile playing at the side of her mouth.

"Weren't here," I finished lamely.

"But there are no other realities, only one, because of the–"

"The collapse of the wave function, I know. I don't know why, but there are other realties. I can remember them."

We'd been taught at ARES that while there were multiple possible realities, there was only ever one actual version. When a Shift was made, the other reality collapsed and the new one took hold.

"How is that possible?" Aubrey said, sounding concerned and confused. "I thought everyone forgot the old realities. And if they didn't, they went mad."

I laughed, a small laugh. "Well, I'm hardly a picture of sanity right now, am I?"

She laughed too, and it felt good. It felt normal. "I'm not sure any of us are all that balanced. Not given the things we've seen. The things we've done. And, bloody hell, if I could remember the other realities, it would tip me over the edge, I'm sure."

"I'm fighting really hard to hang on here," I said.

She chewed at the side of her thumb. I could tell that she wasn't sure whether to believe me or not. And who could blame her? What I was telling her went against everything she'd been told her whole life.

"So, how do you do it?" she said.

"I don't know how it works or why. But I can remember fragments of the other realities. It's just something I can do."

She dropped her hand and sucked in her bottom lip. "And in this other reality, there's no war?"

"Well, there are wars around the world. But nothing in Britain. Nothing like this."

She let out a long sigh. "What was it like?"

"Good," I said, looking at her, drinking in her face. "Wonderful."

She dragged her finger across the wall, tracing the path of a trickle of water. "And you... you know me there?"

"Yes. We're partners. You know, at ARES," I said, quickly deciding that to tell her we were more than that would be too weird right now.

"What am I like?"

"Pretty much like you are here, only–" I gestured to her eye patch.

She raised her hand to touch it. "Oh," she said.

"What happened?"

"It was my first mission," she said. "I'd only been out of training for a couple of weeks when I was sent to the Brighton base. We got word that there had been a Shift in a house on the seafront, but there was no Shifter registered as living there. So I was sent in, as a Spotter, you know."

I nodded to let her know I understood. "What happened?"

"We found this kid there, a girl, freezing in a bathtub, a dead body on the floor next to her."

"She'd killed them?"

"I'd have done the same. The things that had been done to her…" She squeezed her eyes tight, trying to block out the memory. "When I tried to help her, she drew a knife on me. And…" She drew a line across her face.

"You didn't Shift?" I said.

"I wasn't focusing. I was so shocked at what I saw. Rookie mistake."

"I'm sorry."

"Don't be. It was an important lesson. I've never lost focus since." She walked around the room, her boots squeaking on the floor. I watched her, making note of the subtle differences between her and my Aubrey. She held herself differently. Looked less like an animal ready to attack or run, the way the Aubrey I knew always had. She was softer and there was less pain in her expression.

"I bet the other me never did anything that stupid, hey?"

"I don't know. She had pretty suspect taste in men," I said, wondering if I should tell her about the two of us.

"Oh, it sounds like we have that in common, too," Aubrey said, laughing. "I was always a sucker for the bad boys."

I wasn't sure I could ever be thought of as a bad boy, but I decided not to say anything.

"So, there's still ARES, even without the war?"

"As long as there are Shifters, there will be ARES to keep them in line. But it's not like it is here. It's less official. None of the public know about us, for a start."

"Then how do you do your job?"

"You keep it subtle. Under the radar. Mostly, we go about our lives."

"Like normal people?" The side of her mouth turned up the tiniest fraction.

I smiled at the memory of the first night I'd met Aubrey Jones. How she'd taken me to her flat and told me all about what it was to be a Shifter and how all she wanted was to be normal. I'd known then that was never going to be possible.

"Normal compared to here, I guess."

"It sounds good."

"It is."

"And you think there's a way back to that reality? That's why you won't let go of it?"

"I don't know. I've tried, but something is keeping me here." I couldn't admit that that something was her.

"So, why don't you let go of it, then?" She walked over to me. "Why don't you accept that you are here, you are now?"

It was the phrase Frankie had said to me, part of the training we got at ARES to help us deal with reality attacks. If I did let go, if I did give myself completely over to this reality, to this now, how much would I lose?

Memories flashed through my mind: *tucking a lock of Aubrey's hair behind her ear, kissing her, holding her.*

"Because I have to hope that he's wrong. Because it's too good to let go."

"But if there's no way to return, you have to accept that this is the only reality we have. Because if you don't..." She made a corkscrew gesture next to the side of her head.

It was going to send me mad. She was right. But I was going to hold out as long as I could.

"What choice do I have?" I said.

"The only choice any of us have. You fight. Keep fighting till there's an end to this war, and then maybe you can have this normal life again."

"Maybe, but I keep thinking that there's something I can do."

"All Shifters do that. My father told me that it was part of the baggage of being a Shifter. That constant sense of responsibility and guilt."

"Your father?"

"He used to be one of ARES' best Mappers and a colonel in the probabilities office. He'd have liked you." She smiled.

"Used to be? He died?"

"Last year. It wasn't even while on duty. He saw some people raiding a food supply truck and decided to step in. They hit him around the head with a crowbar. Stupid, really. I mean, of all people, he should have seen it coming." It was a bitter joke, but I joined her in laughing anyway.

"Were you close, you and your dad?" I asked.

"As close as possible, what with him in the army and me training at ARES."

Here was yet another of consequence of Frankie's influences having vanished. Aubrey's dad hadn't become the homeless tramp we'd met, driven mad by Frankie's threat of killing his daughter. He'd been a part of Aubrey's life. And a good part, too, judging by the sadness on her face.

"When Mum died, he made sure that he was there for me."

"Your mother is dead," I said, and it wasn't a question.

"All of this is in my file," she said, then shook her head, realising something, "which of course you haven't read, you not being you. She killed herself when I was twelve."

I nodded. It seemed that some things crossed through all realities.

We stood in silence for a while, Aubrey still rubbing her finger on the damp surface of the wall. She seemed to come to a conclusion.

"I won't say anything." She tapped on the wall with her knuckles. "If I had memories like yours," she said, looking up at me, "I'd want to keep hold of them, too."

If only she knew how good the memories were.

"Thanks," I said. "And I'm glad you're in my squad."

"I'm glad, too. You know, I was scared about coming here. I'd heard all this stuff about this amazing Commandant Tyler. The mighty war hero. But now I realise you're just as messed up as anyone."

"Gee, thanks," I said.

"Come on," she said, nudging me with her elbow. "We'd better go, or else Zac will have drunk all the booze."

KIM CURRAN

CHAPTER EIGHTEEN

The party was already in full swing in the barracks by the time Aubrey and I arrived. The men and women of Thirteen squad certainly knew how to enjoy themselves. Music was blasting, some seventies rock song I vaguely remembered Dad used to like. Unwin and Turner appeared to be in some kind of dance-off while the others cheered them on. It was good to see Turner laughing. CP sat on a top bunk, her legs swinging, her hand beating out the rhythm on her leg. Zac was in deep conversation with Williamson, the two of them looking at images on Williamson's tablet. Ladoux stood leaning against the wall, watching it all without joining in. Hedges must have decided to give the celebrations a miss, as he was nowhere to be seen. A metal canteen was being passed from hand to hand. It got to Unwin, who stopped dancing and raised it unsteadily in my direction.

"To the Com," he said loudly.

The rest of the team all stood and echoed his toast. "To the Com."

Unwin took a swig from the bottle and then thrust it into my hand. "Just because we don't remember doesn't mean we don't know," he said, leaning in close. I smelt the bitter heat of the alcohol on his breath. He patted me on the shoulder and then staggered over to the stereo.

I took a swig. The heat of the raw ethanol burnt my throat. I coughed, wiping my mouth with the back of my hand, and handed the bottle to Aubrey. She took it, smiling at me. And we had a moment. A moment like the ones we used to have – where we could say everything without saying a word. Then she took a slug and the moment passed.

"Come on, Com," Unwin shouted, having put on a new song. "Show us your moves."

I held my hands up, shaking my head. "Absolutely no way. I do not dance."

They booed and jeered, but I stood my ground. Zac took the pressure off me by leaping up, grabbing Aubrey by the hand and swinging her into the centre of the room. He proceeded to throw her around, like some kind of crazy Lindy Hop. She laughed, tipping her head back as he spun her in circles. She looked relaxed and happier than I may have ever seen her.

The jealousy I felt every time I saw Zac and Aubrey together bit again, spiking in my stomach. I had to clench my jaws to keep the smile on my face. It was clear these two had history. How much, I wanted to know. And at the same time, I didn't want to know.

I slunk to the back of the room, unable to bear it any more, sickened at my own stupidity, and left them to their fun. Aubrey laughed high and clear as I opened the door.

I sat on the steps of the prefab building that served as the squad's barracks, and rested my head against the railings. When I closed my eyes, the surprised expression on the sniper's face had joined that of Cooper's to haunt me. Who was I? What had I become? I should give it all up and find a way to return to the old reality. Was I really allowing all of this to continue because of the vague hope that Aubrey and I could... could what? Become boyfriend and girlfriend again. It felt pathetic to even think it. But it was true.

I tried to force myself to make a Shift. I thought back to before I'd heard about Frankie, to when I was trying to piece together what I knew about the Shifters, the choice that led me to Benjo, which in turn led me to Frankie. That was the tipping point. I sensed it. If I could undo that, it would all unravel and we'd have just given up on our hunt for the last member of Project Ganymede.

I held it there, that desire to make sure Benjo hadn't survived, and I pushed. Trying to let go of the curiosity that was so often my undoing. I pushed, telling myself to have stayed in bed. I willed that point to flip.

And then I heard Aubrey's laugh, clear and high. The world stayed as it was.

"There has to be another way," I said out loud.

"Another way to what?" I hadn't heard Ladoux open the door behind me. She walked down the steps and stopped at the bottom, leaning against the banister. She had her lighter in her hand again, spinning it around and around in little circles.

"Nothing," I said. "Never mind."

"It's hard, sometimes, accepting this life." She stared up at the dark skies overhead. "We rage against it. 'I am the master of my fate. I am the master of my soul,'" she said.

"What's that?"

She handed me her lighter and I saw the words she had spoken engraved on the casing. "It's from a poem. It was my husband's favourite."

I handed it back to her. "Where is he?"

She looked down at the lighter in her hand. "He died three years ago."

"I'm sorry."

She shrugged. "It feels a long time ago now."

I was surprised at how pragmatic she seemed over the death of her husband. "What happened to him?"

"He was my co-pilot. We were on a drop mission when we were fired upon. The helicopter went down. I walked away. He didn't."

I didn't know what to say. A host of empty platitudes ran through my mind. I settled on a quote I remembered seeing in my flat by an old general. "May God have mercy for my enemies, because I won't."

"Oh, this was not the enemy," she said. "We were fired upon by our own side. A strange English phrase: 'friendly fire'? I can assure you, it really is not that friendly." She slipped the lighter back into her pocket. "It's ironic, I suppose. He was never the master of his own fate. None of us are."

I stared up at her, her small face framed by the red beret. I remember thinking that exact thing when I was lying in a hospital bed, having narrowly missed being blown up on a Tube.

"What's going on here?" It was Zac. "Why do neither of you have a drink in your hands?"

"Ah, what I wouldn't give for some real champagne!" Ladoux said, suddenly changing tone, as if we hadn't just been talking about death.

"When the war is over, I'll get you a magnum of the finest champagne there is!" Zac raised his plastic cup in her direction.

"Ah, but Captain, this war will never truly be over. *Au revoir*, Commandant." And with that, she walked out into the dark.

"I wonder where she's off to," Zac said. "Probably going to find Hedges. The two of them are always sneaking away together."

I didn't say anything. What Ladoux and Hedges got up to was none of my business.

Zac carried on. "She's a funny one." He nudged me with his knee to make room, and sat down on the step next to me. "Almost as weird as you."

I sighed. "Can't you leave me alone?" I snapped, the memory of Aubrey in his arms heating my blood despite the chill of the evening.

"What's got into you?" he said. "I mean, you've been a prickly bastard for the past few years, but I thought you'd started to soften again."

"Nothing's got into me. Why don't you go back inside and carry on showing off?"

"Showing off? *Moi?*" He held his hand to his chest in mock offence. But he wasn't going anywhere. "Is this about the sniper?"

"No. What about him?"

"Only…" He looked down at his fingers. "The barrel on his rifle was loose, as if he'd been dismantling it. There was no way he could have shot you with it."

I stared at him, my head filled guilt and anger.

He held his hands up. "Don't worry, I'm not going to say anything. I know you, Tyler. You had your reasons, I'm sure."

If only he knew that my real reasons had been nothing but cowardice, I'm not sure he would be bothering to talk to me. I stared ahead, hoping that he would leave me alone.

"Come on, Tyler," he said. "You can tell me. Time was, you told me everything. Remember that? When we'd sit around and you'd tell me all about your family, about what girls you liked."

I flinched.

"That's it!" he said, his face lighting up in glee. "It's a girl? Jones!" He held up his finger like Sherlock Holmes coming to a genius conclusion.

I turned away from him, my face too red to bother trying to deny it.

"Do you want me to put a word in? She and I go way back, you know."

"Yes, I know all about you and your history."

"What are you on about, Tyler? Hang on, you don't mean... you're worried about me? And her?" He burst out laughing, clapping his hands together.

"What's so funny?" I said, standing up to get away from him.

"You think... You can't remember..." He could hardly get the words out, he was laughing so much.

"Shut up!" I shouted. The harshness of my tone snapped him out of it.

He stood up, level with me thanks to the higher step he was standing on. "Scott, you have nothing to worry about in regards to me and Aubrey."

"Oh, no?"

"No. Because I'm gay."

It took a moment for what he was saying to sink in. "Gay? But... But you weren't, in my reality."

He rested his hand on my shoulder. "Oh, believe me, Tyler, I am gay in every reality. It's the way I was made. You know, you were much cooler about this the first time I told you."

"I'm cool about it now," I said, embarrassed at myself. "I am. It's only... I always thought that you and Aubrey had been a thing."

"Oh, maybe when I was younger and I was still working this whole sexuality thing out, I might have considered it. You know, she's amazing. But nope. I'm all gay. All the way."

He slapped me gently around the face. "So stop being such a prick and come inside. And if you're really good, I'll tell Aubrey what a great guy you are, OK?"

"I'm such an idiot," I said, shaking my head.

"Don't worry about it," Zac said, looking over my shoulder. "Besides, I think we've got much bigger things to worry about."

I turned to see what he was looking at. Cain strode towards us, a very unimpressed look on his face.

"Busted," Zac said.

"Who wants to explain what is going on here, then?" Cain shouted at us, after we'd all lined up in front of the bunks. "Hmm? No one? Have you all suddenly become mute? Well, that's quite a relief, as it means I won't have to put up with all your tiresome chit-chat when you ask for things like rec time or food."

He strode up and down, his hands clasped behind him.

"What's that?" he said, stopping in front of Turner. "Did you say something?"

Turner flushed and croaked something that I couldn't hear from my end of the line.

"You were celebrating?" Cain roared. "And what exactly were you celebrating? Has the war ended without anyone informing me? Well? Speak up, girl!"

"No," Turner stuttered.

"No, what?"

"No, sir!" Turner shouted.

"I did not think so. Which means that I need every one of my men to be in tiptop condition. The enemy could strike at any point. Do we have a problem, Unwin?"

I risked peering around Zac, who was standing next to me. Unwin looked decidedly green and bit both his lips together as if desperately trying to stop something from escaping out of his mouth. He failed, doubling over and emptying the contents of his stomach onto the floor in front of Cain.

Cain took the longest time to look down, staring straight ahead for, I counted, thirty seconds. He then stepped away, shaking his boot clean.

Unwin was on the floor, spluttering his apologies and trying to wipe the sergeant's boot clean with the sleeve of his shirt. Something within Cain seemed to change. He looked down at Unwin on all fours, and a smile inched across his face. And then he burst out laughing. He laughed so much, he had to bend over and rest both hands on his knees.

A look passed among the squad, not sure what to do. Was this some kind of test?

Cain finally straightened up and wiped a tear from his milky eye. "Someone get this man a glass of water. And while you're at it, get me a glass of whatever hooch you are drinking."

And that was it. The tension vanished, and a few minutes later, the music was blasting again. Cain caught my eye and winked, the action making his whole face fold up like a crumpled ball of paper.

"You want?" Aubrey had joined me in my corner, holding the canteen in her hand.

"God, no," I said. I didn't want to end up like Unwin, who was now lying on the grass outside. "What's that made of, anyway?"

"I find it's best not to ask. There's probably some petrol in it somewhere." She twisted the lid tight on the bottle and laid it on the bunk bed next to us. "How are you holding up?"

"Me? Oh, fine, you know."

"Feeling any less..." She made the corkscrew gesture next to her temple.

"I still don't remember, if that's what you mean."

She nudged me with her hip and smiled. "Good." And with a look that confused the hell out of me while also making my stomach dance, she wandered off to join the party again.

"Not joining in, Tyler?" Cain said.

"I'm not a very good dancer, sir."

"Neither are any of them. But they're having fun. You should try it sometime."

"I'll be sure to do that," I said. "When…"

"When the war's over, hey?" Cain said.

"I guess."

"Well, that may come sooner than you think."

"What they've been saying about the treaty, then, it's true?"

"All I know, *officially*, is that Emperor Tzen is arriving at oh nine hundred tomorrow," he said with a happy smile. "Unofficially, I would say that there will be a lot more celebrating in the days to come. But in the meantime, life doesn't stick around, Tyler. Take it from me. You can wait years hoping for something, all while you miss the fact that what you were looking for was right in front of you all along."

Aubrey was leading the team in some kind of line dance, getting them all to jump left and right. They were all making a complete shambles of it and having a great time doing so.

Cain slapped me on the shoulder so hard, I thought my knees might break. "Don't waste the good times, Tyler."

He nodded towards Aubrey, who was gesturing for me to join in the dance.

"Yes, sir." I stood up to join her, then Unwin came staggering in. He bounced off me.

"Sorry, Com!"

"That's OK."

He bent over, his hands on his knees. "Give me a sec. I'm gonna see if I can Shift myself sober." His Ss all slurred into each other, so I wasn't sure if I'd heard him right.

"What do you mean?" I said.

"Shift," he said, tapping at his beret. "You know? Shhhiiiifffttt."

I grabbed him by the arm and pulled his beret off his head. Under the hat, running across his temple, was a livid red scar.

CHAPTER NINETEEN

I stalked over to Williamson and yanked his beret off, too.

"Oi!" he said, brushing his hair back into place.

I let the hat fall to the floor.

"Com, what's going on?" Zac said.

They were all staring at me like I'd gone crazy. "Nothing," I said. "I... I've had too much to drink."

I pushed Zac aside and ran for the door. I needed some air.

Unwin and Williamson were Shifters. Ladoux and Hedges, maybe? How many others in S3 had been through the process? Shifters and soldiers working side by side, that's what Cain had said. Closer than I could have ever imagined.

I'd been working alongside adult Shifters for days now. The very people I'd been tasked to arrest – the people I'd come to loathe. How hadn't I noticed?

I sensed him there, smiling again.

Took you long enough, he said, mocking me.

I was really, really starting to hate myself.

How could he be this happy about it? What kind of animal had I become? Because, if there were adult Shifters in the army, that could only mean that Project Ganymede was still in operation.

I heard the door open behind me. I didn't need to turn to know it was Aubrey. I could smell her perfume, recognise the sound of her boots on the steps.

"Scott," Aubrey said, resting her hand on my shoulder. "You're scaring me."

"The squad," I said, refusing to face her.

"What about them?"

"They're Shifters."

"And?" she said, as if waiting for the real news. "All of S3 are Shifters."

"The whole division? That's nearly four hundred men!"

"It's why we're called the Special Shifting Service."

I'd been so stupid. I assumed it was soldiers supporting Shifters. Like the Regulators back at ARES. Not that every man and woman in the S3 had the power.

"What's the matter, Scott? I'm scheduled to have the op too, when the time comes. You too, Scott. All senior Shifting officers are."

"No!" I said. "Never."

"Why not, Scott? We need you. You can't let a power like yours go to waste."

"The price is too high."

"The operation? I know it's dangerous, but it's worth it."

Where were they getting the volunteers for their programme now? And then, a horrible realisation dawned.

"The reintegration programme."

"You mean where the kids who flunk out of basic training go? What about it?"

"What is it?" I closed my eyes, hoping that she didn't know. Because if she did know, and if she accepted it, then everything I'd been fighting for over the past few days was worthless. Aubrey wouldn't be the person I wanted her to be.

"I'm not sure. I guess they learn skills to reintegrate into society. It's a place in South London somewhere. But what's this got to do with you not wanting the operation?"

Relief washed over me. She didn't know. She was my Aubrey still. With a heart and a soul that this war hadn't robbed her of, like it was threatening to do to me.

"I need to take you there. You need to see."

"What, now?"

"Yes. Now."

"Scott, I think you should see the doc."

I grabbed hold of her by both arms. "Do you trust me?" I said, looking into her eye.

"You're my senior officer."

"Not like that. I don't mean, will you follow my orders. I mean, do you trust me?"

She scanned my face, as if looking for an answer. "I've only just met you."

"What does your gut say?"

"It says you're probably crazy, but yes, I trust you."

"Then we don't have much time. But first…" I pulled out my phone: army issue, a chunky satellite phone.

"Hello, can I help you?" a clipped voice said.

"Can I speak to Morgan?" I said.

"Mr Morgan is—"

"It's Commandant Tyler," I said, cutting her off. "And I need to speak to him now!"

A few clicks later, Morgan's groggy voice came across the crackling line. "Yes, what is it?"

"Katie Tyler. I want her taken out of the programme and sent to the Hub now. It's mission critical."

"But…"

"But what?"

A cold dread crept its way up my spine. I already knew what he was going to say. "She went through the final test yesterday, and I'm sorry to say that she failed. I tried to coach her through it, but there's only so much that can be done when a child is not willing to—"

I didn't have time for Morgan and his self-importance. "Where is she?"

"She's been sent to the reintegration programme with the other cadets who failed. I'm sure once she's been adequately adjusted, you'll be able to see her."

"Adequately adjusted?"

"Yes. You know, adjusted to become a useful member of society. How to work in shops, that sort of thing."

"You have no idea, do you?" I hung up before he could start to protest.

"What the hell is going on, Tyler?" Zac said, walking down the steps.

"I need the keys to your car," I said.

"No way. No one drives my baby but me."

"Zac," Aubrey said, fixing him with a fierce stare. "Give me the keys."

It felt like forever to get to the address I'd pulled off the files about the reintegration programme. We had to stop at five roadblocks and go through the same boring rigmarole with snarky army officers. I was about to tell Aubrey to drive through the next one when we finally pulled up outside a modern, glass-fronted hospital. In my old reality, the programme had been run out of another hospital called Greyfield's. But this place looked to be three times the size.

"What do you know about what goes on here?" I asked Aubrey as she killed the engine.

"Not much," she said, resting her arm on the steering wheel and peering through the windscreen. "I've heard it called the Bin, you know, where the rejects end up."

"And has anyone ever seen any of the rejects again?" I said.

Aubrey looked up, trying to access her memory. Then she looked at me. "I've never thought about it before, but I don't think I've ever seen a kid that failed after they left."

She leaned forward in her seat again and looked up at the house. "What do they do to them in there?"

I couldn't tell her. She had to see for herself.

"Come on," I said opening the car door. I had to find out if my sister was OK. If she wasn't... I couldn't even think about that.

We walked up to the front door and rang the bell. No sneaking around in the dark like when Cain and I had broken into Greyfield's. Besides, this wasn't the first time I'd been here. Or at least not the first time *he'd* been here. I knew the place as if from a recurring dream.

The door opened, revealing a stern-faced nurse. Her expression switched from annoyance to surprise as soon as she saw me.

"Commandant Tyler," she said. "We weren't expecting you."

"Evening..." It took me the faintest of efforts to pluck her name out of *his* memory, "Marie, I'm sorry I didn't call ahead."

"Oh, not a problem, sir," she said, stepping aside to let me in. "Anything for the S3. We're so proud of your efforts, and to know we'd played our small part."

I forced a smile, when I really wanted to scream abuse in her face. "And you will be justly rewarded for your work," I said.

"Oh, we don't do it for the glory, sir." She rubbed her hands on her bleached white skirt, filled with faux humility.

I glared at her. "Oh, I'm quite sure of that." I coughed. "Anyway, Marie, I'm here because of an issue with one of the latest cadets."

"An issue?" Marie said.

"An administration error over at the academy. You know how it is, what with everything that's been going on. One of the cadets can't be scheduled for surgery."

"Surgery?" Aubrey whispered behind me.

"But some of the cadets have already been processed," Marie said. "We double-checked their results as procedure."

"Has a cadet called Katie been processed?" I said, my voice a dry whisper.

Marie pulled out a small tablet and consulted her list. "We have a Katie…" She paused and looked up at me. "A Katie Tyler. Is she a relation?"

I smiled *his* most enigmatic smile. "I'd like to see her."

"She is about to be prepped for surgery."

I stiffened. "It has to be stopped or there will be consequences." I made that word heavy and threatening.

"Scott, what's going on?" Aubrey said, laying her hand on my arm.

"Take me to her," I said, ignoring Aubrey. "Take me to her now."

Marie huffed and puffed but did as I instructed. She led us up a wide, spiralling staircase and through a bleach-clean corridor, muttering about procedure the whole way.

"The volunteers are in there," she said, stopping in front of a door.

Volunteers. It made me sick. No one ever volunteered for this.

I looked through the hatched glass window to see four kids wearing hospital gowns, perching on the edges of hospital beds. A fifth girl stood, pacing like a caged animal in the zoo.

"Katie!" The relief was overwhelming. I tried to open the door but it was locked. "Open it," I snapped at Marie.

"I'm afraid I need authorisation," she said.

"I am Commandant Tyler, head officer at S3, and this is an S3 facility. What further authorisation do you need?"

"Let me check with–"

I grabbed her by the shoulders before she could reach for her radio and looked deep into her eyes.

"You will open the door. Now," I said, slowly. Clearly.

Her eyes went blank. Whether I'd Forced my will on her or simply scared her into obeying, I didn't know. Either way, she placed her palm against the reader on the door.

"Scott!" Katie said as I threw the door open and charged in.

I scooped her up in my arms. "It's OK," I said. "I'm getting you out of here."

"What's going on?" she said as I put her down. "They said something about surgery."

The other kids had gathered around, looking up at me with terrified eyes. Looking for answers that I didn't know if I could bear to give them.

"It doesn't matter now," I said. "I'm getting you all out of here."

"You can't do that," Marie said, placing herself in the doorway.

"I'm shutting the whole programme down."

"I'm calling Mr Morgan."

"You can call anyone you like," I said, taking Katie's hand and leading her towards the door. "We're leaving. All of us."

Marie made a show of blocking my way: her square jaw set, her arms folded across her chest. But I could tell by the twitch around her eyes that she was close to breaking. All it took was a look from me and she stepped aside.

"Scott," Aubrey said. "You really need to tell us what the hell is going on."

I'd brought her here for this. She needed to see.

"Show them," I snapped at Marie. "Show them the children."

"This is all quite…"

"Now!" I snapped.

Marie flinched before spinning on her heels and leading us further up the stairs.

I let Aubrey go first and followed, playing through my mind the amount of times *he'd* been here, from the first time Abbott brought him here and explained the importance of sacrifice, till the last time he'd come here after Abbott had died to ensure the programme was still running. He was the one who gave clearance on what went on in this place. He was the one responsible.

Marie pressed her palm against a second reader, and a set of double doors swung open.

There were row upon row of beds, hundreds of bodies, each hooked up to a bleeping machine. The bleeps marking their heartbeats were all fractionally out of sequence, creating a sound not unlike birdsong. Dead eyes stared ahead, livid scars ran across small foreheads.

"What is this place?" Aubrey said, her voice small and her eyes wide.

"He calls it the allotment," I said. "A joke – they're all vegetables, you see."

"He?" Aubrey said.

"I mean me."

"But why?" she said.

"This," I said with a wave of my hand, "is the reintegration programme."

"I don't understand," Aubrey said.

"They cut out the part of the brain that's responsible for a Shifter's power and put it in an adult's brain. They lobotomise children."

Some of the kids who had been with Katie were crying. Aubrey covered her mouth with her hand as if she was going to be sick. Katie's skin had gone the colour of off milk. She walked into the room and laid her hand on the cheek of one of the children in the bed. The girl couldn't have been much older than Katie, and judging by the dark stitches in her cut, she'd had the operation recently. I wondered which soldier had ended up with her power. Did I know them? Had I fought alongside them? Had they been one of my men?

Katie turned slowly to face me, a single tear cutting down her cheek. "They were going to do this to me," she said.

I shook my head, trying to stop the idea I knew was forming in her mind.

"The man who took us here told me. He whispered in my ear, with his hot stinking breath, that they were going to cut me open."

"Don't, Katie. Don't think about it."

"But all these kids. Why didn't you stop them?" she said.

Aubrey was looking at me. "You knew about this?" she said.

"Not me," I said, desperately. "*Him.*"

"I don't know why you're trying to deny this," Marie said. "You've been coming here for years, Commandant Tyler." She gave me a smile so bitter and dark, it made me shudder.

Aubrey shook her head and turned away from me.

I tried to think of something to say, something that would make her forgive me. But there was nothing to say.

"I think we'd better get out of here," a boy said, looking out through the window.

"What about them?" Aubrey asked, pointing at the children in the beds.

"I don't think we can be of much help to them, do you?" he said. "But if we don't go, like now, we might be joining them."

Aubrey reached out for Katie's hand. My sister walked past me, her chin held high, refusing to look at me. I laid my hand on her arm and she yanked it away.

She was right. I was despicable. I had done this. Me.

What choices had I made that had turned me into this monster? What had I seen and done that could have possibly led to this? I didn't know whether to pity him or hate him.

We're not so different, he said.

"Go away," I shouted, hitting at my head.

I'm not going anywhere. I belong here. It's you who has to leave.

"Not without a fight," I said, digging my nails into my palms, the pain reminding myself that I was in control.

The children around me stared blankly ahead, mouths open, machines making their chests go up and down like waves. I spotted a mop of sandy hair resting on a pillow.

I had known, even though I hadn't been willing to face it, I'd known what really happened to Jake all along.

I forced myself to look at him now. I brushed aside his fringe, remembering how he used to hate it when I ruffled his hair. His scar was smaller than a lot of the other kids and looked older, as if it had had a while to heal. Had I brought him here? Had he trusted me, believed me, when I fed him lies about valuable contribution to the war effort? His mouth drooped to the side, almost looking like the crooked smile I knew so well.

Any strength I had left flowed out of me as I collapsed to my knees.

They found me like that ten minutes later. Sobbing into Jake's chest. Begging him to forgive me.

When I felt the hand on my shoulder, I reacted, grabbing the man's wrist and twisting so hard, his bones crunched and cracked. While he yelled in pain, a second solider crept forward, uncertain. He wore the S3 uniform. I wondered if he, too, hid a scar under that red beret. It was clear the man knew my reputation. There wasn't a single member of the S3 who didn't. He was right to be wary. But it wasn't going to help him.

I pulled myself to standing and took him out with two swift blows to his chest and throat. The remaining soldiers made the wrong decision in trying to attack me all at once.

My scream of rage was louder than theirs of pain. I kicked, punched, twisted and jabbed till six men lay in a groaning pile.

Then I turned back to Jake and combed his messy hair into place with my bruised and swollen fingers.

"I'm sorry," I said. I reached up and switched his machine off.

One less bleep in the symphony of dying.

"You can't," Marie shouted, stepping over the groaning men. Her instinct to protect her patients was overcoming her fear of me. "He'll die."

"He's already dead," I said, pulling her hand away.

I watched as Jake's chest breathed in, shuddered, and then stopped. His limbs thrashed, fighting for life. This was the point where his brain would be searching for ways out. Where his power to Shift would find a decision to undo. Or it would have if someone hadn't stolen it.

He went still. It was over.

I moved through the rest of the beds, flicking off switches, pulling out tubes, pushing machines to the floor. One by one, the bleeping machines stopped till the only sound was my broken sobbing.

I closed my eyes and covered my face with my hands, allowing the agony of emotion to overtake me. Letting the pain I felt push *him* further and further away. Each tear marked the difference between us two. Him, who felt nothing. Me, who felt it all.

I slumped next to the bed of a small girl, whose hand had fallen over the edge of her bed. I reached up and held it against my cheek. It was still warm.

I didn't see a soldier get to his feet.

CHAPTER TWENTY

Waking from being knocked into unconsciousness is not the same as waking from sleep. There's no cosy transition as your dreams blend with your present reality. No disappointment at being dragged awake when all you want to do is fall back to sleep. One second you're standing fighting with a bunch of men, the next you're sitting in a cold metal chair. With, in my case, your hands shackled and a soft buzz of electricity passing through your body.

I looked down. They'd bound me with the cuffs designed to stop a Shifter from using their powers. Who did they think I was? These things couldn't stop me. Not if I wanted to get out of here.

The room was almost pitch-black, although I sensed shadows moving in the far darkness. Two men. Perhaps the ones who had brought me here. I could hear them breathing. I could also make out a shape next to me. Someone else slumped in a chair.

It smelt of river: damp, second-hand humanity. A cell beneath the Hub, I guessed. Perhaps even the same cell we'd interviewed George in.

I was about to ask them what they thought they were doing, when the bolt clunked and the door opened, creating a rectangle of white light so bright, I had to turn away from it. When I looked back, a figure was outlined in the doorway. A small man, with his arms held stiffly by his sides.

"Please remove the Commandant's cuffs," Vine said, stepping into the room. "And someone turn the light on." He sounded tired, annoyed even.

The heavy-breathing man flicked the light switch, and the room was illuminated with a dull orange glow. It was much easier on the eyes than the light from the corridor outside. The figure next to me was Aubrey. Her head lay on her chest, her eyes closed.

"If you have hurt her..." I said, yanking on my restraints, leaving the threat unspoken.

"Calm yourself, Commandant Tyler. She is perfectly well. See, she is coming to."

He was right. Aubrey stirred, a gentle groan escaping her lips. I watched as she went through the same process as I had, snapping her head up and trying to pull on her cuffs.

"Where am I? What's going on?"

"You are safe, Captain Jones. Both you and Commandant Tyler are under my protection."

Aubrey turned and saw me. Her face went from rage to relief. I tugged again at the cuffs, this time because I wanted to run to her and hold her. To tell her everything would be OK. But then something in her eyes changed. The shame and disgust she'd shown in the hospital returned and she rolled her head away from me.

I went slack in my chair, wanting all of this to be over with.

"Please remove their bonds," Vine said again.

The soldier hesitated before reaching out to undo my cuffs. There's a general rule when it comes to cuffing someone: you do not want to be around when they are let loose. He twisted the key and stepped away as the cuffs clanked to the floor.

I stood up, rubbing at my wrists and fixing him with what I hoped was my most terrifying stare. I was pretty sure I'd Forced Marie in the hospital. And this guy didn't look half as smart as her. My mind flooded with all the images of things I would make him do.

He shuffled away, unhappy about having to turn his back to me to undo Aubrey's cuffs. She sprang up and he leapt away to be clear of her reach.

"I apologise for this, Commandant. My men overreacted somewhat. But you did cause considerable damage to a government facility. Not to mention the damage to my men."

I glanced at the two guards and was not unpleased to notice the beginnings of a black eye on one, while the other held his arm at an awkward angle.

"Would you care to explain?" Vine said.

"That facility, that abattoir," I hissed, "is a disgrace. Do you know what goes on there, Minister? What Project Ganymede really is?"

"I had my suspicions, but Mr Abbott was kind enough to take care of the details so I didn't have to..."

"Get your hands dirty? Is that it? Plausible deniability? Well, excuse me if I call bullshit on that. Because your hands are dirty. My hands are dirty. Everyone in this goddamn place is covered in filth. We are bathed in the blood of innocent children."

Vine didn't even flinch as I unloaded all my rage on him.

"You want to know how the men and women of the mighty Special Shifting Service have their power?" I said. "It's stolen. Kids have their heads cut open and their brains sliced up. How's that for dirty?"

"I see," was all he said.

"That's it? You find out that hundreds of children have been killed and all you can say is 'I see'?"

"This war has forced us all to do terrible things, Commandant Tyler. I think you of all people understand that. After all, you ran the project after Abbott died."

I reeled at this, almost crashing into the chair behind me. "I... what? No, I couldn't have done." There was no denying I'd known about the place. But to have been actually running it... it was too much to take in.

"Oh, I'm afraid so. I've been looking over all the paperwork on the project since I was alerted as to what had happened. And it is your signature on all the procedurals."

I collapsed into the chair and covered my face. I sensed him there, in the back of my mind, smiling.

"Scott," Aubrey said. "He's lying. Tell me he's lying."

I looked up at her, unable to find the words. How could I explain that it wasn't me? I shook my head.

"It certainly looks like your signature on these forms, requesting that the pass mark be changed." Vine held a piece of paper towards me.

Aubrey snatched it away and read it in shaking hands. "Why would you do that? Why would *anyone* do that? Not if they knew... " She crumpled it up into a ball and let it fall to the floor. "Are you charging us?" she said in a flat, dead voice.

"No, of course not, Captain Jones. You are dismissed."

She looked at me, confused and scared, and then ran out of the room. I went to follow when a large hand stopped me. The soldier with the emerging black eye smiled.

"I would like a few more words with you, Commandant," Vine said. He pulled down the edges of his jacket, attempting to straighten the crinkles and failing.

I gazed out the door, listening to Aubrey's hurried footsteps get gradually quieter. Would she ever forgive me?

Would I ever let her? Was it possible that he would have raised the pass grade, sending even more kids into the programme? Was he really so willing to sacrifice so much?

"Commandant?" Vine's voice snapped me back to the room.

"Yes," I said.

"Leave us, please." The two soldiers looked uncertain. Vine sighed. "Don't make me repeat myself."

They stomped out of the room, slamming the door shut behind them.

I waited for what Vine had to say. Was he going to fire me? Can you even fire people from the military?

"I am worried about you, Scott," he said. I noted the switch to my first name. But rather than reassuring me, the intimacy of it unsettled me. Now we were alone, his tone had changed. "I need to know that you are still focused on what matters."

"And what is that? Because I don't think I know anymore."

"Winning this war."

"Don't you mean ending it?" I said.

"No," he said, the strained kindness in his voice totally gone. "I do not. We must win this war, Scott. Win it at all costs."

"But then we become as bad as those we're fighting,"

"Oh, we passed that point long ago. Don't look at me like that, Scott. I thought you understood better than any that there is no black or white in war. There is only victory or defeat. None of us are going to come out the other side of this war clean and without sin. You did what you did for the greater good."

I laughed bitterly at his twisted use of the ARES motto. "Don't try and excuse what I did. I can't."

"You will find a way. We all find a way."

"And if I can't? If I don't want to?" I said.

"Then you bury it deep down inside you and you get on with your job," Vine said, grabbing hold of my arm, his bony fingers digging painfully into my flesh. "You swore an oath, Commandant Tyler," he said, still keeping his voice low. "To protect this country with your life. Your life!" His fingers dug in deeper. "And everything that comes with it, including your soul. So you can drop this childish pretence of a conscience and continue to do your duty." He finally let go of my arm.

I rubbed at where his grip was sure to leave bruises, suddenly afraid of the rage within this quiet man.

"Everything stands on a knife's edge," Vine said, neatening his cuffs. "Tomorrow, the Emperor of China is coming here to sign a treaty of accord. With China as our ally, we will be unstoppable."

I wondered if Tzen knew that Vine wasn't planning on signing the treaty, not to bring about peace but to ensure that Britain came out of this war on top.

Vine continued, "And do you know why he is choosing to come here, to the Hub?"

I shook my head.

"Because he has heard about you. Our super Shifter. He wants to meet you, Commandant. He believes the future of our accord lies with you. I believe he wants you to rule this country as he rules his."

"I don't want to rule. I just want to go home."

Vine ran his tongue over his teeth, making a soft squelching noise. "I am very reassured to hear this. And I suggest you make that quite clear to the Emperor when you meet tomorrow. There might be unfortunate consequences if he wasn't to understand that."

"You're talking to *me* about consequences?" I said with a laugh. I realised what was going on here. Vine wanted the job of ruling for himself. Minister of Defence wasn't enough for him. He wanted to be Prime Minister. "You have no idea who you are dealing with."

"Oh, I think I am perfectly aware of who you are, Tyler. It seems recently that it is you who has forgotten. I think I know more about you than you know about yourself. Like your dealings with the Red Hand. Who do you think sanctioned that? Did you think you were working alone, Tyler?"

I felt the blood draining from my head, and the sound of Vine's voice became muffled and distant.

"I sent you to them. You are nothing but a pawn, Commandant. A powerful one, but a pawn nonetheless."

"Maybe," I said, slowly recovering. "But you know what happens when a pawn crosses over to the other side, Minister?"

Vine swallowed hard. "Defection, Commandant? You don't have it in you."

I stepped closer to him. "Push me, Vine, and you will see what I have in me."

He didn't flinch, but having someone within his personal space, breathing into his face, was clearly making him uncomfortable. "I hear your name whispered in these corridors. Scott Tyler." He said my name in more of a hiss than a whisper. "The men and women of this division call on your name as they would a saint. You give them courage. With their powers, they could rebel at any point. Change their choices to join S3. Alter their past to ensure their individual survival. But with you at the head, they make the right choices. With you as their leader, they choose to protect the country over themselves. Do you know why that is?"

I wasn't going to tell him that there was no mystery to that. It was simply because I Fixed them, not giving them any choices. Like I'd done with Cooper. The idea that the soldiers in this unit took strength from that, that they thought I gave them courage rather taking away their freedom, sickened me.

"You are a symbol, Scott. That is why we have not placed you in the Igloo, where we know you could do plenty of good."

He was threatening me. Toe the line or end up like Benjo. Challenge his position and he would destroy me. I was seeing now why this man had risen to power. Manipulation came as naturally to him as it had Frankie.

"But perhaps your sister…" He stepped away, leaving the sentence hanging. Another warning. Threat upon threat.

"Where is she?"

"Oh, she is quite safe. She is here at the Hub, where she will sit the test again. And this time, I suggest she doesn't fail. Will that suffice?"

I was starting to understand: the key to victory was compromise. "For now," I said. "But after the war is over…"

"We will have no need of adult Shifters, I can assure you. We will close Project Ganymede. You have my word."

He stretched out his hand to me. I took it and we shook, his cold, dry hand closing over my hot, clammy one.

"And my sister?"

"Will no doubt become as valuable a member of the S3 as you have," he said.

"And you won't put her in the Igloo, I have your word?" I said.

"Once the treaty is signed, we may find we have no need of the Igloo, either. As long as we still have our super Shifter."

I nodded. I would do what he asked. I would play along and tell Emperor Tzen what he needed to hear. I would pretend to be the dutiful solider. Because I knew something he didn't. As soon as I was out of here, I was going to find

Aubrey and do what I should done days ago: make sure this war had never started in the first place.

He let go of my hand and knocked on the door. It opened and the two guards peered in, ready to jump to the defence of the Minister if needed.

"Escort Commandant Tyler to his apartment, please." Vine said. "Ensure no harm comes to him."

I knew what that meant. It meant they were to watch me. To make sure I stayed true to my word.

I followed Vine out of the cell and smiled at the men. Let's see if they could keep up.

KIM CURRAN

CHAPTER TWENTY-ONE

It took me three Shifts to shake off my escort. Which was almost disappointing. I was bubbling with so much rage and bitterness, I could do with a fight. But I had to see Aubrey first. The look she'd given me as she'd walked out of the cell burned into my heart. It was the same way she'd looked at me another time, when she'd seen me kissing another girl, only a thousand times worse.

Then, it had taken me days to explain that Frankie had Forced me, for Aubrey to even think about forgiving me. I had no idea what it would take now. Not to mention the fact I had no idea where to find her.

I asked the few people still on duty this late if they'd seen her, and they shrugged, noncommittal. There was someone I was sure would know where she was.

"Zac?" I said, after he picked up.

A croaky voice answered. "It is 2am, Scott. What the hell?"

"Where are Aubrey's bunks?"

There was a pause. And a sigh. "What have you done?" he said.

"Nothing, I mean… something. But I have to explain to her."

"Is it something to do with why you took off from the party? Did you two hook up?" He sounded delighted.

"No. It's not like that. But I screwed up, Zac. Really bad."

"Well, if she's seriously pissed off, she won't be in her bunks."

"Then were will she be?" I asked. He paused again. "Zac, you have to tell me!" I said, the desperation cracking my voice.

"OK. But if you tell her that I told you, I will kill you. That's if she doesn't kill you first."

"I promise."

"There's this place she likes to go to clear her head. She calls it her sanctuary. Have you got a pen?"

Aubrey's sanctuary was on the top floor of an abandoned high-rise building a few miles away from HQ. I arrived, thanked the driver and looked at the building. The bottom floor was a wreck, buckled metal blocking the way in. It must have been hit in a drone strike.

How the hell did Aubrey get in there?

I clambered under the girders, trying to find a way through, but each pathway was blocked. I hit myself on the head when I remembered. We were Shifters, there was always a way through. It was like the poles in training. You just had to keep trying.

The memory of the poles made me try a new approach, getting up high and trying to cross that way. It took a few attempts. With my first, I fell off and was inches away from a large spike piercing my eyeball. In my second, I slipped and ended up hanging by my fingertips. But with the third Shift, I was across.

The lifts, unsurprisingly, weren't working. So I headed for the stairs.

I was out of breath and exhausted by the time I made it to the top floor. I stopped before opening the door to give me time to recover. I was so much frailer in this reality. So much more tired.

That's because you're weak, he said. *Strength isn't in the body. It's in the mind.*

Which is where you are. In my mind.

We both know how this is going to end. There's no escaping me.

Shut up, I said, pressing my head against the door. Shut up shut up shut up. And he was gone. For now.

I opened the door to see a small glow of light, flickering in the darkness. I walked towards it.

Aubrey lay on her back, staring up at the sky, a cigarette held loosely between her fingers. I looked up and was momentarily stunned by the display of stars. I'd never seen anything like it in my life. The light pollution I'd grown up with meant that all I'd ever seen were a handful of stars at best. Now I could see millions, billions of them, swirling in the dark sky. I understood why Aubrey came to this place. I watched as she drew the cigarette to her lips.

"Still smoking?" I said, as she blew out a cloud of pale blue smoke.

She leapt up. "What the...? How?" She pulled the cigarette from her mouth and threw it to the ground. "Zac. I am going to kill him."

"I'm sorry, but I had to see you. I had to explain."

"Don't bother, Commandant. Like I said before, you don't have to explain yourself to me." She turned away from me, staring out across the rooftop.

"Aubrey, please, I need you to listen."

"To what? Some bull about you not being you?" She spun around to glare at me.

"It's true!"

"That was your name on those papers. You did that to those children." She stabbed her finger at me.

"It was him. I wish I could explain better than that. But you have to believe me. I would never, I could never." It was useless. Even as I said the words myself, I realised how stupid they sounded.

"Then how did you know?" she said.

"It's complicated."

"I'll try to keep up," she said, her voice dripping in scorn.

"I found out last year. In my reality," I added quickly as she gasped. "And as soon as I realised, I stopped it. Sergeant

Cain and I, we led a raid on the hospital where they were… they were doing the operation. And we stopped it. I promise you."

She looked at me, her eyebrows drawn together. "I want to believe you. I don't know why, but I do." She returned to looking out at the dark city. "Do they know?"

"Do who know?"

"Cain and the other adults who've had the operation. Do they know where their power has come from?"

"No," I said. "I don't think so. In my reality, when Cain found out, it broke him."

She shook her head. "They should. Everyone should know."

"Vine has promised to shut the programme down once the war is over."

"And you believe him?"

"No. But if he doesn't, I will make him." My hands clenched into fists as I remembered Vine's hidden threat about Katie.

"And how exactly do you plan on doing that?" Aubrey asked.

I paused, the desire to tell her everything, about the depth of my power, bubbling on my lips. Could I trust her? "I'm a Forcer."

Aubrey looked away. "I know," she said with a sigh. "I mean, I guessed. The look on your face when Vine told you about what could happen if a Forcer was put in the Igloo. And then I saw what you did to that nurse."

"Then why didn't you tell anyone?"

She slowly looked at me. "I don't know. I guess I trusted you."

She glared at me and I saw she was fighting back tears. I didn't have the energy to stop mine, so I let them flow.

"You can trust me," I said.

"I believe it," she said, "that there are two of you. I probably shouldn't, but I do believe it. I see it in your eyes sometimes. It's like someone else takes over. I thought it was what you needed to do to get through it all. We all have masks we put up. Walls we hide behind so we don't have to face what we've been through. But that person you become, he scares me."

"He scares me, too," I said, taking her hand, remembering how perfectly it fit in mine.

"Now, it's like, I don't know, you're different." She tilted her head, that expression I knew so well. The look I was able to glimpse in the moments after we'd kissed. When she dropped her guard. When I felt like she'd let me in.

And then it was gone again. She pulled her hand free of mine and walked over to the edge of the building. She kicked a stone off the edge. We watched it disappear into nothing.

"If it's true," she said, something in her softening, "if you're really not from here, if you can remember what it was like before everything went to crap" she waved her arms around, indicating the empty landscape around us "then why don't you Shift back to there so that none of this will have happened?"

"I've tried. But the first rule of Shifting… "

"Damn the rules!" She stared at me. "You break every single rule. Why not that one?"

"Don't you think I've tried? Ever since I found myself here, I've done nothing but try to find a way back to that reality. And sure, there are things I can do, but…"

"So do them!" She walked away from the edge of the roof, circling around me.

"But then I'd lose you!" The words came rushing out before I had a chance to stop them.

She stopped, her mouth half open. "What do you mean, lose me?"

"I mean you die. The last thing that happened before I ended up here was you dying."

I could hardly see her now for the tears in my eyes.

"So what?" she said.

I opened my mouth and shut it again. I couldn't believe what she was saying. I'd just told her that she'd died, and she didn't care.

"So I die. Big deal," she said. "I've spent every day of my life for the past five years facing up to the fact that I may die doing my duty. I made my peace with that."

"But I can't," I said.

"You're not willing to sacrifice one person to save the lives of thousands, millions maybe? One person you only just met, let me add. Then you're a bigger dick that I ever imagined." She walked towards me.

"But you're not just one person, Aubrey. And we didn't just meet. There's a reason I can't let you die."

"It had better be a good one." She was barely a foot away from me now. I could reach out and touch her. Hold her. Kiss her.

"It's because I love you."

Her intake of breath was jagged and sharp. She shook her head, as if trying to shake off my words. "No. You don't even know me."

"It would take a lifetime to truly know you, Aubrey. But I know you better than anyone else. And I love you."

I said it again. I would say it a thousand times until she believed me.

"I don't care. You still have to do it. You still have to make the Shift."

"I can't."

"Why not?"

There was no hiding from the truth now. "You know the way a Shifter can't Shift into a place where their life is in danger?" I said. "It's the same with you. It's like losing you would be worse than dying. I'd die myself in a heartbeat if that would stop all of this. But lose you? Never."

She took a step closer to me. My stomach jolted at the possibility that maybe, maybe she was going to kiss me.

The slap echoed across the rooftops.

"Wha... What was that for?"

"To knock some sense into you, Scott Tyler. You do it. You do it right now, or I swear I will keep hitting you till you do."

She swung her arm again. I blocked it and pulled her towards me.

"I can't," I said, her face only an inch away from mine. "Even if I wanted to, I can't."

She struggled against me. "I'm nothing. Just one girl."

"You're everything to me, Aubrey. Everything."

She stopped struggling and looked at me. Stared deep into me. "If you don't do it," she said, in a whisper, "I will."

She pushed me away, taking a few steps backwards, then lifted her head and looked into the sky, as if enjoying the feeling of a light breeze on her face. She was trying to Shift.

"No!" I shouted, as I realised what she had meant. If I wasn't willing to let her go, she'd do the job herself. Undo some decision that had saved her life.

I focused all of my energies on keeping her here, in this place, this reality. On stopping all other choices. I was Fixing her.

She opened her eyes. "Don't you dare!" she yelled, running at me and hitting me again.

"I told you, I can't let you go." I held her by her arms.

"This isn't your choice to make."

"You're right. It's not. There is no choice." I let her go.

She raised her hand, but instead of hitting me again, she laid it against my face, her fingers curled as if she wanted to claw at my skin. I leant into her and our lips met for the first time. Again.

It was nothing like our first kiss had been. That had been gentle and tentative and filled with promise of tomorrow. This was desperate and lost and fed as much by rage as by passion. And yet it still felt so right.

I wrapped a hand around her waist, the other in her hair, and pulled her into me. Her nails dug into my back. We melted to the floor, a tangle of limbs and discarded clothes and anger at what the world had become. At what it had forced us to become.

In that moment together we found solace. We found oblivion. And the stars looked on.

CHAPTER TWENTY-TWO

We lay on the asphalt, the heat from our bodies seeping into the cold beneath us. I didn't feel it. All I knew was that Aubrey was next to me and the orange-kissed clouds were above. The sun was rising, setting fire to the sky. It could burn the whole world, for all I cared right now.

Maybe the world deserved to burn. Maybe we all did for what we'd done in the name of protecting it. I plucked a blade of grass that had grown up among the concrete and stones. A spore of nature reclaiming the city for itself. I twirled it between my fingers and then threw it into the air. It caught a breeze and danced off.

Aubrey stirred next to me, nuzzling her face deeper into my shoulder.

"Is it morning?" she said, her voice croaky.

"Nearly."

"We'd better get back to the Hub. They'll be wondering where we are."

We stood and started to dress, embarrassedly untangling our clothes from each other's and pulling them on.

She took my hand, her fingers knitting perfectly between mine. Maybe we both knew that we would never be together again, not in this reality, anyway. Or maybe we hoped this would be the beginning of a long life together. Either way, I held her hand like I was never going to let it go.

We walked towards the exit, down the stairs, and helped each other across the assault course of twisted metal. As we made it to the ground floor, I heard a bleeping coming from one of my pockets.

"That will probably be Cain, checking on us," Aubrey said.

I pulled out my tablet, but the screen showed no sign of a call or a message. The bleeping sounded again. It was coming from my inside pocket. I pulled out a phone I didn't recognise. It looked cheap, something you might buy from a corner shop, rather than the high-tech communication devices S3 issued. It bleeped for a third time as the message flashed on the screen.

THE ARCH. 15 MIN. TIME WE MET – S.

"What's that?" Aubrey nodded at the handset.

"Nothing," I said, slipping the phone back in my pocket with shaking hands. I didn't want to admit that I knew exactly who the message was from and why I had a burner phone. I didn't want Aubrey to know the truth about the other me. I'd only just managed to earn her trust, but if she knew who S was and why she was texting me, I might lose that trust. And more than that, I might lose her.

My own cowardice burned like acid in my stomach.

Aubrey watched me. She knew something was up. I could never hide anything from her.

"Scott?"

"It's Katie," I said, quickly. "She's at my place. I need to go and check on her."

"Oh, OK."

I must have become a better liar than I realised. "Will you be all right getting back to the Hub?"

"Don't get all macho on me now." She nudged me with her hip. "I'll be fine. Go see to your sister."

I paused before kissing her, the desire to tell her bubbling up inside me. No. She didn't need to know. *I* was in control now. She never needed to know about what he had done. Or why he was getting texts from Slate, the head of the Red Hand. She could never know.

I kissed her on the forehead and left without saying a word.

The "arch" was an abandoned space near London Bridge, not far from where I'd woken up a few days ago. I knew this because *he* had been there before, when he'd first infiltrated the Red Hand.

A memory flared.

They've placed a black bag over my head, as if that could stop me from working out exactly where I am. I know this city like I know myself, the feel of the cobbles under feet, the smell of the river all around me. I hear our footsteps echo off brick walls. A bridge somewhere. Waterloo? I hear the lapping of water over shale carry on the breeze. London Bridge. They shove me forward, playing like they're the ones in control. But we all know what's going on. I am here because I have chosen to be. I'm led through a door and into a cold room. I hear dripping. Smell damp. They pull the bag off my head, and I have to squint in the sudden light.

"Welcome, Scott Tyler," a robotic voice says. It's coming through a speaker system. Slate has not come herself, but she is watching. I am one step closer to finding her. Destroying her.

I could almost taste the musty damp at the back of my throat. So, he hadn't been working with the Red Hand. He'd been trying to bring them down. And maybe they'd worked that out. Going there alone was a risk. But I had to see it through. I needed to know who Slate was. This could be my chance to stop them and maybe even the war. If there was no going back to my old reality, the only choice I had left was to make this one better.

I approached the checkpoint at the north side of the bridge. Three armed soldiers raised their guns at my approach.

"Report!"

I slowed my pace, holding my hands out from my side to let them know I wasn't a risk. I turned away from the spotlight they were pointing in my direction. "Commandant Tyler. SSS."

They lowered their guns but kept the light on me. "S3, hey?" one of them said. He had a broad forehead and a thick Yorkshire accent. "We've heard about you lot."

"I need to get through." I didn't have time for this. Slate was expecting me.

"No can do, sir." The sir was delivered with an ironic sneer. "We've had our orders. No one gets in or out."

"I appreciate that, Lance Corporal," I said, letting my eyes linger over the single stripe on his arm before returning to stare at him. I outranked him. "But I have official business on the other side of this bridge."

"Of course, you could always magic the barrier away. That's what you lot do, ain't it?" He shared a wink with his colleagues.

I took a step forward, getting out of the full glare of the spotlight. "I'm going to say this one last time. I need to get through."

"Is he gonna get his wand out?" one of the other soldiers said, with a giggle.

"Go on," the lance corporal said. "Show us what makes the S3 so bloody special."

Four minutes left. Three of them. One of me. It was hardly a fair fight.

I took the private who'd made the joke about the wand down with a jab to the throat with my right hand, at the same time kicking out with my left foot, causing the other private to double over in pain. In a blur of movement, both of their weapons clattered to the floor. That left the lance corporal. He fumbled with his rifle, trying to bring it up to point at me. I grabbed hold of it and broke his nose with the butt before looping the strap around his neck and pulling him to the ground.

The three men were on the floor, groaning and disarmed. And I hadn't even needed to Shift.

I crouched down over the lance corporal, who was nursing his bleeding nose. "How's that for a little demonstration?" I hissed, spittle covering his face.

He mumbled something. "What's that?" I said, grabbing hold of his shirt and pulling him closer to me. "Did you have something more to say?" He shook his head vigorously. "Good."

I let go, taking a small pleasure in the sound his head made as it hit the concrete, stepped over him and walked through the barrier.

Maybe that would teach them to show the S3 a little more respect.

A sheet of plywood blocked the doorway into the arch. I could see from the cracks and loose nails that someone had been here before me. I pulled the board aside and squeezed myself through the gap. The dark was all-consuming. I could hear the gentle *drip drip* of water overhead and the rustle of rubbish under my feet. I knew I wasn't alone.

Flick flack. A light flared in the darkness. I should have known.

"Ladoux," I said.

The head of the Red Hand smiled at me, her face warped in the glow of a flame.

CHAPTER TWENTY-THREE

She brought her lighter towards a lantern, transferring the flame. It gave out a weak blue light by which I could see the space we were in. Curved ceilings of black-painted brick were slick with damp. On three of the walls were large paintings of abstract figures that danced in the wavering light.

Ladoux lit a second lantern, then flicked the lighter closed with a snap that echoed around the arches. "I wasn't sure you would come. I thought you might have changed your mind after the lab. Lost the faith."

I'd believed Ladoux was a loyal member of my squad. I was right. But I was wrong about who she was loyal to.

"I'm here, aren't I?" I stepped further into the room.

Once, the trains coming and going from London Bridge's fifteen platforms would have shaken these walls every few minutes. Now there was nothing but the steady drip of water and the sound of my heart pounding in my ears.

"You are." Ladoux turned her back to me and looked up at the largest painting on the wall, a painting of a man's head surround by swirls of red and blue. "And are the rest of the squad going to be bursting in through the doors? Or am I still right to believe?" She turned to face me. I don't know if the fire in her eyes was a reflection from the lantern or something burning from within. Her chin was held high, as if daring me to take her.

"It's just me."

She visibly relaxed, her shoulders slumping. "I was so angry with you after the lab." She wagged a finger at me as if scolding a child. "We had it all so perfectly planned. I was willing to sacrifice myself in order to expose the British government and turn the Chinese Emperor against them so this sham of a peace treaty could be stopped before it started." She spat on the floor, as if her tone wasn't enough to express how much hatred she felt towards the government.

"And releasing the virus would kill all the Shifters within a thirty-mile radius," I said.

Ladoux shrugged. "Better the virus is released that way than let it become another of the government's nasty little secrets, hidden from the world. And as my mother used to say, '*Faire d'une pierre deux coups.*'"

My French was rusty at best. But I understood the meaning. Two jobs. One stone.

"But I see now you were following higher orders," Ladoux continued, the flame in her eyes burning even brighter.

Orders? Did she mean from Vine? As she raised both hands up to the cracked ceiling, I understood. She meant orders from God. Zac had told me the Red Hand were a new religion, doing what they believed their God wanted, which seemed to involve killing a lot of innocent people.

Ladoux disgusted me. Her blazing eyes and crazy mind. My hand twitched next to my holster. It would be so easy to put out that light. Only, my gun wasn't there. I must have left it on the rooftop.

"So, what were your orders?" I said, hoping to keep her talking.

She smiled as if I were teasing her or testing her. "He has guided your hand, Scott. As he has mine. 'Commit your way to the Lord. Trust in him and he will do this: He will make your righteousness shine like the dawn, the justice of your cause like the noonday sun.'"

Now I understood why "shine" had been scrawled on walls around the city. It had been a message from Ladoux and her followers. I also understood that she was insane.

"Did He speak to you? Did He tell you to take the virus back to the Hub?" There was a hungry jealousy in her voice. As if she wanted to be the one that her God spoke to.

I was getting sick of the pretence. Sick of her wide eyes and madness. "No one said anything to me, Ladoux. I did my duty. As you should have done. And now it's over. Or, at least, it will be in less than an hour when the Emperor signs the treaty. The killing will stop. Isn't that what your God wanted?"

"My God?" she said. "What happened to *our* God?"

I'd never believed in God. But did he? Had he really believed in the Red Hand? Had he found some light in the darkness? I searched inside of myself and saw the truth staring back at me. He'd not believed any more than I had. He'd lied and used Ladoux and the Red Hand, just like he had everyone else. But for what?

"I've had a change of heart," I said finally.

Ladoux's expression changed from hope to disgust; her painted lips curled up in a sneer. She spun away, unable to look at me any longer. "You said I might have to walk this road alone," she said. And I knew she wasn't talking to me any longer. "That others would fall by the wayside. But I won't fail You."

"Come on, Ladoux," I said, tired and uncomfortable with her fervent faith. I'd known people who were believers. Kind, patient people, who found their religion a comfort. But for Ladoux, her faith was a hot brand she wanted to burn everyone with. "I'm going to take you back to the Hub, where you can stand trial."

She laughed. "You think I have been through what I have been through, done the things I have done, to give up now?" She looked down at her hands, her nose wrinkling in revulsion, as if they were dripping in something foul. "The sacrifices I have made, Scott, all in His name. The lives I have taken. Going through with that evil operation, even though I knew it would make me an abomination like you." She rubbed at the scar with the heel of her hand as if she could wipe it and what it represented away. "I had to become the very thing I despised. I had to become a monster. His monster. We were never meant to have this power. The power to change His plan. We should be faithful to Him. Surrender ourselves to His will." She lifted her face as if basking in the sunlight, even though it was dark and gloomy in here. It was the same expression I'd seen on the face of plenty of Shifters when they were trying to change a decision and bring about a new reality. A mix of focus and hope, that whatever world they found themselves in would be better.

I didn't know if she was trying to Shift or not. It was irrelevant. She wasn't going anywhere.

Her eyes snapped open. The fire was white-hot now. "Plans and backup plans, I have been working towards this day for years. And I will not stop till every Shifter is destroyed."

I didn't need a psych eval to know that Ladoux was having a psychotic attack. Like the man I'd seen on the Tube, calling everyone sheep, moments before his head blew up. Like Glenn, the cage fighter I'd brought down. I sighed and reached for my cuffs. It was just like bringing in the remaining members of Project Ganymede all over again.

"Starting with me?" I said.

Ladoux's face split into a grin. "I thought you were a believer, Scott. I thought He had brought you to us. The most powerful Shifter fighting for us."

"I'm sorry to disappoint you." I unclipped my cuffs. "Now, are you going to come quietly?"

I don't know why I was even bothering saying it. They never came quietly.

Ladoux threw a lantern at me and it went crashing to the floor, spilled oil instantly catching. I leaped over the pool of fire and grabbed Ladoux's arm. She twisted out of my grip and followed through with a punch aimed for my head. I blocked it with ease, grabbing her arm again and twisting it around her back. I kicked the back of her knee and drove her down onto the floor. She cracked her head against the cold floor and it was over.

I slapped one cuff around her wrist and fixed the other to a water pipe running up the wall, then pulled off my jacket and used it to douse the flames.

"It's over, Ladoux," I said, throwing my ruined jacket to the floor. "The Emperor will be signing the treaty any moment. You failed your country and now you've failed your God. You're too late."

She lay on the floor, her blood mixing in with the puddles of water. "You are the one who is too late," she said, laughing.

"What do you mean?"

"The Emperor won't get a chance to sign the treaty! He will be trapped in the Hub along with a virus designed to kill everyone there. It's perfect. It's His design!"

"But the virus was destroyed. Frankie destroyed all of the twenty vials."

"There were twenty-one," Ladoux said, cackling now like a crazed witch. "Twenty-one!"

I stepped away from her, racking my brain. Hedges had carried the vials for Frankie.

Phrases swam around my head.

The two of them are always sneaking away together.

They've turned a loyal member of S3.

Hedges. It was his information that led us to X73 in the first place. We'd been so disturbed by his scars that we'd not even stopped to think whether he was still loyal to us.

And now he was back at the Hub, waiting for the arrival of the Emperor. With the last vial.

I checked my watch. I had fifteen minutes till the Emperor arrived at the Hub. Fifteen minutes to stop Hedges from killing everyone in S3.

"It's too late," I heard Ladoux call out as I ran for the door. She rocked back and forth, the steady clanking of her cuffs on the pole like a slow clap. "You're too late."

KIM CURRAN

CHAPTER TWENTY-FOUR

Outside, I tried to calm my breathing and work out what to do. You knew, didn't you? I thought to myself.

Not this. I thought the Red Hand could be controlled. I was wrong.

"You were wrong?" I shouted, my voice echoing between the arches. "That's all you have to say?" I hated him. Hated myself. How was it possible that we were the same person? With the same parents and same childhood? *But we are not the same person, Scott.*

There was no escaping him. *You could never make the choices I have had to.*

"You sound like Ladoux, you know that?"

She understood the nature of sacrifice. I respected that. Towards the true way, that's what it's always been about. Every choice I've made, I've made it for the greater good. You say those words, but you never really understood what they meant.

God, I hated myself. I was so righteous. So right.

Screw you, I thought. Screw you and your patronising know-it-all bullshit. You know what? You're right; I'm not you. And I never want to be you. I'll never be as certain as you are. I'll always doubt myself, but that's what makes me the better person. I would find my own way.

I had less than fifteen minutes to get back to the Hub and stop Hedges.

"Captain Black," I said, pressing the button on my collar and waiting to be connected.

"S'up?" Zac replied.

"How quickly can you get to London Bridge?"

I heard Zac cough over the radio. "Actually, I'm already there."

"What?"

"Aubrey sent me after you. She saw Katie at the Hub and knew you were up to something. But if she'd come after you herself, it would make her look like a stalker."

"Where are you?"

Headlights flared in the dark. "Opposite you."

I ran over to Zac's car and wrenched open the door. "Back to the Hub. Now!"

My expression must have been all the explanation Zac needed. He hit the accelerator, turning the car in a tight circle and speeding off towards the bridge.

"Captain Jones," I said. I was hoping to hear Aubrey's voice – so I could warn her and explain why I'd lied – but all I was getting was static. The panic rose in my chest.

"Yeah, the network is down," Zac said. "Must be a glitch at base."

This was more than a glitch. It was Hedges putting his plan into action.

"Oh, you have to be kidding me."

I saw what had caused Zac to slow down: the army roadblock up ahead. Three soldiers were on guard. I didn't need to look at my watch now. The countdown ticked in my head as if the digits had been burned into my brain. We had less than fourteen minutes. I considered what to do for a moment, then decided.

"Go through it." Zac opened his mouth to protest. "Go through it!" I said again.

He slammed on the pedal. The engine roared in response, like a caged animal wanting to be let loose. The soldiers barely had time to react before we crashed through. The barriers shattered under the impact, bouncing off the windscreen and cartwheeling away. Through the rear-view mirror I saw the soldiers get to their feet and raise their guns.

"Zac…" I said in a warning tone.

"I know." He downshifted into third and the car lurched forward, just as the pops of gunfire sounded behind us.

Bullets slammed against the rear window like someone performing a drum solo on the car. But the glass held.

"Come on, baby," Zac said, willing the car on like a jockey might his horse.

The gunfire slowed. The car rolled on. We'd escaped. I looked to Zac and we shared a moment of victory. But then I checked the rear-view mirror again and my smile faded. I saw one of the soldiers running out of the guard box, carrying a rocket launcher. He raised the launcher to his shoulder and...

Everything became heat and noise and pain. The car was thrown into the air, spinning once, twice before crashing back down on the concrete. I reached out for the last decision I'd made. And the world flipped.

We were still at the checkpoint. This time, I'd told Zac to stop. We still had thirteen minutes till the Emperor was scheduled to arrive. There was still time.

One of the soldiers tapped on the window. I nodded to Zac and he wound it down.

"Can't you read?" the solider said, leaning forward. "You can't come through this way." I recognised the Yorkshire accent. It was the lance corporal from earlier. The one I had left with a bloodied nose. I detected a certain muffle in his voice that suggested it was still causing him trouble.

I turned away, hoping he wouldn't see me.

"We're on S3 business," Zac said, leaning his arm out of the window so that the lance corporal could see his S3 tattoo.

It was probably the worst thing he could have done. These guys did not like S3.

"Get out the car," the lance corporal shouted.

Zac's brow furrowed. "I don't think you heard me. I am Captain Black of the SSS. I suggest you let us through."

The barrel of a rifle appeared at Zac's temple. "Easy, now." Zac raised his hands slowly away from the steering wheel, opened the door, and stepped out. They'd be coming for me next. And if they recognised me, it would all be too late. I stared at the digits on my watch as if I could fix them in place as easily as I could a Shifter. But time was something I had no control over.

I heard the exchange of loud voices: Zac trying to reason with the soldiers. One of them walked around to my side of the car.

Before he had a chance to bend down, I slammed the door open, knocking him onto his back, rolled out and came up holding his rifle. It was an LMT sharpshooter's rifle. Heavier than the ones we were issued at S3. Older and less reliable, too. I could see why the army resented us so much. Tough.

The corporal's eyes widened in angry recognition. "You!"

"Yes. Me. Place your weapons on the ground and there's a chance this won't go as badly for you as it did last time," I said.

His eyes tightened in defiance. I clicked off the safety, just to make sure he knew how serious I was.

"The future of this country depends on what you do next, Lance Corporal. Make the right choice."

He lowered his weapon and laid it on the ground, muttering obscenities as he did. His fellow squaddies did the same, without the swearing.

"Zac, can you reach into the guard box and remove the rocket launcher they have in there?"

"The what?" Zac said. But didn't bother to ask again. He walked into the box and came out holding the launcher in his arms like a baby. "Now, what are you boys doing with a big gun like this?"

"Protecting the motorcade," the lance corporal said through gritted teeth.

As if on cue, I heard rumbling engines and saw flashing lights as a line of black cars streaked past on the opposite side of the river. The Emperor and his escort.

"We have to go!"

Zac threw the launcher onto the back of the car and leapt into the driver's seat. I ejected the clip from the rifle and dropped in on the chest of the solider who still lay on the ground.

"This ain't over," the lance corporal shouted, as we burned away.

I only hoped he was right.

Seven minutes. We were racing behind the last car of the Emperor's escort as it headed for the Hub.

"Overtake them," I said.

"Not a good idea." Zac pointed to a helicopter overhead. It was bristling with weapons, covering the motorcade from the sky. He was right. If we tried to get ahead, they'd blow us away before we had a chance to say "Trap!"

I pushed the button on my throat mic. "Captain Jones," I said. Still nothing but static. "Sergeant Cain." Nothing. Did they know, I wondered, that they were already under attack? "Shit," I said, slamming my hand on the dashboard.

"You want to tell me what the hell is going on?"

"Ladoux was working with the Red Hand."

"Ladoux! I don't believe it. She saved my life."

"Ladoux and Hedges, too. And he's got the X73 virus and he's going to release it in the Hub when the Emperor arrives."

Zac blinked. "But they tortured him. I saw the scars."

"They turned him," I said. "And we have less than six minutes to stop him."

Zac's hands tightened on the steering wheel. "And the network?"

"I think he's got to it."

Zac nodded. "It's the first thing I'd do. OK, try to intercept the Emperor's security channel."

I pulled out my tab and tried scanning for a different frequency. I picked up old radio channels broadcasting propaganda messages and music, but nothing in Chinese.

The escort pulled off the road. We were nearly at the Hub. The front car pulled to a halt outside the bunker. I jumped out before Zac even had a chance to slow the car down.

"Stop!" I shouted, running forward. "It's a trap!" But my voice was drowned out in the *thump* of helicopter blades.

I headed for the middle car, the one I assumed the Emperor Tzen and his Shifter guards – the *Banjai Gonsi* – would be travelling in. When they saw me, they would do what they were trained to do: Shift and get the Emperor out of here.

Car and van doors opened. Men wearing black and carrying large weapons piled out and pointed everything at me. I held my hands up, to show I wasn't a threat, while I scanned the vehicles, looking for Tzen. Neither he nor his Little Guards were anywhere to be seen. I heard a low groan of machinery and turned to see the large doors to the Hub close with a booming slam.

"Where's the Emperor?" I shouted at one of the bodyguards, a thick-necked man with a shaven head.

He grinned. "He is already inside. So, if you planned on harming him, you are too late."

"The motorcade was a diversion," I heard Zac say, from behind me.

The big man nodded, proud of himself and his work.

"You have got to get him out," I said. "It's a trap!"

The bodyguard looked unsettled, unsure of what to do. And my panic wasn't helping things.

"This is Commandant Tyler of the S3," Zac said. "We have intel that someone inside the Hub is planning on…" He turned to me, unsure if he should continue.

I finally calmed down enough to take charge. "Planning on assassinating the Emperor and everyone else inside there. So we have to get those doors open."

The man lowered his weapon, his face pallid and tight. It was his job to protect the Emperor, and if I was to be believed, he had just failed.

I ran toward the doors, where two S3 soldiers stood looking confused and uneasy. "We have to get the doors open."

"No can do, Com. They open from the inside only. And we've been told they're on lockdown till the treaty is signed."

I slammed on the metal sheets. Ten inches thick and capable of withstanding a bomb strike. But there had to be a way of opening them. Any minute now, Hedges would release the virus. A virus that tore straight through the brain faster than anyone would have time to Shift. The images of Frankie's slideshow flashed through my mind. But instead of the faces of strangers, I saw Aubrey and Katie. Their eyes bleeding. Their bodies giving up. Their mouths crying for help.

"What can we do?" the Emperor's guard said, laying his hand against the metal.

"Step aside, please."

I turned around to see Zac with the rocket launcher we'd taken off the men at the roadblock readied against his shoulder.

I nodded and pulled the guards out of the way. I waved at everyone to get back. We took cover behind the row of cars and waited.

It took Zac an infuriatingly long time to work out how to operate the launcher. I was almost about to take it off him and do it myself when there was a *whoosh* and the rocket blasted out of the barrel, throwing Zac off his feet.

It exploded on impact with the doors, creating a fireball ten-feet high. Metal blackened. Stone shook. But when the flames died down, the doors were still intact.

I ran back to the door. The metal was too hot to touch, and when I tried, my hand came away covered in soot. I looked around for something, anything, that I could use to pry the doors open. There was nothing but rubble and dying fires. I ignored the heat and clawed at the hair-thin crack between the doors with my fingernails. Some of the guards tried to help, all of us tugging and banging on the doors, trying desperately to get in.

I felt a hand on my shoulder. One of the guards spoke to me. I didn't understand what he was saying, but I understood the gesture. A hand to his ear. *Listen.*

I stopped banging and leaned in, closer to the door. There was a noise coming from the other side. Thudding and screaming. I closed my eyes and pressed my forehead against the still-hot metal. I didn't care about the pain. It was nothing compared to what my friends inside were going through.

There had to be something I could do.

CHAPTER TWENTY-FIVE

This time, I didn't even bother calling Zac.

I'd run out of the arch, leaving Ladoux rocking and laughing inside, and I'd kept running.

I had two miles to cover in fifteen minutes. When I used to run home from ARES HQ before... before all of this, the best I could do was an eight-minute mile. But I was stronger then – I didn't have a body that had grown up on rations or gone through week after week where I was lucky enough to grab a couple of hours' sleep at a time. Not to mention the bullet hole in my leg. But I'd also never had something driving me like this.

I ran, jumping over burned-out cars and through the rubble of buildings. Under precarious bridges and over the ruins of roads.

You can make it. You can make it, I kept hearing him, over and over, pushing me on. Faster and Faster. For the first time since I'd woken up in this reality with his voice in my head, we wanted the same thing.

I'd ignored the screaming of my muscles, the vomit rising in my throat, and I ran. As I had done when Frankie commanded me to. Only this time, I was the one in control.

I'd thought of Frankie, down in the Hub, an innocent doctor doomed to die with all the other Shifters. Had it been her screams I'd heard through the doors?

If only I was able to undo the choice I'd forced on her that night, I wouldn't be here – the broken landscape of London blurred around me – none of this would be here. Then why was I still fixed in this place, in this reality? Why couldn't I just give up and go back to the world I knew – the safe, peaceful world?

Because you have a job to do.

I thought it at exactly the same time as I heard his voice say it. I almost laughed at the irony of us being on the same side for once. Because I knew there was still a chance I could stop this. And as long as there was a chance, I would see this though.

I'd pounded past a road sign, which hung by one screw from a wall. I was near the Embankment. If I kept up the pace, I could still make it. But my limbs were starting to scream in revolt.

It's just pain.

To my right, I'd seen the Emperor's motorcade gliding past. Hedges might already be getting ready. I had to make it this time.

I dug deep within me, to a place I'd been trying so hard to block out and found strength. His strength. I put on a burst of speed.

I raced across the street, past a plain car parked to the left of the doors. And somehow I knew the Emperor was already here. The doors were already closing. They were a quarter closed. A half. I threw my feet out from under me, ignoring the warnings from the sentries, and skidded under the closing gap, scraping my back off the rough ground as I slid inside the Hub.

The door clanged closed behind me. Whatever was going to happen next, I was locked in here with everyone else.

"Commandant?" I looked up to see a solider standing over me. "Are you OK?"

I pushed myself to standing. "Get a message out, we're under attack," I shouted, racing through the hangar, past the row of vehicles and for the lift. I placed one hand on the keypad and slammed on the wall with the other. "Come on!"

It seemed to take forever for the lift to arrive, and even longer for the doors to close once I was inside. In the agonisingly slow seconds it took for the lift to descend one hundred feet, I paced inside the silver box, like a caged animal.

When the lift doors finally opened, I ran out and scanned the Hub. It was packed with S3 officers and support staff. They'd all come out to see the Emperor arrive.

"Emperor Tzen," I shouted, pushing people out of the way.

At last I saw him standing on the far side of the hall, surrounded by his Shifter guards. They all turned to me, their bodies poised for a fight. Tzen just smiled at my approach. But the smile didn't last long.

"Get out!" I'd shouted, staggering towards him. My legs were finally giving up. "It's a trap!"

I saw a look of concentration begin to form on the faces of the *Banjai Gonsi*. They were going to Shift and at least they would be safe. And without the Emperor here, maybe Hedges wouldn't go through with the plan.

"*Stop*," Tzen said, resting his hand on the shoulder of one of the Little Guards, who was about a foot taller than him. "Commandant Tyler, I would say it is good to finally meet you. But judging by your expression, this does not seem to be the case."

"I don't have time," I said, scanning the gathering crowd for Hedges. "You have to get out of here. It's not safe."

The boy next to Tzen started pleading with him in rapid Chinese, his face tight with concern.

Tzen held his hand up and the boy stopped. "This treaty is more important than me."

I rolled my eyes. This was not the time for honour. If he got out of here, the treaty could be signed tomorrow. Or the day after. If he stayed here, he would die with the rest of us.

I pushed him aside, to the outraged grunts of his guards. If he wasn't going to leave, I only had one choice. Find Hedges.

I didn't need to look for long.

Hedges stood in the middle of the room, a look of beatification on his scarred face. He was a man at peace, a man ready to embrace his destiny. What had happened to him? What had turned him from loyal S3 solider to holy warrior? I would never know. He pulled his hand out of his pocket and something flashed purple in the light. He raised his fist to shoulder height and lifted his first finger.

I patted my belt for my pistol. I'd forgotten it was missing.

I saw Aubrey push her way through the crowd.

"Scott, what's going on?" She took hold of my hand, trying to get my attention, but I didn't take my eyes of Hedges. He lifted his second finger.

I yanked Aubrey towards me, grabbed the gun from her belt and raised it. Time seemed to slow as the bullet cut its way across the room. Hedges had time to lift his third finger from the vial before the bullet punctured his forehead, just above his left eyebrow. Blood sprayed out as the bullet drilled deeper into his skull. His eyes widened in shock. His last act before his brain shut down was to raise his last finger.

The vial spiralled to the floor as he toppled backwards. It bounced once, twice, three times on the hard, tiled floor of the Hub and rolled away towards the shocked onlookers. Cain stopped it under the toe of his boot.

No one in the Hub moved. They just stared from Hedges' dead body, pooling blood, to me, the gun still pointed straight ahead, to the vial under Cain's foot. For a terrible moment, I wondered if Cain was part of Ladoux's plan. All he needed to do was tip his weight forward onto the vial and it would all be over.

Cain bent down, lifted his foot a fraction of an inch at a time, as if removing his foot from a landmine, and picked the vial up from the floor.

There was a small crack in the glass. But the vial was still sound. The virus hadn't escaped. We were saved. Cain looked up at me, his face filled with questions, as my legs finally gave way.

Aubrey helped me to my feet. "You're bleeding," she said, nodding to a widening patch of blood on my thigh. I must have torn my stitches running. But it didn't matter; everyone was safe. I wrapped my arm around Aubrey, on the pretence of letting her take my weight, but really, I wanted to hold her in my arms. If the whole of S3 hadn't been watching us, I would have kissed her and not stopped till I ran out of breath.

"What in the name of sweet baby Jesus is going on, Tyler?" Cain shouted. "And what was Hedges doing with this?" The vial lay in his open palm, as if he was frightened to close his hand around it.

"He was working with the Red Hand. Ladoux, too."

I explained to the room about their plans for the X73. There were gasps and mutterings as they realised how closely they'd all come to dying. The reactions from the *Banjai Gonsi* had a slight delay, as the boy Tzen had spoken to earlier quickly translated what I was saying.

"We're lucky you made it in time, Tyler." Cain's face was a picture of open pride and admiration.

"Only on the third try."

"What do you mean?" Aubrey said.

"Twice. I didn't make it twice."

The shock of understanding passed through the crowd. I heard my name being whispered over and over.

CP made her way through the crowd, dragging a crate. "You look like you could use a sit-down, sir."

I nodded in gratitude and collapsed onto the upturned crate.

"The doctor should see to your leg," Aubrey said.

"In time."

Tzen walked forward. With me on the crate, we were eye to eye. He looked so much older than the last time I'd seen him, even though I knew it was only a few weeks ago. The grief of losing his father and the weight of being the leader of his country had hardened his once-soft features. He had the haunted look that I recognised from looking in the mirror. He'd seen terrible things, and yet I also saw hope in his eyes.

He placed one fist into the other and bowed. I copied it as best as I could.

"It appears you have saved my life, Commandant Tyler."

"You should have got out when I told you," I said.

Tzen pursed his lips, trying to stop himself from smiling. "I am afraid I am not very good at being told what to do. For example, my advisors said that I should not have come here today. I told them that wherever Commandant Tyler was, I would be safe. I am glad to have been proved right." Tzen threw a look at the tall boy behind him, who bowed his head in apparent contrition. "I hope we will get a chance to speak later, Commandant. I think we have much to discuss."

I remembered Vine's warning. Could Tzen really want me to lead Britain as he led China? If so, he was going to be very disappointed.

"But now," he continued, "if you will excuse me, I have a treaty to sign and a war to end."

Cain stretched out one hand. "The Minister is this way, Your Majesty."

Tzen nodded at me and turned to follow Cain, ignoring the body of the man who had attempted to assassinate him.

The crowd closed in around him.

Aubrey crouched down next to me. Her eye was wide with concern and more, a light I'd seen in the eyes of *my* Aubrey.

No, I corrected myself. This was my Aubrey. When the choice came, I made it. To stay here and die with her if necessary. And soon, the war would be over and we could build a new life for ourselves. Just like we'd always promised each other.

"We need to get you to the doc," Aubrey said.

"She's not going to be too impressed I messed up her stitches."

"I think she'll forgive you." She helped me to my feet and I staggered towards the infirmary.

Frankie was changing the bandages on the girl with one arm when we walked in.

She turned and looked at me, an eyebrow raised in mild irritation "And what have you done to yourself now, Commandant?"

"Run two miles. In fifteen minutes."

"On that leg?" She snorted in exasperation. "Well, better let me look at it, then."

I hopped up on one of the beds and allowed Frankie to administer to my wound. Aubrey watched me the whole time, smiling. I desperately wanted to be alone with her again. But we'd have to wait.

"I go out for five minutes," Zac strode through the doors of the infirmary, "and I miss all the excitement."

"What excitement?" Frankie asked, threading the needle through my skin.

"Just Tyler saving the world. Again."

Frankie looked at me as Zac, Aubrey and I burst out laughing.

It was one of those perfect moments. The three of us together. I felt the warm glow of good friendship. Or maybe it was the drugs kicking in. Whatever, I felt more at peace that I had done in days. Perhaps even months.

Frankie shook her head and finished tying off the last of the new stitches.

As if the moment couldn't get any better, I saw the door open and two small figures walk through. It was Katie and CP. Katie hesitated at the door as if she wasn't sure if she should be there.

CP pushed her forward gently. "Get in there."

I pulled Katie into a tight, shameless hug as soon as she was within reach.

"They said you nearly died," she whispered into my neck, her voice chocked in emotion.

I didn't correct her that we had *all* nearly died and tightened my hug. "It's OK," I said. "Everything is going to be OK."

I had my sister and my friends around me. Life was good.

Which was when I heard the first explosion.

CHAPTER TWENTY-SIX

A second explosion followed quickly after, shaking the walls of the infirmary. Dust rained down on the white floor. We all stood there staring up at the ceiling.

"What the…" Zac said.

Plans and backup plans, that's what Ladoux had said. It appeared the Red Hand had yet another in store.

"We have to get to the command room." I jumped off the bed, ignoring Frankie's complaints that I needed to keep the weight off my leg, and ran for the door, Zac, Aubrey and the others trailing after me.

The Hub was a flurry of activity as everyone in S3 prepared for attack. I watched them as they armed themselves, checked their equipment and tried to stay focused and calm as yet another explosion rocked overhead. Some of them had clearly been woken and were still pulling on their uniforms. How many of them could be trusted? How far had the Red Hand infiltrated our ranks?

Everyone stopped as another, louder explosion was quickly followed by the sounds of screeching metal, as if a great beast was clawing at the doors overhead.

I crossed the Hub, ignoring the red stain where Hedges' body had been, and pushed open the doors of the command room.

The scene that greeted me was one of barely contained panic. The intel officers were scrambling around, pushing buttons. The large screens were broadcasting feed from the security cameras showing what was happening on the streets meters above our heads.

On the live footage I saw the Emperor's helicopter on its side, blades still turning, clawing gashes in the side of the building. Swarms of figures in red scarves surrounded the entrance to the Hub, armed with machine guns. The Emperor's security force were putting up a good fight, but they were outnumbered. We watched as the last of them fell to the bullets of the Red Hand. And then a tank rolled into frame, a large Red Hand painted on its side.

"The bastards," Zac said. "That's one of ours. They could at least have the decency to not kill us with our own bloody tanks."

I wondered if this was a touch of irony from Ladoux, revenge for the friendly fire that had killed her husband.

The only thing stopping the Red Hand from getting into the hangar was ten inches of steel. Only minutes ago, I'd been praying for those doors to buckle, cursing them for not letting me in. Now I was praying that they would hold and keep our enemy out.

The turret on the tank twisted, pointing straight at the doors. They'd withstood a rocket launcher, but could they stand against a tank shell? No one breathed as the tank fired. The impact shook the walls again and plaster rained down on our heads.

"How long will it hold?" Cain had entered the command room.

"Honestly," one of the intelligence officers said – his name was Philips, I seemed to remember – "I don't know."

Cain slammed a red button with his hammer fist. A blasting klaxon sounded and all the lights in the Hub turned red. Not that anyone needed the level five protocol to let us know we were in deep shit. "Radio the army," Cain said. "We need backup."

"The network is down," Philips said.

I'd forgotten about how I'd not been able to get through to Aubrey earlier. And now it seemed we were unable to get any messages out.

"Then get them back up again!" Cain shouted, pounding his fist on a table.

Phillips ripped a panel off the wall. Red, black and blue wires spilled out like guts. He started trying to trace the wires back.

"What other means of communication do we have?" I asked.

The intel officers all shared a look. None, it seemed.

"What about Morse code?" Katie stepped forward. "I was trained on it last week. Mr Morgan said it was how messages were sent in the old days."

Philips jumped up. "Yes! I think I know where there's a hard-wired transmitter left over from the last war."

"Then get a message through to Morgan. Tell him the Hub is under attack and we need help."

"I actually don't know Morse code," Phillips said, shame turning his cheeks pink.

I looked at Katie. "I only know SOS," she said.

"Then send that," I said.

Katie and Phillips ran out of the room as we all turned back to the screens. The tank was firing over and over. The doors would give any moment, and then they would be heading for the lift. We would have to be ready.

"How many of S3 are here?" I said, turning to Cain.

"All of them."

Three hundred trained men and women. Most of them Shifters. Up against an army. Only, all our heavy artillery was in the hangar above our heads.

"What weapons do we have?" I asked.

"Let's go find out."

The shelling was almost constant now; a deafening pounding that shook my teeth. We were all covered in plaster dust, and great cracks had appeared in the ceiling.

The armoury was empty. We'd handed out every last gun, grenade and knife. And the men and women of S3 were bristling with an arsenal of weapons.

"What can we do, sir?" Williamson said, stepping forward, slipping his head through a belt of quantum grenades. His dark eyes glittered with a mixture of fear and excitement. Unwin stood next to him, the straps of at least three guns criss-crossing over his chest. His jaw worked frantically at a piece of gum.

"You can start building a barricade in front of the lifts, in case they get through."

"Message sent," Katie said, skidding to a halt in front of us. "I don't know if it got through, though."

"We'll just have to hope it did," I said, pulling her into a half hug.

"What's going on?" Vine appeared, Tzen at his side. They were covered in dust.

"We're under attack, sir," Zac said, stating the obvious.

"You and the Emperor need to get into the Igloo and lock yourself up. It's the safest place here."

"I do not hide," Tzen said.

"You do today," I said. "Without you, this treaty will crumble and everything we have been fighting for will have been for nothing."

"But I can fight."

"I know you can," I said. "You are one of the best fighters I've seen." I remembered how the two of us had gone up against each other in the golden tip of the Pyramid while his father watched. "But a great warrior knows when to pick his battle. And this is not yours."

Tzen sucked on his bottom lip, suddenly looking like the young boy he really was. He was scared and fighting not to show it. Just like we all were. He breathed in and then nodded. "I will go."

I turned to Vine. I still hated him for everything he had done. For the way he'd tried to use my love of my sister to manipulate me. But his safety was more important than my desire for revenge. "Take your most trusted men with you. When they break through, they will head for the Igloo."

"I am looking at my most trusted man," he said.

I shook my head. "I'm staying here."

"Then I am sure I have nothing to fear." He reached out his hand.

Even now, when there was an enemy army breaking in overhead, he was still worried about appearances. I took his hand and shook it, taking pleasure in squeezing it as tightly as I could. If we made it out of here, I was going to make sure that Vine went down.

But first, I had to stay alive.

Vine led Tzen to the Igloo and I turned back to my squad. I was about to issue an instruction when a huge lump of masonry crashed down in the space between Williamson and me. We looked at it for a moment. It had narrowly missed our heads.

"They've broken through."

"And they'll bring the whole place down on us at this rate," Zac said, looking up at the large hole in the ceiling. "We're sitting ducks down here."

"You suggest we take the fight to them, Captain?" Cain said.

Zac blinked. I knew he was calculating the odds, plotting the outcomes. "Only ten at a time can go up through the lifts."

"We'd be cut to shreds as soon as we stepped out of the box," Aubrey said.

What other choice did we have? Sit down here and wait to be crushed under falling bricks, or try and take a few of them out with us?

"If I could get to the Rhino," CP said. "It's DNA-coded to me, so they won't be able to access it."

"There's no way you're coming up with us," I said.

"Maybe the lift isn't the only way up." Katie pointed up at the airshafts. They were only a foot wide. Only enough room for a small child.

"No," I said, realising what she was suggesting.

"Yes!" CP said, catching on. "Someone get a grappling gun."

"Cancel that," I said, grabbing CP by the shoulders. "It's not going to happen, Finn," I said. "That's an order."

"Well, with the greatest of respect, sir," CP said, digging her small fists into her hips, "but screw orders."

"The shaft comes out at the rear of the hangar," Zac said, following the path of the silver tube as it twisted along the walls and up. "She might just make it."

"And if not, I just Shift. It's what I was trained for, Com."

I hesitated and then realised she was right. "OK. Get the grapple."

"I'm going with her," Katie said. I looked down and saw she was pulling on a pair of oversized gloves.

I was about to protest when she punched me in the arm. "Stop acting like a brother and start thinking like a solider. They'll have Shifters on their side too, right?"

"I don't know. Maybe."

"Then CP will need a Fixer to cover her. And unless you can squeeze through that hole, I don't see another Fixer around here, do you?"

"She's right, sir," CP said. "And I promise, if it doesn't go to plan, I'll get us both back here to safety."

I looked from CP to my little sister. I crouched down so that she and I were on eye level. "I want you to think about this moment. Right here and now. I want you to really think about your decision to go up there. That goes for you too, CP."

CP pulled off her salute: two fingers brushing against her long fringe. "Yes, sir."

Unwin and Williamson seemed to be fighting over who would get to fire the grappling gun. Unwin won and took aim. The hook soared through the air, dragging the rope behind it, and slammed into the brickwork a few inches away from the shaft opening. Williamson rolled his eyes, there was that ripple as a new reality took over, and suddenly, Williamson was holding the gun. He pulled the trigger and the harpoon shot clear through the hole and to the top of the shaft.

CP tugged on the rope. It held. Unwin and Williamson helped the two girls clip on. Acid bubbled in my throat as I watched CP work her way up the rope and disappear inside the shaft.

Katie was up next. Williamson tightened the clip on her harness. I could see her hands were shaking too much to do it herself.

"Remember, Katie," I said, checking over the harness myself, "the slightest hint—"

"And I Shift. I get it." She pushed my hands away. "They retested me, you know? This time, I didn't try and fail. I scored a twelve."

Unwin chuckled next to me. "She beat your record, Com."

Katie beamed. I leant forward and kissed her on the forehead. "Show-off," I said.

Williamson lifted her up so she could grab hold of the rope, and we watched as she winched herself into the air.

"Break some balls," Unwin said, just as she eased her way inside the shaft. She winked back down in response.

"OK," I said, taking a deep breath and trying to forget about the danger my little sister was about to face. "We'll give the girls five minutes, and then we're going up. A squadron at a time. Starting with Thirteen."

The men and women of S3 split off and began organising themselves into their squads. Of my squad, there were only Aubrey, Zac, Williamson, Unwin and Turner left. I was overwhelmed by a sense of pride and love for each and every one of them.

"You appear to be a few men short."

I turned to see Sergeant Cain. He was fully suited and carrying a shotgun. He pumped the forestock, slotting a round into the barrel. "Permission to volunteer for the Lucky Thirteens, Commandant."

I smiled at my old instructor. "Permission very much granted." I reached out my hand and he shook it.

"Two minutes and counting," Zac said, handing me a gun.

"Weapon check." I said

"Check," Aubrey said,

"Check," Zac said.

"Check," Williamson and Unwin said in unison.

Turner was the last to speak up. She was tucking a gold medallion under her shirt. I recognised it as the one Cooper used to wear. "Check," she said finally.

I ran through the process of ensuring my gun was loaded and not jammed without even thinking. "Check," I said at last.

Whatever happened next, we were ready. "Thirteen squad. Are you ready to break some balls?"

"Yes, sir!" they echoed.

The rest of S3 were equally primed. Zac had been right when he said they were the best of the best. Today, they'd prove that to the world.

I heard a high screech and *whoomp* from above.

"You gotta love the Rhino's plasma cannon," Unwin said.

"They made it!" Aubrey said, clutching my arm.

"Now! Now! Now!" I shouted and we ran towards the lift.

"Wait!"

I turned to see a red-faced Carl jogging towards us.

"Unless you're joining us, Carl, I suggest you take cover."

"That's not the only way up." He bent forward, clutching his knees, fighting to get his breath back.

"We know about the shafts," Zac said, pulling him to standing by his arm.

"Not them."

"Then why the hell didn't you tell us? My sister is up there right now and you're telling me there's another way?" I grabbed him by his damp Led Zeppelin T-shirt.

"Because I was getting it ready," he squeaked.

I let him go. "Getting what ready?"

He held up what looked like a remote detonator in his hand. "The platform."

KIM CURRAN

CHAPTER TWENTY-SEVEN

"The whole floor rises up?" Aubrey said, looking down at the tiled pattern beneath our feet.

"It used to. But when the place was shut down after the last war, they had the pistons concreted up. I did try to tell you," he said, fixing me with an irritated look.

"So, how do we get it operational?" Cain said.

"Four controlled explosions at the base of each of the pistons might – might, I stress – clear the cement from the mechanism. I've already set one of them." He waved the detonator again.

"Williamson, take two more men and get Carl here to show you where to place the explosives. You've got one minute and then we're going up anyway."

"I need more time," Carl said, a drip of sweat rolling down his forehead.

I rested my hand on his shoulder. "I trust you, Carl. You can do it."

His lips tightened in a line of determination. He nodded and pulled off the worst salute I'd ever seen. "Sir, yes, sir!"

He jogged away with Williamson and two more members of S3.

"All right, listen up," I shouted, my voice carrying across the assault still raging up above. "In under a minute, this whole floor is going to rise up and we're going to face the enemy. There are people up there who believe that Shifters are an abomination. That we should be wiped off the face of the planet. And they are willing to do anything and everything to make sure that each and every last Shifter is destroyed. But we are not going to allow that to happen.

"I wish I could promise that you will make it. But I'm not going to insult you by lying. Some of us will die today. Even those of us who have the power to change our decisions will be forced to make the ultimate choice."

Fear and emotion made my words crack. I looked down at my shaking hands.

You can do it.

I looked around to see who had said that. Then realised it was him. He was here again. Only this time, instead of sneering at me, judging me and criticising me, he was willing me on. And I realised with an overwhelming certainty that he cared about the people in this room as much as I did. Unsurprising, now I thought about it. He'd fought alongside them all these years. He'd gone into battle and led them home time after time. He was the one that they believed in.

Every choice he'd made, whether I agreed with it or not, he'd done to protect them. To protect what this place and the people in it stood for. Whereas I was willing to sacrifice my life for the people I loved, he'd sacrificed his soul. Did that make him a better man? I didn't know. It made him a better soldier. He was focused and ruthless where I was distracted and driven by emotion. But maybe, just maybe, together we might be worthy of leading these men and women.

I sensed the divide between us start to fade, like words in sand. There wasn't him and me anymore. I was one person, with a clear job ahead of me and the people behind me I needed to get it done. Today, this would end.

"We have been given our power for a reason," I said, my voice taking on a tone and strength new to me. "To protect this country. And today, that is what we will do. Even if we have to lay down our bodies so that those left can crawl over us to reach our goal. We will do our duty. We will prove to those who doubt us that we are stronger than they can imagine. We will prove to those up on the surface who want to make our home our grave that our power is a gift, not a curse. We will be braver than they can comprehend. More powerful than a thousand tanks or missiles. If you follow me today, I can't promise that I will lead you to safety, but I will lead you to victory."

The men and women in the room saluted in unison. I returned the gesture. "Towards the true way," I said.

The motto of ARES was taken up by everyone in the room, repeated over and over.

"Well, that was impressive," Zac said when the echo had died down. "Have you been practising it long?"

"For weeks," I said, smiling at him.

He returned it, bigger and brighter, and looked up at the cracked ceiling. "So, one way or another, this is it. A life free of ARES, can you imagine it? I wonder what I would do with myself."

"Become star striker for Chelsea Football Club?"

Zac looked pleased at the idea. "You know, that might just work."

"Just stay alive, OK?"

"I'll do my best."

I reached my hand out to him to shake it. Zac pushed it out of the way and pulled me into a big hug.

I'd never found making friends easy in my old reality. And here I was with a friend. A real friend who was willing to follow me into death. Whatever happened today, that was something I was grateful to this reality for.

Zac let me go and saluted, the first genuine salute he'd given me.

I felt Aubrey's fingers entwine with mine. "Hello, you."

I didn't understand what she meant. "Er, hello yourself?"

She laughed. "There's a change in you. Not as scary as when that coldness takes over you. Something else. It's like you're finally here."

"And I'm not going anywhere till this is over." I reached out and tucked a lock of her blonde hair behind her ear.

"In position." I heard Williamson's voice over the radio.

"Do it."

Four soft thuds shook the floor under our feet.

"Yes!' I heard Carl's voice being picked up by Williamson's mic.

"Report," I said.

"He seems happy, sir. He's doing a sort of dance."

I imagined him playing air guitar. "Tell him to knock it off and get us up there."

A moment later, I heard the whirring of machinery.

"Form a circle!" I shouted, remembering what I'd read about battle formations in my military strategy books.

My command was repeated over and over, till the whole of S3 were standing facing the walls as a crack ran in a perfect circle around the whole of the Hub, and slowly the floor began to rise. I looked at Aubrey on my right and Zac on my left. The two people I trusted most in the world, more even than I trusted myself. They believed in me. Them and the whole of S3. It was about time I did the same.

We got closer and closer to the ceiling, till it was just feet above our heads. For a moment, I worried that we would be crushed against it, when it split down the middle and slid across. The sound of the gunfire and the plasma cannons was almost deafening.

"Bring the rain!" I shouted, and all hell broke loose.

Grenades were thrown. Machine guns fired through the gap in the ceiling. Bodies of Red Hand soldiers fell through the breach and tumbled down onto the platform. If they weren't dead when they fell, they were a few moments later as they were picked off by the S3.

The platform rose, bringing us up inside the hangar, and I came face to face with our enemy for the first time. I set my gun against my shoulder and fired into the front row of the Red Hand.

It was a hail of bullets on all sides as both sides tore into each other. Men and women next to me went down, holes opening in their chests, limbs being blown off. But a blink later and they were back on their feet, firing – this time having dodged the bullet. This was what it meant to go up against a Shifting army. Bullets didn't work.

All around me was that weird, jerking, blurring of movement you saw when Shifters fought. It had never looked more beautiful.

I slapped in a new magazine and started to walk forward in line with the rest of my squad. I took a bullet in the side, but the pain didn't even have time to register before I Shifted clear of its path. I saw Aubrey next to me take one in the chest, the bullet passing clear through her heart. The image of her dying in my arms came back so raw, and a scream of rage formed on my lips. But before it had a chance to escape, she simply closed her eyes and was whole once more. The man who had shot her, however, was missing his head.

The Red Hand were clearly panicking, not understanding why they didn't seem to be able to kill us.

Then one of them worked it out. "Headshots!" they cried.

That was the sure way to kill a Shifter. I watched as a man next to me fell, a neat hole in his helmet. His eyes stared straight ahead. The Red Hand must be using armour-piercing rounds. Another solider went down behind me. They were picking us off one by one and there was nowhere for us to run. No chance of retreat. We were trapped inside the hangar. What have I done? I thought. I've led my men into a massacre.

A third soldier went down next to me, blood pooling out of the hole in his head. I had to do something.

Then I heard a peal of gunfire coming from ahead of us, from behind the line of the Red Hand. They were being attacked from behind.

"The army is here," I heard Cain shout in delight.

But it wasn't the army.

As a path cleared in the enemy lines, I saw small figures dressed in black, with too-large helmets bouncing on their heads. They were firing rifles, the front row kneeling down so the row behind could get a clear shot. Just like we'd been taught in training.

The cadets were here.

"Fire!" I saw Morgan at the head of the troop, dressed in his ARES uniform, gold brocade glinting in the light. And the cadets fired.

It was clear that the Red Hand didn't want to return fire, not at a bunch of kids. They spun in confusion, not knowing whether to run or to fight back. The cadets were focused, trained and composed. And the men and women of the Red Hand fell under the shots of the children they believed to be an abomination.

I saw the Rhino roll forward. The front line of the Red Hand scattered in front of it. Those who didn't make it in time were ground into the dirt under its tracks. They were being attacked from the front and the back. A perfect pincer manoeuvre. We pushed them back, out of the hangar and into the open. We had them. I turned to Zac and we smiled. The day was ours.

I heard the *thump* of blades and looked up to see a helicopter hovering overhead. It spun till the nose was pointed at us, and I saw Ladoux behind the controls. She was grinning, a look beyond mania contorting her face. I should have killed her when I had the chance.

I aimed for the glass covering the cockpit and opened fire. Zac and Aubrey did the same, but our bullets pinged off.

"Bring it down!" I shouted, directing all fire towards the gunship as its rocket launchers slotted into place. She was going to finish us off.

All the weapons around me pointed at Ladoux's helicopter. A shot found its home, tearing a hole in the tail. It began to circle wildly. But she let a rocket loose before spiralling away and crashing into the side of the Hub in a ball of fire. Ladoux was dead. I didn't even have time to feel happy about that.

"Get clear," Zac shouted. He tried to hold me back, but I broke free of his grip and ran towards the Rhino, shouting my sister's name as Ladoux's rocket soared towards its target.

Everything moved as if in molasses. The people around me fighting and dying all faded away. All I could see was the missile cutting through the blue sky like a paper aeroplane thrown by a child.

I raced through the options, looking for something to Shift before I had to watch it collide. But in my panic, nothing came to me. My mind had gone totally blank.

I raised my hand, as if I could reach out and grab the missile out of its trajectory. Then the world exploded in heat and fire.

I was thrown off my feet by the explosion. Time returned to normal as I hit the ground. Fragments of concrete and dirt rained down on me, filling my mouth and eyes. I sat up, spluttering, trying to clear my vision. The Rhino was upside down, tracks still whirring, like a turtle on its back. Exposed and vulnerable.

I tried to pull myself to my feet but collapsed as white-hot pain cut through me. I looked down to see a shard of metal protruding from my right calf. My right arm, too, was a bloody mess.

There was a groaning from next to me. Unwin covered his face with his hands. Blood poured down what was left of his face. I could see the white of bone jutting through the ragged flesh, teeth exposed from where his cheek had been. He was dead. He just didn't know it yet.

I struggled to my feet again, yanked out the shard of metal, and stumbled towards the Rhino. There was still a chance. And that was the only thing that was stopping me from lying down and joining Unwin.

I could hear screams from inside the Rhino. I couldn't tell if it was Katie or CP crying out for help. I scrambled through the smoke towards the tank, dipping and dodging the few bullets that were still being fired. I clambered up onto the belly of the tank and tore at the hole left by the missile, trying desperately to widen it enough to get inside. I shredded the skin on my hands, but I didn't care. I could still hear a girl's voice crying out for help. Whoever it was, why didn't they Shift?

"Stand back." Zac was up on the tank next to me, an axe in his hands. He swung it and buried the head into the metal of the tank. Again and again he hacked till a hole appeared. White smoke billowed out, and then a small hand reached through. I grabbed it. I knew it was Katie's hand as soon as my fingers closed around it. I pulled her free of the hole and into my arms. I held her so tight, I might have crushed her. "Why didn't you Shift?" I said. "Why didn't you Shift?"

She was coughing, struggling to say something. I let her go enough so she could speak. "CP!"

I let her down and pushed my head through the hole and looked into the dark interior of the tank.

CP was still at the controls, hanging upside down by the straps, a shard of shrapnel sticking out of her head.

"No."

Rage poured into me, filling the hole that had torn through my soul, like it had the night I'd watched Aubrey die. Bringing with it a power stronger than I had ever known. I let it storm through me. I made myself remember Jake, Cooper, Unwin, Ward. Everyone I had ever lost. I let all of the grief and anger that I had been holding back break free.

"No!"

KIM CURRAN

CHAPTER TWENTY-EIGHT

My command passed over the battle like a tidal wave, touching every person here. Guns clattered to the floor. Soldiers on both sides fell to their knees. Their will was mine now. And I wanted the fighting to end.

Faces that had snarled in rage softened and went still. Every man, woman and child froze exactly where they were, unable to so much as lift a finger. I looked around at the blood-splattered faces of the Red Hand. I was filled with so much hatred that I considered Forcing them all to die. To pick their guns back up and put them in their mouths. I saw the image in my mind and knew with utter certainty that I could make it happen. But then I saw the body of a cadet lying in the dust, and the hot anger faded into grief. And I let them all go.

My control over them had only lasted for a matter of seconds. But it was enough. It was over.

The understanding that the battle had ended and they were still alive came as a relief to some. A weight to others. They had lived, whereas others had not.

I didn't know how I felt about it. All I knew was that I had lost a friend. I looked down at CP's tiny body, her eyes wide open and staring at the sky as if she was looking for shapes in the clouds.

I could Shift. I could find a way for this not to have been. I could bring CP back to life.

I felt a hand on my arm. Katie was standing next to me.

"It's done," she said.

She was right. I could Shift. But the question was, should I? I looked around at the forces picking their way through the burning rubble. The fighting was over. CP's death had given me the strength to Force my will on them all. If I saved CP, I wasn't sure I'd find that strength again.

Sacrifice.

He understood it, and maybe I did now.

I didn't know what that said about me, that I was willing to sacrifice CP in a way I wasn't willing to let go of Katie or Aubrey. How had I become the kind of person who ranked the value of people's lives?

I moved CP in my arms so she was lying over my shoulder, and allowed Katie to lead me off the tank and back onto the ground. Frankie ran forward, her white coat covered in blood. She tried to take CP off me, to see if there was anything that could be done. I pushed her away. There was nothing.

"Let her," Katie said.

Reluctantly, I handed CP to Frankie. She laid her on the ground and called for a stretcher while taking her pulse.

Checking her for signs of life. It was a waste of energy. The stretcher arrived and CP was carried away.

"Let me see to your leg," Frankie said, softly. She cleaned and bandaged it quickly and then stood up. "You'll live."

I nodded my thanks as Frankie moved on to tend to the wounded.

Katie took my hand and we moved through the crowds. S3 soldiers were gathering up what remained of the Red Hand forces and corralling them inside the hangar. They didn't even need to bother marching them at gunpoint or cuffing them. The Red Hand walked seemingly of their own volition. Holy warriors whose God had abandoned them.

"Scott!"

I turned to see Aubrey running toward me. She leapt off the ground, throwing her arms around my neck. She was shaking and kept saying my name over and over.

"It's OK," I said. "I'm here."

"I thought you were dead. I saw the explosion," she said into my neck.

We pulled away from each other. Her face was covered in what looked like freckles. I looked closer; they were speckles of blood. I stroked her cheek with my thumb, smudging the blood and leaving a dark trail.

"What happened?" she said, looking around. "One second, everyone was fighting and then…"

"It doesn't matter," I said. "All that matters is that it's over."

I wrapped my left arm around her and took Katie's hand again with my right. The men and women of S3 swarmed around me. Some called out my name, others saluted. Others still reached out and touched me, as if that would bring them luck or protection. Like they were touching a statue.

Scott Tyler, saint of the S3. It sickened me.

They laid hands on Katie too, as if she was also some mascot for the unit. I shoved away the first couple of people who did it, but she shook her head, telling me it was OK.

"I have to get out of here," I said to Aubrey.

She understood. She led me to a sleek black limo. It had been one of the Emperor's cars and looked relatively undamaged.

I opened the back door for Katie, then got into the passenger's seat. I slammed the door on the sound of my name being passed through the troops like a chant.

"Tyler. Tyler. Tyler."

Aubrey hotwired the ignition, fired up the engine, and slowly pulled away. I watched the smoking ruins of the Hub grow smaller in my rear-view mirror.

Katie was curled up in the back. Her shoulders quivered, and I was sure that she was crying. I wished I could do the same. I wished that I could feel something. Anything.

I watched Aubrey. She stared straight ahead at the road.

"Where are we going?" I said.

"Somewhere that nobody can find us."

I let out a long breath, feeling the tightness in my chest lighten a little. "That sounds good. Just for a while."

"Just for a while."

She drove across the river, pausing only to talk to some guards at a roadblock.

Yes, she told them, the treaty had been signed. No, she said, she didn't know what was going to happen next.

Katie's sobs had quietened, and when I looked back, she was asleep.

I reached my hand out and wrapped it around the back of Aubrey's neck. She settled her head against it. "What are you going to do?" I said.

"What do you mean?"

"Now the war is over."

"I don't know," she said. "I never really bothered thinking beyond tomorrow. The future always seemed so far out of reach. What will you do?"

"Go and see my parents, I guess. Spend some time with Katie. Get to know you."

I watched her smile. "I thought you already knew me," she said.

"I know the other you. The one from the other reality. I know your favourite book is *The Wonderful Wizard of Oz*."

"Same! My father gave me that book!" she said, sounding delighted. "He used to read it to me whenever he was home. What else do you know about me?

"I know you had your first cigarette with Adam Jackson."

"Never heard of him. Different! What else?"

"I know you like your coffee with vanilla sprinkles."

"Vanilla sprinkles?" she said, laughing. It was like the sound of rain in the desert.

"Yeah, you always said a coffee wasn't complete without vanilla sprinkles. I mean the other you did."

"I'll have to try it sometime. But different. What else?" It was like a guessing game, how much did she share with her other self?

"I know that you love me."

She looked over at me, scanning my face, as if she was trying to find the answer to a question there. Then she turned back to the road. "Same," she said, finally.

Aubrey stopped the car in front of a familiar tower block.

"Your sanctuary?" I said.

"Our sanctuary now," she said, getting out of the car.

I left Katie asleep in the back and followed Aubrey through the twisted metal and up the stairs till we were back on the roof, looking down on the city.

It was so huge, stretching out as far as anyone could see. As the wind whipped around me, I thought about how big the city was and how small I was. Rather than making me feel scared or lost, it felt so good. Because what did my problems or my experiences matter against something that huge? I was just one life among millions. And soon, the city would recover and thrive and I could disappear into the crowd.

Since arriving in this place, I'd felt nothing but a crushing responsibility to fix everything. To fix the world. But now, I was a boy holding the hand of a girl he loved. And nothing else mattered.

"I thought I lost you," Aubrey said, tightening my hand.

"I'm hard to kill."

"No, I thought you were going to Shift back to your old reality. To save yourself."

I looked down. I didn't want to say that I was still considering it.

"But what about me?" Aubrey said, reading my expression. I was never able to hide anything from her.

"You'd be there with me, I'd make sure of it."

"But that would be a different me. I'd still be here."

"No, you wouldn't. There's only one reality, like we were told." I thumbed her cheek.

"But you said you can remember the other realities. And that means they must exist, doesn't it? Somewhere, somehow, they don't collapse like we've always been told. So if you return to your reality, I'll have never known you. And I'll still be here, fighting."

Was it possible that what we'd been taught about there being a single version of reality was wrong? Were there multiple versions existing alongside each other? Were there thousands, billions of other Scotts out there, living their lives? Thousands of other Aubreys? How many versions were there? How many different choices?

It didn't explain why I could remember the alternatives when no one else could. But it did explain why with every choice I'd made, I felt weaker. As if I'd left part of myself in that other reality. And the only thing that stopped me from disappearing altogether was her, the girl in front of me. She had always been my anchor in the storm. The one person I kept coming back to. The one person that made me feel whole.

"As long as I'm with you," I said. "I am home."

Maybe we stood there for hours. Or maybe it was only minutes. Eventually, I heard Katie call my name from the street below.

"We'd better go back," Aubrey said.

And I knew she didn't only mean back to the car. As glorious as it was to imagine we could stay here for the rest of our lives, we had to return to the Hub. They'd come looking for us eventually.

One more day, I thought. One more day and then I can finally keep the promise I made to Aubrey what seemed like a lifetime ago. Quit ARES and get on with the rest of our lives.

Just one more day.

CHAPTER TWENTY-NINE

By the time we made it back to the Hub, the streets were filled with people, cheering and waving the strange version of the Union flags. It was hard not to be infected by their shared joy and relief.

'Is it possible?" Aubrey said as she stopped the truck. "Can it really be over?"

I'm not sure it would ever be over. Not really. As long as there were men like Vine in power and people like Ladoux willing to oppose them, the rest of us would constantly be caught in the middle. But at least the fighting had stopped. And for now, that would have to be enough.

"One way to find out," I said, opening the car door.

As soon as I stepped out, I was scooped up into a bear hug so tight, I couldn't breathe. Finally, I was put down.

Cain beamed at me, his broken face twisted by the huge smile. "I couldn't be prouder of you than if you were my own son, Tyler," he said. His good eye became as clouded as his damaged one as a single tear traced the ragged path of his scar. "What a day," he said, wiping the tear away.

"What a day!" He wrapped his arm around my shoulder. "Come on, Vine is about to address the troops."

I was subjected to so many congratulatory pats as Cain led me back down into the Hub that my shoulders were stinging by the time we made it down the lifts.

The platform had been lowered once more and the whole of the S3 was packed into the hall along with the cadets. Some of the soldiers had lifted little kids onto their shoulders so they could see. Morgan stood in the corner with a gaggle of young women around him hanging on his every word. He'd earned it.

There was a buzz of excitement and happiness that I wished I could feel. But all I felt was worn thin. Tired and broken. The only thing I really wanted right now was to sleep.

The chatter silenced and all faces turned in the same direction. Vine walked up onto a raised platform where a lectern waited for him. He was dressed in a brown suit, an attempt, I guessed, to give his look a military flair. But all it managed to do was remind me that he was a man who had never seen action.

He rested his hand on the edge of the podium, the other tucked in his suit pocket. A pose perfectly orchestrated to create an image of a man in control. It was, I was sure, an image cribbed from great leaders of the past. A bit of Churchill, some Lincoln, perhaps some of the great dictators, too. Everything about this was had been planned by Vine, an attempt to give the perfect message. His leadership election campaign was already under way for when the dust of the war had settled and Britain had to rebuild herself. What kind of a country would we become? A country built on fear and control? Or a country that swore "never again"?

I knew which I hoped for. But that would take leaders who believed in humanity. Vine was not that leader.

"Today," Vine said, his voice screeching slightly through the speakers, "a treaty has been signed that has brought an end to this war. But that treaty would have been nothing but dust had it not been for your bravery. The courage and sacrifice of each and every man, woman and child today has saved thousands, millions of lives. But this victory was not without its costs. I know you stand here marked not only with your own blood but with the blood of your brothers and your sisters."

I looked at my hands. I'd not cleaned CP's blood off them, and it had started to harden and crack like old paint. I felt that wiping them clean would be a betrayal to her. So I clasped my hands behind my back.

"But their sacrifice," Vine continued, "will not be forgotten. You are soldiers of uncertainty; you have lived your whole lives built on the moving sands of a power I cannot comprehend. But this is one event that will not change. It will not alter. You have made history today. And your actions will echo throughout the ages."

Cheers and supportive murmurs passed through the crowd.

"They pushed us and we pushed back. They wanted to tell us what was right or wrong, they wanted to force us to follow their God rather than our own conscience. And we said no. No more. This is the line and no further. We have been a sleeping dragon for too long. Well, the dragon has been awoken. And they have felt our fire. Let them run. Let them hide from our wrath. We will chase them to the ends of the Earth so that none shall ever push us again. The tide has turned and we shall ride the wave of victory till our country is safe once more. The war is over. The war is won!"

There was a deafening roar as every voice in the room picked up his chant, "The war is won!"

Vine pulled off his beret and raised it into the air. One after the other, the men and women of S3 did the same, removing their berets or unclipping helmets and holding them up in salute. Some threw theirs into the air like mortar boards on graduation day.

On the blood-splattered face of almost every adult here, one thing repeated over and over and over. A single scar across the foreheads. The cost of our victory today was deeper than any of them truly knew.

This is what it means to be a man. His voice was so clear now. *To be able to make tough choices.*

Perhaps I was a child – if that meant being unwilling to accept the death of innocent children as a necessity. If being a man meant living in a grey winterland – where there was no right or wrong, only survival, no absolutes to hang onto – then I didn't want to grow up.

I remembered the words that Zac had sprayed onto the outside of the old ARES HQ. *"We don't stop playing because we grow old. We grow old because we stop playing."*

It wasn't that I thought this was all some big game. I wasn't in the playground, shooting my friends with stick guns. There were real bullets. Real deaths. But that didn't mean I had to accept them. I didn't have to measure lives in terms of collateral. There were some sacrifices that I wasn't willing to make.

I rubbed at my face, trying to wipe some of the agony away. But as soon as I closed my eyes, the images threatened to swamp me. Explosions and limbs being torn off. And blood, so much blood.

When I opened my eyes, Vine was staring straight at me. He smiled at me across the sea of soldiers in a way that troubled me more than any look he'd given me since I'd met him. I was about to walk away when I felt a heavy hand on my shoulder.

"The Minister would like a word." It was Vine's guard. The one I'd punched when he'd tried to stop me at the hospital. His black eye was turning purple.

I shook his grip off. "Maybe later," I said.

"Now," he said.

I looked over to Aubrey. She had her hand resting on Katie's shoulder. She tilted her chin at me. *Go on*, the look said. *We'll be here when you're done.*

I laid my hand over the large palm on my shoulder, applying just the right amount of pressure in the right spot. The man winced and pulled his hand away. "Come on, then," I said. "Let's get this over with."

Vine's office was coated in a thin layer of white plaster dust, but he was carrying on as if it wasn't there. Keeping up appearances, just like always. He sat behind his desk, hands pressed down on the green leather as if he were trying to stop the table from floating away. The small smile on his face reeked of smugness. I'd proven to be his puppet after all.

"Congratulations, Commandant Tyler," he said as I walked in.

I didn't bother replying. I wanted out of this office as quickly as possible.

He wasn't put off by my silence. "Can you leave us, please?" he said to the guard who had led me here. The man nodded and closed the door behind him. I heard the bolting of locks.

"I admit," Vine said, standing up. "I was worried that the Red Hand would be victorious. But I should have kept the faith."

I let out a small laugh at the irony. The Red Hand were supposed to be the faithful ones, after all. If Vine understood what I found funny, he didn't let on. He just smiled that thin, stretched smile. I wanted to hit him. Hit him and keep hitting him till there was nothing left of his smug face.

"Our super Shifter is always victorious, after all."

"Don't!" I shouted, the rage I'd been trying to push down bursting to the surface again. I slammed my fist into the wall next to me, leaving a crack in the wood panelling. Vine flinched, the first genuine reaction I think I'd ever seen from him. I looked down at my hand. There were long splinters of mahogany sticking out of my knuckles. I pulled them out without even feeling a thing.

"I know it's not been easy," Vine began.

"Don't," I said again, more softly. "Just don't." I couldn't bear this.

"The safety of the nation…"

I fixed him with a glare and he stuttered into silence.

"Can I go?" I said.

"I suppose so. There is still much to be done."

"I mean, can I go home?"

"Are you asking to be discharged?"

"I don't know what the term is. Resign. Abandon my post. Quit. But yes, whatever it is, I want out."

Vine looked down and rubbed at a small bubble under the leather covering on his table. "I have one more duty I would like you to perform."

"Just one?"

"Yes, but after that, I promise you that your country will ask no more of you."

"And Aubrey and Katie?"

"No harm will come to them, I promise you."

I didn't know what this duty would be. One last child to kill? One last slice off the humanity I had remaining? It couldn't be worse than anything I'd been through today.

"One last duty," I said.

"Very good." He stood, straightening his jacket. "Then it truly is over."

I didn't like the way he said that. Or the way he called for the guard to come in. When the door opened again, there were six armed men standing there.

"Commandant Tyler is under arrest for conspiring with the enemy," Vine said.

I barely had time to open my mouth to protest when I was hit in the chest by a taser and fifty thousand volts of electricity surged through my body.

CHAPTER THIRTY

The cell was the same one we'd put George in. I could tell from the foul graffiti he'd scratched into the brickwork. I wondered where he was now. Had his execution already taken place? Just one more dead Shifter.

As I lay on the bed, staring up at the rough rock overhead, I thought about what Vine had said. One more duty to perform and then I would be free. One more duty and Aubrey and Katie would be safe.

The shock from the taser had stopped me from Shifting at the time. And now, as I banged my head against the wooden slab underneath me, I found I didn't have the energy to try to make another.

The hours passed slowly. I closed my eyes and tried to sleep. But despite exhaustion radiating from my bones, I couldn't drift off. I sat up. I paced. Added some graffiti of my own using the coin from my pocket. Lay on the bed again before working out that the floor was more comfortable. I listened to the muffled sounds coming from the corridor outside and the vibrations in the rocks, and I thought.

I'd not really stopped to think ever since I'd arrived here. I'd been so busy just trying to survive. Now, it seemed as if I had nothing but time.

It was stupid of me to assume I could just walk away from this life. Vine was never going to allow it, for a start. He was scared of me and my power. But if he wasn't going to let me go free, then all of the sacrifices I'd made would be for nothing.

I'd chosen to stay in this reality, giving up everything in my old life, just to be with Aubrey. But if he was going to take that away, there was nothing holding me here anymore.

In the silence of the cell, it became clear just how selfish I had been, how many people had died, and all because I wasn't willing to let go of Aubrey.

Maybe it wasn't too late to put it right. Maybe I could still find a Shift that could undo all of this.

I sifted through everything that had happened since I'd woken up on the banks of the Thames with the fake gongs of Big Ben sounding. Back further, to my encounter with Frankie, meeting Aubrey's father, the fight with Glenn. And back even further to Abbott and Benjo and joining ARES. There had to be a weak point. A fracture I could put pressure on to bring this whole reality down on top of itself but which kept Aubrey alive.

I felt like the answer was there, somewhere. An itching in my mind. If only I could reach it. I was so close…

Wait.

"This might be my only chance."

You know what Vine is planning. We have to go through with it.

"No. Anything but that." I couldn't bear to think it. But he was right. I'd known exactly what Vine had in store for me ever since he'd shown me that room.

It's what I've been working towards since the start. It's the only way. Together, we can do this. One thought, and there will never be a war again.

I knew he was right. But I was scared. "It would mean me staying here."

No. Only I need to stay here.

"There has to be a way for both of us to be happy. You can get out of here. Run away. Be with Aubrey."

That's a lovely dream. But it's time to wake up.

If I went through with this, there was no guarantee it would work. Maybe both of us would be trapped here forever. And even if I did make it back, I'd be leaving this side of me – the side that knew how to command, that had accepted the burden of impossible choices – in this reality. My mind had become like Schrödinger's box. Two possibilities existing in one space. Him and me. It was time to open the box.

"Do you think Vine knows what it will really mean?

No. He's so blinded by his fear.

It was beautiful, really. The thing he thought would destroy me would also tear him down.

"OK," I said. "Let's do this."

At that moment, the door rattled and opened. "Tyler, you've got a visitor."

I scrambled to my feet as the bolts on the door slid open to reveal Vine. He readjusted his tie and brushed a speck of dirt off the cuff of his sleeve with the faintest of movements, so soft that if there had been any dust there, I doubt it would have dislodged it.

"Thank you for seeing me, Scott," he said, acknowledging that me being here at all was my choice. "I assume it is OK if I call you Scott? I think the time for ranks and formalities is past."

"What should I call you, then? Prime Minister?"

He laughed, faking humility. "Oh, I think it's a little early for that. But perhaps..." He adjusted the cuff of his shirt. "This country needs a strong leader. Someone who understands the true cost of peace. If only you had grasped that."

"You don't know me like you think you do. All I've ever wanted is to live a peaceful, boring life."

"What we want and what we must do are rarely the same thing. Can I sit down?" He gestured to the bunk.

I moved out of his way, pressing against the wall, wondering what his game was now.

"My friends..." I said.

"All safe and free."

"And the programme?"

"Shut down, and all the remaining children are to be sent to care centres. I've been overseeing the process myself," he said, touching his perfectly knotted tie again.

"So what now?

I waited. Pretending I didn't know exactly what he wanted of me.

"Doctor Goodwin says Benjo Green doesn't have much longer to live. A few hours at most."

I'd known what his plan was, but I played along. "You want to put me in the Igloo?"

"It is a regrettable decision, but the only choice available to us at this time. You are the only Fixer left, Scott. Doctor Goodwin has said she will do everything she can to make the process as quick and painless as possible."

"You said the war was over. Why do we even need the machine now?"

"This war is over. But there will be others. New enemies who wish to destroy us. That machine has become the thin red line."

"You're asking me to sacrifice myself? After everything you've done to me?"

"I'm asking you to sacrifice yourself to save countless lives. So that the people of this country can rebuild their lives without the shadow of terror. So that your friends and family can."

The way he said the words "friends and family" made it perfectly clear what his real offer was. Step into the machine and Aubrey and Katie and the others remain safe. Fight him and he would bring them down. I gave a quick, bitter laugh. For a Shifter, I'd not had a hell of a lot of choices lately.

"I'll do it. But I want one thing from you first."

"Yes?"

"It's like you said; I've been through a lot. Before I do this thing, before I give myself up completely to the Igloo, I need to be certain of who I am. I want access to a simulator before…"

Before I'm subjected to Frankie's 'delicate balance of chemicals', I didn't bother to add.

Vine's eyes tightened. He was pleased with me. "I think that would be a very good idea. It will give you a chance to lay your ghosts to rest."

What it will give me, I thought, is a chance to play out my options.

Frankie waited, her tablet pressed to her chest under folded arms, a stern expression on her face. She turned without saying anything as I was escorted into the room, and went to stand next to the large chair with a headset dangling over it. I glanced at Vine. Beneath the usual mask of blank expression I sensed tension, urgency. Well, he could wait.

I walked slowly over to the chair, taking in my surroundings. The grey walls, the bright lights overhead. Would these be some of my last memories?

The soft leather of the seat hissed air as I sat down. It was surprisingly comfortable. Frankie pulled the headset down and eased it onto my head.

"If only you'd come to me sooner, Tyler," she whispered in my ear as she fiddled with the straps. "I said I could have helped you."

"There's only one person who can help me."

She waited for me to elaborate, but I didn't bother. She sighed and lowered the glasses over my eyes, blocking out all light. "We're ready."

"You have half an hour, Tyler," Vine's voice echoed around the room. "After that, you will need to take Green's place."

I hoped this would work.

Frankie bustled about, fine-tuning the controls. She smelt of antiseptic and coffee. "Are you ready?"

I nodded, causing the wires on the headset to rattle against each other.

There was a blinding light and then...

I'm holding a phone in my hand, shaking fingers attempting to dial a number from a black business card with the letter ARES punched out. Forget it, I think, and put the phone down. I don't need their help. I can do it alone. I crumple up the card and throw it in the bin.

I rode the ripples from my decision to join ARES and it led to me sitting in another jail, arrested for Shifting without a licence. And while I was there, I heard stories from the guards on duty about the death of a Shifter. Found hanging from chains in an abandoned warehouse, part of her brain missing.

I tried another decision.

I'm standing outside the wooden doors of St Sebastian's. I'm here to warn Aubrey that ARES are coming for her. But she doesn't want to see me. She made that clear. I turn around and walk down the street, rain soaking through my clothes.

But it was too late; I'd already lead ARES to their door. Aubrey and Zac had been arrested, just like before. Only, this time, there was nobody there to find out about Greyfield's. Nobody to stop Abbott's plan. Or to save Aubrey from becoming another Ganymede volunteer.

I hunted for another pivot point.

I'm peering in through the broken glass at a warehouse. I've forgotten to bring a jacket and I'm already freezing. There's nothing in there but darkness. Benjo Green is dead. I'm a fool to think

*otherwise. I should never have bothered coming here
at all. I close my eyes and I'm in my bed.*

Yes! I thought. If I'd never gone after Benjo, I wouldn't have learned about Frankie Anderson or her children. Never have put Aubrey in danger. This new reality filled me with a sense of hope. But then the consequences of turning my back on Benjo revealed themselves. Hiding in his dark warehouse, Benjo had gathered his strength, his mind twisting around a single thought. Revenge. Against the boy who had destroyed his life. And what better way to destroy me than to take away the person I loved?

There had to be another way. The images playing about my head suddenly stopped, like someone switching a TV off. But it was OK. I knew what I had to do. It was so perfect, I couldn't believe I hadn't thought of it from the start.

"Time's up," Frankie said. She raised the helmet and took the glasses off my face, looking into my eyes. "Are you with us, Tyler?"

I nodded. "I'm here." A strange sort of calmness had come over me. I'd accepted everything that was going to happen. It felt good not having to fight anymore. I couldn't remember the last time I wasn't fighting against something. The enemy. Myself. I was finally at peace.

"And you know where you are?"

"I'm in the Hub. Home to the S3. And you are Doctor Francesca Goodwin, and you are about to put me in the Igloo," I said.

Her skin blanched and her lips tightened. "Yes," she said.

She gave me her hand and helped me to my feet. Vine and the armed guards were all watching me.

"Well," I said. "What are we waiting for?"

They led me through winding corridors. I knew Vine hoped to keep my arrest as quiet as possible. If any of the S3 found out that he planned on putting put their saviour in the Igloo, it might all kick off. I would play along. I wasn't going to be here for much longer.

When we arrived at the Igloo, there was a second coffin in the centre of the room, its lid open wide, ready for me. I walked towards it, glancing down at Benjo in the coffin next to the one that would be mine. His pale face was shrivelled, his black eyes sunken like hot coals in the snow.

"We'll make the switch once you're hooked up," Frankie said, her voice forced through clenched teeth.

I looked at Vine. This small man who wore power like another man's suit. Who'd become addicted to it. Twisted by it. Soon, I'd be setting us both free.

Once I was hooked up, I would Force him to stand down. I would Force every leader in the world to obey my commands. No more senseless death. No more profit above people. No more war.

Unaware of my plans, Vine nodded, unable to keep a smile from twitching at the corners of his mouth. I nodded in return.

I eased myself into the box and lay down in the padded interior. At least they'd tried to make things comfortable.

Frankie held up a glass bottle containing clear liquid. She pushed a syringe into the rubber seal and drew the liquid into it. It made a tiny squeaking noise as she pulled it out, as if the rubber didn't want to let go of the needle. She held it upright and squeezed a bubble of air out of the syringe, so precise that no liquid escaped. She rolled up my sleeve, revealing my arm with the S tattoo on it. I remembered the day I'd had that done now. Remembered the itching burning of the ink being scratched into my skin and how proud I felt. How proud I was to do my duty.

Frankie lowered the needle into the crook of my arm, an inch above my tattoo. As it pricked my skin, I smiled.

"I wish there was another way," Frankie said, more to herself than to me, I thought.

"It's OK," I said, resting my hand over hers. "It was always going to come to this."

What she didn't know was that once I committed to the machine, I would have the power to push my will on anyone. It would amplify my thoughts and send them all across the world.

Everything *he* had done led to this. As soon as he'd learnt about the capabilities of the Igloo, he'd known there was only one way to stop the madness that had infected the world. He'd worked to earn Vine's trust so the Minister would think him his loyal soldier, then pushed him enough so he would be willing to sacrifice his most powerful pawn to this machine. It had been a delicate game of actions and consequences. And he had played it masterfully. I'd almost ruined it all by turning up at the most crucial moment. I'd been fighting so hard against him, I couldn't see what was really happening.

Now both of us had a job to do to put things right. Him in this reality. Me in mine. Neither of us were going to have the happy endings I had naively hoped for. Maybe there's no such thing.

Goodbye, Scott.

"Goodbye."

Frankie flinched at the word she thought was for her, then composed herself, blinking away the tears that threatened to cloud her vision. She pushed down on the syringe, the thick, clear liquid pumping under my skin, mixing with my blood. I lay on the pillow, which suddenly felt like the softest pillow in the entire world.

Frankie started to count down from twenty.

I knew what I had to do. But it was hard, giving up on everything I loved. Knowing I would never see my family again. Aubrey again. But it was the right thing.

"Thirteen."

He taught me that; he had given me the strength to follow it through. Or maybe I had that strength within me all along?

"Nine."

I was going to have to hold on to that certainty. To override the biology that would fight to keep me alive. This was mind over matter.

"Five."

I let myself drift back to that night.

"One."

To that very first night.

The electricity pylon looms over me like a monster against the night sky. They're all chanting my name, but I can tell now that they're doing it to mock me, rather than because they actually believe I'm going to go through with this. But they don't really know me at all.

I jump, leaping up to grab onto the first strut. It feels cold under my fingers, the sharp edges of the metal digging into my flesh. It hurts, but it's only pain. I pull myself up to the next rung.

Voices call up to me, bored by the game, wanting me to come down so they can get on with drinking. But I ignore them. This isn't about them anymore. The only person I have anything to prove to is myself. I'm fourteen, fifteen rungs up. And I've never felt more confident in my life. Like I have finally found the place where I belong. I reach out for the next metal rod. My hand closes around it.

The snap of metal is like the sound of a coffin lid slamming shut.

Final and certain and inescapable.

It was always going to come to this.

I close my eyes, giving in to gravity and fate and whatever else has brought me here.

And let myself fall, a smile on my face.

CHAPTER THIRTY-ONE

I jolted awake. I was blind: a white fogginess obscuring my eyes. Panicked, I reached up and realised there was something stuck to my face. I peeled it off, blinking sleep-glued eyes. It was a page of paper covered in scribbled notes. Typed across the top was a question.

Nucleus X is B. Deduce the number of protons and the number of neutrons in nucleus Y.

Beneath it, after the series of dots marking out where the answer should be written, were more questions. About pair production, excited atoms, the ionisation energy of hydrogen.

It was a physics exam paper.

There were scatterings of more pages, along with physics textbooks, piled on top of other books about chemistry and advanced mathematics. I was at home. In my bedroom. It was 7.43am on the fourteenth of April, judging by my digital clock.

"But," I said out loud, "I should be dead."

I tried to stand up, and pain shot through my thigh and all the way up my spine. Was it the injury from the battle?

I sat back down. I was wearing a grey tracksuit and trainers, but there was something strange about my left leg. I pulled up the trouser. Sticking out of my trainer, where my calf should have been, was something that looked like a leg. It was the colour of skin and had the shape and form of a leg. I poked it. It was rubbery plastic. I continued to poke all the way up till I got to my thigh. That was all flesh. The simple pressure of my finger was enough to make me wince.

I leaned back in my chair, trying not to panic. Trying to make sense of what was going on.

First things first. I was alive. That was a surprise. When I undid my very first shift, made the night I fell from the electricity pylon, I assumed it would have resulted in my death. It did, however, seem that I now only had one leg. I patted the rest of my body. Tenderness in my lower back, stiffness in my shoulder, which, I saw as I pulled my T-shirt down, was covered in a neat crisscross of scars.

I probed my memory. I'd fallen from the pylon and shattered my pelvis, my femur, broken my scapula, my humeral head and a list of other bones I couldn't remember. But I'd lived.

I remembered how I'd been stretchered out of the park, with Hugo, my supposed best friend, crying and blaming himself while a blonde girl with big boots and dark eyeshadow looked on. She was the most beautiful girl I'd ever seen. And I dumbly asked for her number as the paramedics pushed me into the ambulance, the drugs they'd given me for the pain making me brave and stupid.

I hadn't seen her after that night.

I tried standing again, remembering how to find my balance on my artificial limb. It was awkward at first, and I needed to lean on the walls to help me along. But I made it down stairs.

"About time," my mother said as I shuffled into the kitchen. "I was about to come and check on you. You have to leave in half an hour."

I leaned against the doorway, watching my mum busy herself with the kettle and toaster.

"You look sick," she said when she turned around, mug of steaming tea in her hand. "Are you sick?" She pushed the mug into my hand and pressed her palm against my head. "If you have another infection, I swear I will sue that hospital."

I held her hand. "It's fine, Mum. I'm fine."

"Well, you had better be. You can't miss any more school with your exams coming up."

I spat out the mouthful of tea I'd taken. "Exams?"

"Oh, Scott. You're not having another of your turns, are you?"

"No, I'm good," I said.

"He's just trying to get out of going to school," a voice said behind me. Katie pushed me out of the way and sat at the table. It was all I could do to stop myself from hugging her and never letting her go.

"What?" she said. "Have I got something on my face?" She grabbed a spoon and turned it around to look at her reflection in the curved bowl.

"No. You're perfect," I said, fighting down the tears.

"You're a freak, Scott." She plunged the spoon into a bowl of cereal and shoved it into her mouth. "I can't believe we have to go to the same school."

I laughed. It seemed like everything was back to normal. As if the last year of my life had never happened. I'd never joined ARES, never met the people who were to become my friends. I didn't even know if any of them were still alive.

"Where are you off to?" Mum said.

"I have to check on something," I said, walking as quickly as I was able on my new leg up the stairs.

I sat at my desk, opened my laptop and rested my fingers on the keyboard. "Please remember," I said.

I punched in the URL for the ARES intranet and took a deep breath when the login screen appeared. I typed in Carl's password.

CARLSEXGOD

It hadn't changed.

I paused before choosing who to search for first. It was like I couldn't bring myself to search for her, not yet. I began with Jake Bailey.

There were a few tense moments while the system loaded, then his face appeared. That crooked grin was still there, but the sandy mop of hair was no more. Cropped into a neat buzz cut. He looked older than I remembered. I scanned his files. He'd quit ARES three months before, was going to school and living with his sister. I clicked through to check her file. She was under surveillance as a possible rogue and suspected member of the SLF – the Shifter Liberation Front – although no evidence had been found to prove it. But both of them were safe – that's all that mattered.

Next, I searched for Zac.

Isaac Black – suspected leader of the SLF. Now believed to be living in America.

Probably a millionaire already, I thought, smiling.

I closed his file and searched for CP. As I waited for the results to show, I mentally unpicked the events of the last year and a half. Her file loaded and my heart contracted when I read the words.

Cleopatra Finn. Volunteer – Project Ganymede.

"No!" I screamed, picking my laptop up in my hands and shaking it, as if I could somehow wipe away those words.

Did that mean the project was still up and running? I did a search, and the agony over CP softened slightly when I saw that the programme had been shut down a year ago. Sergeant Cain had, the report said, uncovered what had been going on, and Abbott had been arrested and was now in prison for life.

Another click and I pulled up Cain's file.

Sergeant Charles Cain: Deceased. Killed on Duty.

Like before, he'd given his life to stop Abbott. Only this time, he'd been too late to save CP.

Cain and CP gone. Jake, Zac and Rosalie safe.

I couldn't put it off any more.

My hands shook as I typed the eleven letters. I closed my eyes. "Please," I said. "Please. Please. Please."

When I opened them again, I was looking at Aubrey's face. It was the picture from her ARES ID, where she was scowling at the camera. I reached out and touched it, small rainbows of colour pooling out from where my fingers touched the screen.

**Aubrey Jones, Spotter, 4th Class. Retired.
Commendation for her work leading to the uncovering
of Project Ganymede. Suspected ties to the SLF.
Observation recommended.**

Aubrey was alive. She was out of ARES. And it seemed like she had been responsible for leading Cain to Greyfield's. I tried to work out how she could have known about the project. Then I remembered. The night I'd gone to speak to her and Zac in the church, the night that ARES had followed me and arrested them all, she and Zac had been looking over plans of the hospital. They hadn't needed me. Aubrey hadn't needed me.

But that didn't mean that I didn't still need her.

I read through the rest of her file, to see if her address was still the same. It was, but it also gave a place of work.

I closed the laptop and stared at my wall. It was covered with pictures I didn't recognise, including a photo of me looking uncomfortable next to Hugo and some girl. The girl, who was pretty enough, had her arm wrapped around mine and was gazing up at me with a worrying expression on her face.

Oh, God, I thought. Don't let it be what it looks like.

There was only one way to find out. I rifled around on the papers on my desk and found my mobile phone. It was weird, looking at it. A model I didn't recognise and so slim compared to the satellite phones I'd been using. It took me a few seconds to work out the unfamiliar operating system. I found Hugo's number and hit dial.

He answered after a few rings.

"Scotty!" he said, in his usual posh drawl.

"Hugo, you have no idea how good it is to hear your voice."

"Oh, funny, funny. Missing me after a few hours?"

I tried to laugh, but the truth was, hearing his voice was enough to make me want to sob.

"Are you OK, Scott?" Hugo said, genuine concern in his voice. "You're not still upset over Emily? I thought you were relieved when she ended it."

The girl in the picture. Emily. Yes, it fit. I hunted out the memory. We'd dated for a month, and she'd ended it last week. I could remember the relief. I'd not had the guts to do it myself.

"No," I said, coughing to clear my throat. "It's not that. It's just…" How could I even begin to explain to Hugo? It's just I've spent the last week watching people die, watching the whole country burn, and now I was back in a place where everything was safe and there was no war and I was aching to get back to that other reality because the girl I loved was there? There was no point in even trying.

"It's just this physics homework is killing me," I finished, finally.

"Well, that will serve you right for taking sciences, Scotty. You should have done humanities like me. Plenty more girls do humanity."

I laughed. "Promise me something, Hugo?"

"What's that?"

"Never change."

"As if. Why would I mess with perfection?"

I laughed again. "I'd better go."

"Catch you on later. And Scott," he said, as I was removing the phone from my ear to hang up, "are you sure everything's OK?"

"Everything is fine. Everything is perfectly fine," I said, and hit the end call button.

I should be happy, I thought, as I struggled to clamber onto my bed, still clumsy on the false leg. The world was a better place because of the Shift I'd finally been able to make. Only... Only.

"Aubrey," I said. And it came out as a sigh.

I would be a stranger to her. I should try to forget about her. Move on with my life and let her move on with hers.

Like that was going to happen.

KIM CURRAN

CHAPTER THIRTY-TWO

It was an achingly cool café in Shoreditch, East London, filled with men with preposterous beards and women in jeans that looked like they'd been sprayed on. The walls had all been painted in blackboard paint, and quotes had been scrawled in yellow chalk.

I read one of them and raised an eyebrow.

I have measured out my life with coffee spoons. T.S. Eliot

What did that even mean? Were coffee spoons different than tea spoons?

"Are you in the queue?" a man grunted at me.

I mumbled an apology and stepped out of the way, promptly banging into a long table and spilling someone's coffee. They were too engrossed in a book of poetry to even notice. I'd still not got the hang of walking with my prosthetic leg. I got into the queue while looking around.

There were three staff members: two men behind the counter and a young, dark-haired woman serving the tables.

Maybe the file was wrong. Maybe she no longer worked here. I was about to turn and leave when she came out of the kitchen carrying a try of steaming muffins.

"Mind your backs," she said, "hot stuff coming through."

This made everyone around the counter laugh, as if it was an old joke shared among them.

Her hair was pushed away from her forehead and tied with a blue-and-white scarf, making her look like a little like a 1940s Land Girl. Her face was perfect. No scar from Benjo. No missing eye. She looked exactly like she had the very first day I had met her. She nudged a barista out of the way with her hip and placed the muffins in the glass counter, then wiped her hands on a white apron tied around her waist. She looked beautiful. She looked happy.

The plan had been to come here and see her, then go. And I'd done the first. I should turn around and leave her to her new life. I had brought her nothing but pain. She would be better off without me, I was sure of it. But my feet refused to listen to me. I kept staring at her as she came to stand behind the tills and started taking orders. I couldn't take my eyes off her, even as the person behind me coughed loudly to suggest I move forward in the queue. Then she turned to look at me, fixing me with the full wattage of her smile. And I had no choice.

"Next," she said.

I staggered forward and tried to think of what to say. What words could convey everything my heart felt? How could I make her realise who I was, who she was to me, who we were together? It would take days, months, and I had only seconds.

"What can I get you?" she said.

"A large latte with vanilla sprinkles," I managed to say.

The male barista scoffed at my order. "We only do black and flat whites here, mate. If you want crap like that, you'll have to go to the chain across the road."

But Aubrey wasn't laughing. She cocked her head to one side and smiled at me. "Vanilla sprinkles?" she said.

"A coffee's not complete without vanilla sprinkles."

This made her laugh, a warm, friendly laugh that sent a wave of happiness flooding over me.

"The best I can do you is a white coffee and a splash of vanilla essence. Will that do?"

"For now," I said.

She told me the price, took my money and poured my change into my hand, then busied herself with making my order.

I moved along the line, watching her over the chrome coffee maker. She kept glancing up at me, then down to the coffee.

"Vanilla sprinkles," she said again, shaking her head.

She poured milk from a silver jug into the black cup of coffee, wiggling the flow of milk to make a pretty leaf pattern.

"Hang on," she said, then disappeared into the kitchen. She returned a moment later with a small brown bottle. She twisted off the lid of the vanilla essence and let three droplets fall onto the white foam, then popped a plastic lid on top and handed it over to me.

Our fingers met as she handed it to me, and she flinched, as if getting a static shock.

We stood there, both of us holding the cup, staring at each other. The moment was broken when a customer banged into me, causing me to spill a drop of the hot coffee over Aubrey's hand.

"I'm sorry," I said as she shook the liquid off.

"Don't worry about it. Enjoy your coffee."

She hesitated. I knew that she was about to go back to her work and I would never see her again. I racked my brain trying to think of something to say. I could tell her that I was a Shifter. That I knew all about ARES. All about her.

But I didn't have to. She turned to me and looked me up and down through narrow eyes.

"Do I know you?" she said.

"No," I said, with a smile. "But you will."

ACKNOWLEDGEMENTS

Writing the last book in a trilogy is a bittersweet moment. It's been an amazing, thrilling rollercoaster of a ride. But I'm sad I won't get to live with these characters any more. I like to think Scott and Aubrey and the others have lots of adventures ahead of them, it's just that I won't be the one to write them.

The publication of this book has had its own rocky journey. For a while there, I didn't think I it would happen. Endless thanks to Calee Lee and the team at Xist for making it happen. I couldn't have found a better home for the book. To Lou Morgan, for talking me off a cliff when I was about to burn the whole book and run away and become a Mongolian Eagle Hunter. To Laura Lam for your feedback and pointing out my obsession with the word 'just'. To Regan Warner, who is the best work partner anyone could ask for. And to Chris, my husband, for your patience – I know I've really tested it this time around.

But the most important person to thank is you, the reader, for sticking with me and Scott over the last three books. I hope you've enjoyed reading it as much as I have loved writing it. And I hope you stick with me with whatever I write next.

About the Author

Kim was born in Dublin and moved to London when she was seven. She got her first typewriter when she was eight, had a poem she wrote about a snail published in a magazine when she was nine, and that was it – Kim was hooked on writing.

Because she never thought she'd actually be able to make a living as a writer, she decided she needed a trade to fall back on. So, naturally, she went to Sussex University to study philosophy.

While Kim's plan of being paid big bucks to think deep thoughts never quite worked out, she did land a job as a junior copywriter with an ad agency a week after graduating. She's worked in advertising ever since, specialising in writing for videogames.

She can be found at www.kimcurran.co.uk and on Twitter @KimeCurran.